*"Murder. What a beastly soft sound
the word makes!"*

"Have you thought carefully about this?" Alleyn asked. "Do you realize you're starting something you may want to stop and—not be able to stop?"

"I'm living in a nightmare," Losse insisted.

"I just think I ought to warn you. I'm a bit of state machinery. Anyone can start me up, but only the state can shut me off. You have been warned."

Died in the Wool

Ngaio MARSH

BERKLEY PRIME CRIME, NEW YORK

This Berkley Prime Crime Book contains the complete text of the original hardcover edition.

DIED IN THE WOOL

A Berkley Prime Crime Book / published by arrangement with Little, Brown and Company

PRINTING HISTORY
Little, Brown and Company edition published 1945
Five previous paperback printings
Jove edition / December 1981
Berkley Prime Crime edition / November 1994

ISBN: 0-425-14469-0

Berkley Prime Crime Books are published by The Berkley Publishing Group, 200 Madison Avenue, New York, New York 10016. The name BERKLEY PRIME CRIME and the BERKLEY PRIME CRIME design are trademarks belonging to Berkley Publishing Corporation.

PRINTED IN THE UNITED STATES OF AMERICA

10 9 8 7 6 5 4 3

For the Lexicographers

Died in the Wool

PROLOGUE

1939

"I am Mrs. Rubrick of Mount Moon," said the golden-headed lady. "And I should like to come in."

The man at the stage-door looked down into her face. Its nose and eyes thrust out at him, pale, all of them, and flecked with brown. Seen at close quarters these features appeared to be slightly out of perspective. The rest of the face receded from them, fell away to insignificance. Even the mouth with its slightly projecting, its never quite hidden, teeth was forgotten in favour of that acquisitive nose, those protuberant exacting eyes. "I should like to come in," Flossie Rubrick repeated.

The man glanced over his shoulder into the hall. "There are seats at the back," he said. "Behind the buyers' benches."

"I know there are. But I don't want to see the backs of the buyers. I want to watch their faces. I'm Mrs. Rubrick of Mount Moon and my wool clip should be coming up in the next half-hour. I want to sit up here somewhere." She looked beyond the man at the door, through a pair of scenic book wings to the stage where an auctioneer in shirt-sleeves sat at a high rostrum, gabbling. "Just there," said Flossie Rubrick, "on that chair by those painted things. That will do quite well." She moved past the man at the door. "How do you do?" she said piercingly as she came face to face with a second figure. "You don't mind if I come in, do you? I'm Mrs. Arthur Rubrick. May I sit down?"

She settled herself on a chair she had chosen, pulling it forward until she could look through an open door in the proscenium and down into the front of the house. She was a tiny creature and it was a tall chair. Her feet scarcely reached the floor. The auctioneer's clerks, who sat below his rostrum, glanced up curiously from their papers.

1

"Lot One-seven, six," gabbled the auctioneer. "Mount Silver."

"Eleven," a voice shouted.

In the auditorium two men, their arms stretched rigid, sprang to their feet and screamed. "Three!" Flossie settled her furs and looked at them with interest. "Eleven-three," said the auctioneer.

The chairs proper to the front of the hall had been replaced by rows of desks, each of which was labelled with the name of its occupant's firm. Van Huys. Riven Brothers. Dubois. Yen. Steiner. James Ogden. Hartz. Ormerod. Rhodes. Markino. James Barnett. Dressed in business men's suits woven from good wool, the buyers had come in from the four corners of the world for the summer wool sales. They might have been carefully selected types, so eloquently did they display their nationality. Van Huys's buyer with his round wooden head and soft hat; Dubois's, sleek, with a thin moustache and heavy grooves running from his nostrils to the corners of his mouth; old Jimmy Ormerod who bought for himself, screamed like a stallion, and turned purple in the face; Hartz, with horn-rimmed glasses, who barked; and Mr. Kurata Kan of Markino's with his falsetto yelp. Each buyer held printed lists before him, and from time to time, like a well-trained chorus ensemble, they would all turn a page. The auctioneer's recital was uninflected and monotonous yet, as if the buyers were marionettes and he their puppet master, they would twitch into violent action and as suddenly return to their nervously intent immobility. Some, holding the papers before their eyes, stood waiting for a particular wool clip to come up. Others wrote at their desks. Each had trained himself to jerk in a flash from watchful relaxation into spread-eagled yelling urgency. Many of them smoked continuously and Flossie Rubrick saw them through drifts of blue tobacco clouds.

In the open doorways and under the gallery stood groups of men whose faces and hands were raddled and creased by the sun and whose clothes were those of the countryman in town. They were the wool growers, the run holders, the sheep cockies, the back-countrymen. Upon the behaviour of the buyers their manner of living for the next twelve months would depend. The wool sale was what it all amounted to: long musters over high-country; nights spent by shepherds in tin huts on mountain-sides; late snows that came down into lambing paddocks; noisy rituals of dipping, crutching, shearing; the final down-country journey of the wool bales—this was the brief and final comment on the sheepman's working year.

Flossie saw her husband, Arthur Rubrick, standing in a doorway. She waved vigorously. The men who were with Arthur pointed her out. He gave her a dubious nod and began to make his way along a side aisle towards her. As soon as he reached the steps that led from the auditorium up to her doorway she called out in a sprightly manner. "Look where I've got to! Come up and join me!" He did so but without enthusiasm.

"What are you doing up here, Floss?" he said. "You ought to have gone down below."

"Down below wouldn't suit me at all."

"Everyone's looking at you."

"That doesn't embarrass me," she said loudly. "When will he get to us, darling? Show me."

"Ssh!" said her husband unhappily and handed her his catalogue.

Flossie made play with her lorgnette. She flicked it open modishly with a white-gloved hand and looked through it at the lists. There was a simultaneous flutter of white paper throughout the hall. "Over we go, I see," said Flossie and turned a page. "Now, where are we?"

Her husband grunted urgently and jerked up his head.

"Lot One-eighty," gabbled the auctioneer.

"Thirteen."

"Half!" yelled old Ormerod.

"Three!"

"Fourteen!"

The spectacled Mr. Kurata Kan was on his feet yelping a fraction of a second quicker than Ormerod.

"Top price," cried Flossie shrilly. "Top price! Isn't it, darling? We've got top price, haven't we? That dear little Jap!"

A ripple of laughter ran through the hall. The auctioneer grinned. The two men near the stage-door moved away, their hands over their mouths. Arthur Rubrick's face, habitually cyanosed, deepened to a richer purple. Flossie clapped her white gloves together and rose excitedly. "Isn't he too sweet?"

she demanded. "Arthur, isn't he a pet?"

"Flossie, for God's sake," Arthur Rubrick muttered.

But Flossie made a series of crisp little nods in the direction of Mr. Kurata Kan and at last succeeded in attracting his attention. His eyelids creased, his upper lip lifted in a crescent over his long teeth and he bowed.

"There!" said Flossie in triumph as she swept out at the stage-door, followed by her discomfited husband. "Isn't that splendid?"

He piloted her into a narrow yard. "I wish you wouldn't make me quite so conspicuous, my dear," he said. "I mean, waving to that Jap. We don't know him or anything."

"No," cried Flossie. "But we're going to. You're going to call on him, darling, and we shall ask him to Mount Moon for the week-end."

"Oh, no, Flossie. Why? Why on earth?"

"I'm all for promoting friendly relations. Besides, he's paid top price for my wool. He's a sensible man. I want to meet him."

"Grinning little pip-squeak. I don't like 'em, Floss. Do you in the eye for tuppence, the Japs would. Any day. They're our natural enemies."

"Darling, you're absolutely antediluvian. Before we know where we are you'll be talking about the Yellow Peril."

She tossed her head and a lock of hair dyed a brilliant gold slipped down her forehead. "Do remember this is 1939," said Flossie.

ii

1942

On a summer's day in February, 1942, Mr. Sammy Joseph, buyer for Riven Brothers Textile Manufactory, was going through their wool stores with the storeman. The windows had been blacked-out with paint, and the storeman, as they entered, switched on a solitary lamp. This had the effect of throwing into strong relief the square hessian bales immediately under the lamp. Farther down the store they dissolved in shadow. The lamp was high and encrusted with dust: the faces of the two men looked cadaverous. Their voices sounded stifled, there is no echo in a building lined with wool. The air was stuffy and smelt of hessian.

"When did we start buying dead wool, Mr. Joseph?" asked the storeman.

"We never buy dead wool," Joseph said sharply. "What are you talking about?"

"There's a bale of it down at the far end."

"Not in this store."

"I'm good for a bet on it."

"What's biting you? Why d'you say it's dead?"

"Gawd, Mr. Joseph, I've been in the game long enough, haven't I? Don't I know dead wool when I smell it? It pongs."

"Here!" said Sammy Joseph. "Where is this bale?"

"Come and see."

They walked down the aisle between ranks of baled wool. The storeman at intervals switched on more lights and the aisle was extended before them. At the far end he paused and jerked his thumb at the last bale. "Take a sniff, Mr. Joseph," he said.

Sammy Joseph bent towards the bale. His shadow was thrown up on the surface, across stencilled letters, a number and a rough crescent.

"That's from the Mount Moon clip," he said.

"I know it is." The storeman's voice rose nervously. "Stinks, doesn't it?"

"Yes," said Joseph. "It does."

"Dead wool."

"I've never bought dead wool in my life. Least of all from Mount Moon. And the smell of dead wool goes off after it's plucked. You know that as well as I do. Dead rat, more likely. Have you looked?"

"Yes, I have looked, Mr. Joseph. I shifted her out the other day. It's in the bale. You can tell."

"Split her up," Mr. Joseph commanded.

The storeman pulled out a clasp-knife, opened it, and dug the blade into the front of the bale. Sammy Joseph watched him in a silence that was broken only by the uneasy sighing of the rafters above their heads.

"It's hot in here," said Sammy Joseph. "There's a nor'west gale blowing outside. I hate a hot wind."

"Oppressive," said the storeman. He drew the blade of his knife downwards, sawing at the bale. The strands of sacking parted in a series of tiny explosions. Through the fissure bulged a ridge of white wool.

"Get a lungful of that," said the storeman, straightening himself. "It's something chronic. Try."

Mr. Joseph said: "I get it from here, thanks. I can't understand it. It's not bellies in that pack, either. Bellies smell a bit but nothing to touch this." He opened his cigarette case. "Have one?"

"Ta, Mr. Joseph. I don't mind if I do. It's not so good, this pong, is it?"

"It's coming from inside, all right. They must have baled up something in the press. A rat."

"You will have your rat, sir, won't you?"

"Let's have some of that wool out." Mr. Joseph glanced at his neat worsted suit. "You're in your working clothes," he added.

The storeman pulled at a tuft of wool. "Half a sec', Mr. Joseph. She's packed too solid." He moved away to the end wall. Sammy Joseph looked at the rent in the bale, reached out his hand and drew it back again. The storeman returned wearing a gauntleted canvas glove on his right hand and carrying one of the iron hooks used for shifting wool bales. He worked it into the fissure and began to drag out lumps of fleece.

"Phew!" whispered Sammy Joseph.

"I'll have to hand it to you in one respect, sir. She's not dead wool."

Mr. Joseph picked a lock from the floor, looked at it, and dropped it. He turned away and wiped his hand vigorously on a bale. "It's frightful," he said. "It's a God-almighty stench. What the hell's wrong with you!"

The storeman had sworn with violence and extreme obscenity. Joseph turned to look at him. His gloved hand had disappeared inside the fissure. The edge of the gauntlet showed and no more. His face was turned towards Joseph.

The eyes and mouth were wide-open.

"I'm touching something."

"With the hook?"

The storeman nodded. "I won't look any more," he said loudly.

"Why not?"

"I won't look."

"Why the hell?"

"It's the Mount Moon clip."

"I know that. What of it?"

"Don't you read the papers?"

Sammy Joseph changed colour. "You're mad," he said. "God, you're crazy."

"It's three weeks, isn't it, and they can't find her. I was in the last war. I know what that stink reminds me of. Flanders."

"Go to hell," said Mr. Joseph, incredulous but violent. "What do you think you are? A radio play or what?"

The storeman plucked his arm from the bale. Locks of fleece were sticking to the canvas glove. With a violent movement he jerked them free and they lay on the floor, rust-coloured and wet.

"You've left the hook in the bale."

"——the hook."

"Get it out, Alf."

"——!"

"Come on. What's wrong with you? Get it out."

The storeman looked at Sammy Joseph as if he hated him. A loose sheet of galvanized iron on the roof rattled in the wind and the store was filled momentarily with a vague soughing.

"Come on," Sammy Joseph said again. "It's only a rat."

The storeman plunged his hand into the fissure. His bare arm twisted and worked. He braced the palm of his left hand against the bale and wrenched out the hook. With an air of incredulity he held the hook out, displaying it.

"Look!" he said. With an imperative gesture he waved Mr. Joseph aside, leant forward, and vomited comprehensively. The iron hook fell at Sammy Joseph's feet. A strand of metallic-gold hair was twisted about it.

CHAPTER I

ALLEYN AT MOUNT MOON

May 1943

A service car pulled out of the township below the Pass. It mounted a steep shingled road until its passengers looked down on the iron roof of the pub and upon a child's farm-animal design of tiny horses tethered to verandah posts, upon specks that were sheep-dogs and upon a toy sulky with motor-car wheels that moved slowly along the road, down-country. Beyond this a system of foot-hills, gorges, and clumps of *Pinus insignis* stepped down into a plain fifty miles wide, a plain that rose slowly as its horizon mounted with the eyes of the mounting passengers.

Though their tops were shrouded by a heavy mask of cloud, the hills about the Pass grew more formidable. The interval between cloud roof and earth floor lessened. The Pass climbed into the sky. A mountain rain now fell.

"Going into bad weather?" suggested the passenger on the front seat.

"Going out of it, you mean," rejoined the driver.

"Do I?"

"Take a look at the sky, sir."

The passenger wound down his window for a moment and craned out. "Jet-black and lowering," he said, "but there's a good smell in the air."

"Watch ahead."

The passenger dutifully peered through the rain-blinded windscreen and saw nothing to justify the driver's prediction but only a confusion of black cones whose peaks were cut off by the curtain of the sky. The head of the Pass was lost in a blur of rain. The road now hung above a gorge through whose bed hurried a stream, its turbulence seen but not heard at that height. The driver changed down and the engine whined and roared. Pieces of shingle banged violently on the underneath of the car.

9

"Hullo!" said the passenger. "Is this the top?" And a moment later—"Good God, how remarkable!"

The mountain tops had marched away to left and right. The head of the Pass was an open square of piercing blue. As they reached it the black cloud drew back like a curtain. In a moment it was behind them and they looked down into another country.

It was a great plateau, high itself, but ringed about with mountains that were crowned in a perpetual snow. It was laced with rivers of snow water. Three lakes of a strange milky green lay across its surface. It stretched bare and golden under a sky that was brilliant as a paladin's mantle. Upon the plateau and the foot-hills, up to the level of perpetual snow, grew giant tussocks, but there were no forests. Many miles apart, patches of *Pinus insignis* or Lombardy poplars could be seen and these marked the solitary homesteads of the sheep farmers. The air was clear beyond belief, unbreathed, one would have said, newly poured out from the blue chalice of the sky.

The passenger again lowered the window, which was still wet but steaming now, in the sun. He looked back. The cloud curtain lolled a little way over the mountain barrier and that was all there was to be seen of it.

"It's a new world," he said.

The driver stretched out his hand to a pigeon-hole in the dashboard where his store of loose cigarettes joggled together. His leather coat smelt unpleasantly of fish oil. The passenger wished that his journey was over and that he could enter into this new world of which, remaining in the car, he was merely a spectator. He looked at the mountain ring that curved sickle-wide to right and left of the plateau. "Where is Mount Moon?" he asked. The driver pointed sweepingly to the left. "They'll pick you up at the forks."

The road, a pale stripe in the landscape, pointed down the centre of the plateau and then far ahead forked towards the mountain ramparts. The passenger could see a car, tiny but perfectly clear, standing at the forks. "That'll be Mr. Losse's car," said the driver. The passenger thought of the letter he carried in his wallet. Phrases returned to his memory. " . . . the situation has become positively Russian, or, if you prefer the allusion, a setting for a modern crime story. . . . We continue here together in an atmosphere that twangs with stretched nerves. One expects them to relax with time, but no ... it's over a year ago. ... I should not have ventured to make the demand upon your time if there had not been this preposterous suggestion of espionage ... refuse to be subjected any longer to this particular form of torment..." And, in a pointed irritable calligraphy, the signature— "Fabian Losse."

The car completed its descent and with a following cloud of dust began to travel across the plateau. Against some distant region of cloud a system of mountains was revealed, glittering spear upon spear. One would have said that these must be the ultimate expression of loftiness, but soon the clouds parted and there, remote from them, was the shining horn of the great peak, the Cloud Piercer, Aorangi. The passenger was so intent upon this unfolding picture that he had no eyes for the road and they were close upon the forks before he saw the signpost with its two arms at right angles. The car pulled up beside them and he read their legends: "Main South Road" and "Mount Moon."

The air was lively with the sound of grasshoppers. Its touch was fresh and invigorating. A tall young man wearing a brown jacket and grey trousers came round the car to meet him. "Mr. Alleyn? I'm Fabian Losse." He took a mail-bag from the driver, who had already begun to unload Alleyn's luggage, and a large box of stores for Mount Moon. The service car drove away to the south in its attendant cloud of dust. Alleyn and Losse took the road to Mount Moon.

ii

"It's a relief to me that you've come, sir," said Losse after they had driven in silence for some minutes. "I hope I haven't misled you with my dark hints of espionage. They had to be dark, you know, because they are based entirely on conjecture. Personally I find the whole theory of espionage dubious, indeed I don't believe in it for a moment. But I used it as bait."

"Does anyone believe in it!"

"My deceased aunt's nephew, Douglas Grace, urges it passionately. He wanted to come and meet you in order to press his case, but I thought I'd get in first. After all it was I who wrote to you and not Douglas."

The road they had taken was rough, little more than a pair of wheel tracks separated by a tussocky ridge. It ran up to the foot-hills of the eastern mountains and skirted them. Far to the west now, midway across the plateau, Alleyn could still see the service car, a clouded point of movement driving south.

"I didn't expect you to come," said Fabian Losse.

"No!"

"No. Of course I wouldn't have known anything about you if Flossie herself hadn't told me. That's rather a curious thought, isn't it? Horrible in a way. It was not long before it happened that you met, was it? I remember her returning from her lawful parliamentary occasions (you knew of course that she was an M.P.) full of the meeting and of dark hints about your mission in this country. 'Of course I tell you nothing that you shouldn't know but if you imagine there are no fifth columnists in this country . . .' I think she expected to be put on some secret convention but as far as I know that never came off. Did she invite you to Mount Moon?"

"Yes. It was extremely kind of her. Unfortunately, at the moment . . ."

"I know, I know. More pressing business. We pictured you in a false beard, dodging round geysers."

Alleyn grinned. "You can eliminate the false beard, at least," he said.

"But not the geysers? However, curiosity, as Flossie would have said, is the most potent weapon in the fifth-column armoury. Flossie was my aunt by marriage, you know," Fabian added unexpectedly. "Her husband, the ever-patient Arthur, was my blood uncle, if that's the correct expression. He survived her by six months. Curious, isn't it? In spite of his chronic endocarditis, Flossie, alive, did him no serious damage. Dead, she polished him off completely. I hope you don't think me very heartless."

"I was wondering," Alleyn murmured, "if Mrs. Rubrick's death was a shock only to her husband."

"Well, hardly that," Fabian began and then glanced sharply at his guest. "You mean you think that because I'm suffering from shock I adopt a gay ruthlessness to mask my lacerated nerves?" He drove for a few moments in silence and then, speaking very rapidly and on a high note, he said: "If your aunt-by-marriage turned up in a highly compressed state in the middle of a wool bale, would you be able to pass it off with the most accomplished *sang-froid?* Or wouldn't you? Perhaps, in your profession, you would." He waited and then said very quickly, as if he uttered an indecency, "I had to identify her."

"Don't you think," Alleyn said, "that this is a good moment to tell me the whole story, from the beginning?"

"That was my idea, of course. Do forgive me. I'm afraid my instinct is to regard you as omniscience itself. An oracle. To be consulted rather than informed. How much, by the way, do you know?"

Alleyn, who had had his share of precious young moderns, wondered if this particular specimen was habitually so disjointed in speech and manner. He knew that Fabian Losse had seen war service. He wondered what had sent him to New Zealand and whether, as Fabian himself had suggested, he was, in truth, suffering from shock.

"I mean," Fabian was saying, "it's no use my filling you up with vain repetitions."

"When I decided to come," said Alleyn, "I naturally looked up the case. On my way here I had an exhaustive session with Sub-Inspector Jackson who, as of course you know, is the officer in charge of the investigation."

"All he was entitled to do," said Fabian with some heat, "was to burst into sobs and turn away his face. Did he, by any chance, show you his notes?"

"I was given full access to the files."

"I couldn't be more sorry for you. And I must say that in comparison with the files even my account may seem a model of lucidity."

"At any rate," said Alleyn placidly, "let's have it. Pretend I've heard nothing."

He waited while Fabian, driving at fifty miles an hour, lit a cigarette, striking the match across the windscreen and shaking it out carefully before throwing it into the dry tussock.

"On the evening of the last Thursday in January, 1942," he began, with the air of repeating something he had memorized, "my aunt by marriage, Florence Rubrick, together with Arthur Rubrick (her husband and my uncle), Douglas Grace (her own nephew), Miss Terence Lynne, her secretary, Miss Ursula Harme, her ward, and me, sat on the tennis lawn at Mount Moon and made arrangements for a patriotic gathering to be held, ten days later, in the wool-shed. In addition to being our member, Flossie was also president of a local rehabilitation committee, set up by herself, to propagate the gospel of turning good soldiers into bewildered farmers. The meeting was to be given tea, beer, and a dance. Flossie, stationed on an improvised rostrum hard by the wool press, was to address them for three quarters of an hour. She was a remorseless orator, was Flossie. This she planned, sitting in a deck-chair on the tennis lawn. It may give you some idea of her character when I tell you she began with the announcement that in ten minutes she was going to the wool-shed to try her voice. We were exhausted. The evening was stiflingly hot. Flossie, who was fond of saying she thought best when walking, had marched us up and down the rose garden and had not spared us the glass-houses and the raspberry canes. Wan with heat, and already exhausted by an after-dinner set of tennis, we had trotted at her heels, unwilling acolytes. During this promenade she had worn a long diaphanous coat garnished with two diamond clips. When we were at last allowed to sit down, Flossie, heated with exercise and embryonic oratory, had peeled off this garment and thrown it over the back of her deck-chair. Some twenty minutes later, when she was about to resume the garment, one of the diamond clips was missing. Douglas, blast him, discovered the loss while he was helping Flossie into her coat and, like a damned officious booby, immediately came over all efficient and said we'd all look for it. With fainting hearts we suffered ourselves to be organized into a search-party; this one to the rose beds, that to the cucumber frames. My lot fell among the vegetable marrows. Flossie, encouraged by Douglas, was most insistent that we separate and cover the ground exhaustively. She had the infernal cheek to announce that she was going off to the wool-shed to practise her speech and was not to be disturbed. She marched off down a long path, bordered with lavender, and that, as far as we know, was the last time she was seen alive."

Fabian paused, looked at Alleyn out of the corners of his eyes, and inhaled a deep draught of smoke. "I had forgotten the classic exception," he said. "The last time she was seen alive, except by her murderer. She turned up some three weeks later at Messrs. Riven Brothers' wool store, baled up among the Mount Moon fleeces, poor thing. Did I forget to say we were shearing at the time of her disappearance? But of course you know all that."

"You followed her instructions about hunting for the clip?"

Fabian did not answer immediately. "With waning enthusiasm, on my part, at least," he said. "But, yes. We hunted for about forty-five minutes. Just as it was getting too dark to continue, the clip was found by Arthur, her husband, in a clump of zinnias that he had already ransacked a dozen times. Faint with our search, we returned to the house and the others drank whisky-and-sodas in the dining room. Unfortunately I'm not allowed alcohol. Ursula Harme hurried away to return the clip to Flossie. The wool-shed was in darkness. She was not in her drawing-room or her study. When Ursula went up to her bedroom she was confronted by a poisonously arch little notice that Flossie was in the habit of hanging on her door handle when she didn't want to be disturbed.

> *Please don't knock upon my door,*
> *The only answer is a snore.*

"Disgusted but not altogether surprised, Ursula stole away but not before she had scribbled the good news on a piece of paper and slipped it under the door. She returned and told us what she had done. We went to our beds believing Flossie to be in hers. Shall I go on, sir?"

"Please do."

"Flossie was to leave at the crack of dawn for the mail car, thence by train and ferry she was to travel to the seat of government where normally she would arrive, full of kick and drive, the following morning. On the eve of these departures she always retired early and woe betide the wretch who disturbed her."

The track descended into a shingle bed, and the car splashed through a clear race of water. They had drawn nearer to the foot-hills and now the mountains themselves were close above them. Between desultory boulders and giant tussocks, coloured like torches in sunlight, patches of bare earth lay ruddy in the late afternoon light. In the distance, spires of Lombardy poplars appeared above the naked curve of a hill and, beyond them, a twist of blue smoke.

"Nobody got up on the following morning to see Flossie off," said Fabian. "The mail car goes through at half-past five. It's a kind of local arrangement. A farmer eight miles up the road from here runs it. He goes down to the Forks three times a week and links up with the government mail car that you caught. Tommy Johns, the manager, usually drove her down to the front gate to catch it. She used to ring up his cottage when she was ready to start. When he didn't hear from her, he says, he thought one of us had taken her. That's what he says," Fabian repeated. "He thought one of us had taken her and didn't bother. We, of course, never doubted that she had been driven down by him. It was all very neat when you come to think of it. Nobody worried about Flossie. We imagined her happily popping in and out of secret sessions and bobbing up and down at the Speaker. She'd told Arthur she had something to say in open debate. He tuned in to the House of Representatives and appeared to be disappointed when he didn't hear his wife taking her usual energetic part in the interjections of 'What about yourself?' and 'Sit down' which are so characteristic of the parry and riposte of our parliamentary debates. Flossie, we decided, must be holding her fire. On the day she was supposed to have left here the communal wool lorry arrived and collected our bales. I watched them load up."

A shower of pebbles spattered on the windscreen as they lurched through the dry bed of a creek. Fabian dropped his cigarette on the floor and ground it out with his heel. The knuckles of his hands showed white as he changed his grip on the wheel. He spoke more slowly and with less affectation.

"I watched the lorry go down the drive. It's a long stretch. Then I saw it turn into this road and lurch through this race. There was more water in the race then. It fanned up and shone in the sunlight. Look. You can see the wool-shed now. A long building with an iron roof. The house is out of sight, behind the trees. Can you see the shearing shed?"

"Yes. How far away is it?"

"About four miles. Everything looks uncannily close in this air. We'll pull up if you don't mind, I'd rather like to get this finished before we arrive."

"By all means."

When they stopped the smell and sounds of the plateau blew freshly in at the windows; the smell of sun-warmed tussock and earth and lichen, the sound of grasshoppers and, far away up the hill-side, the multiple drone of a mob of sheep in transit, a dream-like sound.

"Not," said Fabian, "that there's very much more to say. The first inkling we had that anything was wrong came on the fifth evening after she had walked down the lavender path. It took the form of a telegram from one of her brother M.P.'s. He wanted to know why she hadn't come up for the debate. It gave one the most extraordinarily empty and helpless feeling. We thought, at first, that for some reason she'd changed her mind and not left the South Island. Arthur rang up her club and some of her friends in town. Then he rang up her lawyers. She had an appointment with them and hadn't kept it. They understood it was about her will. She was prolific of codicils and was always adding bits about what Douglas was to do with odds and ends of silver and jewelry. Then a little procession of discoveries came along. Terry Lynne found Flossie's suitcase, ready packed, stowed away at the back of a cupboard. Her purse with her travel pass and money was in a drawer of her dressing table. Then Tommy Johns said he hadn't taken her to the mail car. Then the search-parties, beginning in a desultory sort of way and gradually getting more organized and systematic.

"The Moon River runs through a gorge beyond the homestead. Flossie sometimes walked up there in the evening. She said it helped her, God save the mark, to think. When, finally, the police were brought in, they fastened like limpets upon this bit of information and, after hunting about the cliff for hours at a time, waited for poor Flossie to turn up ten miles down-stream where there is a backwash or something. They were still waiting when the foreman at Riven's wool store made his unspeakable discovery. By that time the trail was cold. The wool-shed had been cleaned out, the shearers had moved on, heavy rains had fallen, nobody could remember with any degree of accuracy the events of the fatal evening. Your colleagues of our inspired detective force are still giving an unconvincing impersonation of hounds with nose to ground. They return at intervals and ask us the same questions all over again. That's all really. Or is it?"

"It's a very neat résumé at all events," said Alleyn. "But I'm afraid I shall have to imitate my detested colleagues and ask a great many questions."

"I am resigned."

"Good. First, then, is your household unchanged since Mrs. Rubrick's death?"

"Arthur died of heart trouble three months after she disappeared. We've acquired a housekeeper, an elderly cousin of Arthur's, called Mrs. Aceworthy, who quarrels with the outside men and preserves the proprieties between the two girls, Douglas and myself. Otherwise there's been no change."

"Yourself," said Alleyn, counting. "Captain Grace, who is Mrs. Rubrick's nephew, Miss Ursula Harme, her ward, and Miss Terence Lynne, her secretary. What about servants?"

"A cook, Mrs. Duck, if you'll believe me, who has been at Mount Moon for fifteen years, and a man-servant Markins, whom Flossie acquired in a fashion to be related hereafter. He's a phenomenon. Men-servants are practically non-existent in this country."

"And what about the outside staff at that time? As far as I can remember there was Mr. Thomas Johns, the manager, his wife and his son Cliff, an odd man—is roustabout the right word?—called Albert Black, three shepherds, five visiting shearers, a wool classer, three boys, two gardeners, a cow-man and a station cook. Right?"

"Correct, even to the cow-man. I need tell you nothing, I see."

"On the night of the disappearance, the shearers, the

gardeners, the boys, the station cook, the classer, the shepherds and the cow-man were all at an entertainment held some fifteen miles away?"

"Dance at the Social Hall, Lakeside. It's across the flat on the main road," said Fabian, jerking his head at the vast emptiness of the plateau. "Arthur let them take the station lorry. We had more petrol in those days."

"That leaves the house-party, the Johns family, Mrs. Duck, the roustabout, and Markins?"

"Exactly."

Alleyn clasped his long hands round his knee and turned to his companion. "Now, Mr. Losse," he said tranquilly, "will you tell me exactly why you asked me to come?"

Fabian beat his open palm against the driving wheel. "I told you in my letter. I'm living in a nightmare. Look at the place. Our nearest neighbour's ten miles up the road. What do you think it feels like? And when in January shearing came round again, there were the same men, the same routine, the same long evenings, the same smell of lavender and honeysuckle and oily wool. We're crutching now and getting it all over again. The shearers talk about it. They stop when any of us come up, but every smoke-oh and every time they knock off it's The Murder. What a beastly soft noise the word makes. They're using the wool press of course. The other evening I caught one of the boys that sweep up the crutchings squatting in the press while the other packed a fleece round him. Experimenting. God, I gave them a fright, the little bastards." He swung round and confronted Alleyn. "We don't talk about it. We've clamped down on it now for six months. That's bad for all of us. It's interfering with my work. I'm doing nothing."

"Your work. Yes, I was coming to that."

"I suppose the police told you."

"I'd heard already at Army Headquarters. It overlaps my job out here."

"I suppose so," said Fabian. "Yes, of course."

"You realize, don't you, that I'm out here on a specific job? I'm here to investigate the possible leakage of information to the enemy. My peace-time job as a C.I.D. man has nothing to do with my present employment. But for the suggestion that Mrs. Rubrick's death may have some connection with our particular problem I should not have come. It's with the knowledge and at the invitation of my colleagues that I'm here."

"I got a rise with my bait then," said Fabian. "What did you think of my brain child?"

"They showed me the blueprints. Beyond me, of course. I'm not a gunner. But I could at least appreciate its importance and also the extreme necessity of keeping your work secret. It is from that point of view, I believe, that the suggestion of espionage has cropped up?"

"Yes. To my mind it's an absurd suggestion. We work in a room that is locked when we're not in it and the papers and gear—any of them that matter—are always shut up in a safe."

"We?"

"Douglas Grace has worked with me. He's done the practical stuff. My side is purely theoretical. I was at Home when war broke out and took an inglorious part in the now mercifully forgotten Norwegian campaign. I picked up rheumatic fever but, with an extraordinarily bad sense of timing, got back into active service just in time to get a crack on the head at Dunkirk." Fabian paused for a moment as if he had been about to say something further but now changed his mind. "Ah well," he said, "there it was. Later on still when I was supposed to be fairly fit they put me into a special show in England. That's when I got the germ of the idea. I cracked up again rather thoroughly and they kicked me out for good. While I was still too groggy to defend myself, Flossie, who was Home on a visit, bore down upon me and conceived the idea of bringing her poor English nephew-in-law back with her to recuperate in this country. She said she was used to looking after invalids, meaning poor old Arthur's endocarditis. I started messing about with my notion soon after I got here."

"And her own nephew? Captain Grace?"

"He was actually taking an engineering course at Heidelberg in 1939 but he left on the advice of some of his German friends and returned to England. May I take this opportunity of assuring you that Douglas is not in the pay of Hitler or any of his myrmidons, a belief ardently nursed, I feel sure, by Sub-Inspector Jackson. He enlisted when he got to England, was transferred to a New Zealand unit, and was subsequently pinked in the bottom by the Luftwaffe in Greece. Flossie hauled him in as soon as he was demobilized. He used to work here as a cadet in his school holidays. He's always been good with his hands. He'd got a small precision lathe and some useful instruments. I pulled him in. It's Douglas who's got this bee in his bonnet. He will insist that in some fantastic way his Auntie Flossie's death is mixed up with our eggbeater, which is what we ambiguously call our magnetic fuse."

"Why does he think so?"

Fabian did not answer.

"Has he any data—" Alleyn began.

"Look here, sir," said Fabian abruptly. "I've got a notion for your visit. It may not appeal to you. In fact you may dismiss it as the purest tripe, but here it is. You're full of official information about the whole miserable show, aren't you? All those files! You know, for example, that any one of us could have left the garden and gone to the shearing shed. You may even have gathered that apart from protracted irritation, which God knows may be sufficient motive, none of us had any reason for killing Flossie. We were a tolerably happy collection of people. Flossie bossed us about but more or less we went our own way." He paused and added unexpectedly: "Most of us. Very well. It seems to me that, as Flossie was murdered, there was something about Flossie that only one of us knew. Something monstrous. I mean something monstrously out of the character that I, for one, have conceived of as being 'Flossie Rubrick'—something murder-worthy. Now that something may not appear in any one of the Flossies that each of us has formed for his or her self, but to a newcomer, an expert, might it not appear in the collective Flossie that emerges from all these units put together? Or am I talking unadulterated bilge?"

Alleyn said carefully: "Women have been murdered for some chance intrusion upon other people's affairs, some idiotic blunder that has nothing to do with character."

"Yes. But in the mind of the murderer of such a victim she is forever The Intruder. If he could be persuaded to talk of his victim, don't you feel that something of that aspect of her character in his mind would come out? To a sensitive observer?"

"I'm a policeman in a strange country," said Alleyn. "You mustn't try me too high."

"At any rate," said Fabian with an air of relief that was unexpectedly naïve, "you're not laughing at me."

"Of course not, but I don't fully understand you."

"The official stuff has been useless. It's a year old. It's just a string of uncorrelated details. For what it's worth you've got it in these precious files. It doesn't give you a picture of a Flossie Rubrick who was murder-worthy."

"You know," said Alleyn cheerfully, "that's only another way of saying there was no apparent motive."

"All right. I'm being too elaborate. Put it this way. If factual evidence doesn't produce a motive, isn't it at least possible that something might come out of our collective idea of Flossie?"

"If it could be discovered."

"Well, but couldn't it?" Fabian was now earnest and persuasive. Alleyn began to wonder if he had been very profoundly disturbed by his experience and was indeed a little unhinged. "If we could get them all together and start them talking, couldn't you, an expert, coming fresh to the situation, get something? By the colour of our voices, by our very evasions? Aren't those signs that a man with your training would be able to read? Aren't they?"

"They are signs," Alleyn replied, trying not to sound too patient, "that a man with my training learns to treat with extreme reserve. They are not evidence."

"No, but taken in conjunction with the evidence, such as it is?"

"They can't be disregarded, certainly."

Fabian said fretfully: "But I want you to get a picture of Flossie in the round. I don't want you to have only my idea of her, which, truth to tell, is of a maddeningly arrogant piece of efficiency, but Ursula's idea of a wonder-woman, Douglas' idea of a manageable and not unprofitable aunt, Terence's idea of an exacting employer—all these. But I didn't mean to give you an inkling. I wanted you to hear for yourself, to start cold."

"You say you haven't spoken of her for six months. How am I to break the spell?"

"Isn't it part of your job," Fabian asked impatiently, "to be a corkscrew?"

"Lord help us," said Alleyn good-humouredly, "I suppose it is."

"Well then!" cried Fabian triumphantly. "Here's a fair field with me to back you up. And, you know, I don't believe it's going to be so difficult. I believe they must be in much the same case as I am. It took a Herculean effort to write that letter. If I could have grabbed it back, I would have done so. I can't tell you how much I funked the idea of starting this conversation, but, you see, now I have started there's no holding me."

"Have you warned them about this visitation?"

"I talked grandly about 'an expert from a special branch.' I said you were a high-up who'd been lent to this country. They know your visit is official and that the police and hush-hush birds have a hand in it. Honestly, I don't think that alarms them much. At first, I suppose, each of us was afraid—personally afraid, I mean, afraid that we should be suspected. But I don't think we four ever suspected each other. In that one thing we are agreed. And, would you believe it, as the weeks went on and the police interrogation persisted, we got just plain bored. Bored to exhaustion. Bored to the last nerve. Then it stopped, and instead of Flossie's death fading a bit, it grew into a bogey that none of us talked about. We could see each other thinking of it and a nightmarish sort of watching game set in. In a funny kind of way I think they were relieved when I told them what I'd done. They know of course that your visit has something to do with our X Adjustment."

"So they also know about your X Adjustment?"

"Only very vaguely, except Douglas. Just that it's rather special. That couldn't be helped."

Alleyn stared out at the clear and uncompromising landscape. "It's a rum go," he said, and after a moment: "Have you thought carefully about this? Do you realize you're starting something you may want to stop and—not be able to stop?"

"I've thought about it *ad nauseam*."

"I think I ought to warn you. I'm a bit of state machinery.

Anyone can start me up but only the state can switch me off."

"O.K."

"Well," Alleyn said, "you have been warned."

"At least," said Fabian, "I'll give you a good dinner."

"Then you're my host?"

"Oh, yes. Didn't you know? Arthur left Mount Moon to me and Flossie left her money to Douglas. You might say we were joint hosts," said Fabian.

iii

Mount Moon homestead was eighty years old and that is a great age for a house in the Antipodes. It had been built by Arthur Rubrick's grandfather, from wood transported over the Pass in bullock wagons. It was originally a four-roomed cottage, but room after room had been added, at a rate about twice as slow as that achieved by the intrepid Mrs. Rubrick of those days in adding child after child to her husband's quiver. The house bore a dim family resemblance to the Somersetshire seat which Arthur's grandfather had thankfully relinquished to a less adventurous brother. Victorian gables and the inevitable conservatory, together with lesser family portraits and surplus pieces of furniture, traced unmistakably the family's English origin. The garden had been laid out in a nostalgic mood, at considerable expense and with a bland disregard for the climate of the plateau. Of the trees old Rubrick had planted, only Lombardy poplars, *Pinus insignis* and a few natives had flourished. The tennis lawn, carved out of the tussocky hill-side, turned yellow and dusty during summer. The pleached walks of Somerset had been in part realized with hardy ramblers and, where these failed, with clipped fences of poplar. The dining-room windows looked down upon a queer transformation of what had been originally an essentially English conception of a well-planned garden. But beyond this unconvincing piece of *pastiche*—what uncompromising vastness! The plateau swam away into an illimitable haze of purple, its boundaries mingled with clouds. Above the cloud, suspended it seemed in a tincture of rose, floated the great mountains.

At dinner, that first night, Alleyn witnessed the pageant of nightfall on the plateau. He saw the horn of the Cloud Piercer shine gold and crimson long after the hollows of the lesser alps, as though a dark wine poured into them, had filled with shadow. He felt the night air of the mountains enter the house and was glad to smell newly lit wood in the open fire-places.

He considered once again the inmates of the home.

Seen by candlelight round the dining-room table they seemed, with the exception of the housekeeper-chaperon, extremely young. Terence Lynne, an English girl who had been Florence Rubrick's secretary, was perhaps the oldest, though her way of dressing her hair may have given him this impression. It swept, close-fitting as a cap, in two black wings from a central parting to a knot at the nape of her neck, giving her the look of a *coryphée*, an impression that was not contradicted by the extreme, the almost complacent, neatness of her dress. This was black, with crisp lawn collar and cuffs. Not quite an evening dress, but he felt that, unlike the two young men, Miss Lynne changed punctiliously every night. Her hands were long and white and it was a shock to learn that since her employer's death she had returned to Mount Moon as a kind of land girl, or more accurately, as he was to learn later, a female gardener. Some hint of her former employment still hung about her. She had an air of responsibility and was, he thought, a trifle mousy.

Ursula Harme was an enchanting girl, slim, copper-haired and extremely talkative. On his arrival Alleyn had encountered her stretched out on the tennis lawn wearing a brief white garment and dark glasses. She at once began to speak of England, sketching modish pre-war gaieties and asking him which of the night clubs had survived the blitz. She had been in England with her guardian, she said, when war broke out. Her uncle, now fighting in the Middle East, had urged her to return with Mrs. Rubrick to New Zealand, and Mount Moon.

"I am a New Zealander," said Miss Harme, "but all my relations—I haven't any close relations except my uncle— live in England. Aunt Flossie—she wasn't really an aunt but I called her that—was better than any real relation could have been."

She was swift in her movements and had the silken air of a girl who is, beyond argument, attractive. Alleyn thought her restless and noticed that, though she looked gay and brilliant when she talked, her face in repose was watchful. Though, during dinner, she spoke most readily to Douglas Grace, her eyes more often were for Fabian Losse.

The two men were well contrasted. Everything about Fabian Losse—his hollow temples and his nervous hands, his lightly waving hair—was drawn delicately with a sharp pencil. But Captain Grace was a magnificent fellow with a fine moustache, a sleek head and large eyes. His accent was slightly antipodean, but his manners were formal. He called Alleyn "sir" each time he spoke to him and was inclined to pin a rather meaningless little laugh on the end of his remarks. He seemed to Alleyn to be an extremely conventional young man.

Mrs. Aceworthy, Arthur Rubrick's elderly cousin who had come to Mount Moon on the death of his wife, was a large sandy woman with an air of uncertain authority and a tendency to bridle. Her manner towards Alleyn was cautious. He thought that she disapproved of his visit and he wondered how much Fabian Losse had told her. She spoke playfully and in quotation marks of "my family" and seemed to show a preference for the two New Zealanders, Douglas Grace and Ursula Harme.

The vast landscape outside darkened and the candles on the dining-room table showed ghostly in the uncurtained window-panes. When dinner was over they all moved into a comfortable, conglomerate sort of room hung with faded photographs of past cadets and lit cosily by a kerosene lamp. Mrs. Aceworthy, with a vague murmur about "having to see to things," left them with their coffee.

Above the fire-place hung the full-dress portrait of a woman.

It was a formal painting. The bare arms, executed with machine-like precision, flowed wirily from shoulders to clasped hands. The dress was of mustard-coloured satin, very *décolleté*, and this line was repeated in the brassy high lights of Mrs. Rubrick's incredibly golden *coiffure*. The painter had dealt remorselessly with a formidable display of jewelry. It was an Academy portrait by an experienced painter, but his habit of flattery had met its Waterloo in Florence Rubrick's face. No trick of understatement could soften that large mouth, closed with difficulty over protuberant teeth, or modify the acquisitive glare of the pale goiterous eyes which evidently had been fixed on the artist's and therefore appeared, as laymen will say, to "follow one about the room." Upon each of the five persons seated in Arthur Rubrick's study did his wife Florence seem to fix her arrogant and merciless stare.

There was no other picture in the room. Alleyn looked round for a photograph of Arthur Rubrick but could find none that seemed likely.

The flow of talk, which had run continuously if not quite easily throughout dinner, was now checked. The pauses grew longer and their interruptions more forced. Fabian Losse began to stare expectantly at Alleyn. Douglas Grace sang discordantly under his breath. The two girls fidgeted, caught each other's eyes and looked away again.

Alleyn, sitting in shadow a little removed from the fireside group, said: "That's a portrait of Mrs. Rubrick, isn't it?"

It was as if he had gathered up the reins of a team of nervously expectant horses. He saw by their startled glances at the portrait that custom had made it invisible to them, a mere piece of furniture of which, for all its ghastly associations, they were normally unaware. They stared at it now rather stupidly, gaping a little.

Fabian said: "Yes. It was painted ten years ago. I don't need to tell you it's by a determined Academician. Rather a pity, really. John would have made something terrific out of Flossie. Or, better still, Agatha Troy."

Alleyn, who was married to Agatha Troy, said: "I only saw Mrs. Rubrick for a few minutes. Is it a good likeness?"

Fabian and Ursula Harme said: "No." Douglas Grace and Terence Lynne said: "Yes."

"Hullo!" said Alleyn. "A divergence of opinion?"

"It doesn't give you any idea of how tiny she was," said Douglas Grace, "but I'd call it a speaking likeness."

"Oh, it's a conscientious map of her face," said Fabian.

"It's a caricature," cried Ursula Harme. Her eyes were

fixed indignantly on the portrait.

"I should have called it an unblushing understatement," said Fabian. He was standing before the fire, his hands on the mantelpiece. Ursula Harme turned to look at him, knitting her brows. Alleyn heard her sigh as if Fabian had wakened some old controversy between them.

"And there's no vitality in it, Fabian," she said anxiously. "You must admit that. I mean she was a much more splendid person than that. So marvellously alive." She caught her breath at the unhappy phrase. "She made you feel like that about her," she added. "The portrait gives you nothing of it."

"I don't pretend to know anything about painting," said Douglas Grace, "but I do know what I like."

"Would you believe it?" Fabian murmured under his breath. He said aloud: "Is it so great a merit, Ursy, to be marvellously alive? I find unbounded vitality very unnerving."

"Not if it's directed into suitable channels," pronounced Grace.

"But hers was. Look what she did!" said Ursula.

"She was extraordinarily public-spirited, you know," Grace agreed. "I must say I took my hat off to her for that. She had a man's grasp of things." He squared his shoulders and took a cigar case out of his pocket. "Not that I admire managing women," he said, sitting down by Miss Lynne, "but Auntie Floss was a bit of a marvel. You've got to hand it to her, you know."

"Apart from her work as an M.P.?" Alleyn suggested.

"Yes, of course," said Ursula, still watching Fabian Losse. "I don't know why we're talking about her, Fabian, unless it's for Mr. Alleyn's information."

"You may say it is," said Fabian.

"Then I think he ought to know what a splendid sort of person she was."

Fabian did an unexpected thing. He reached out his long arm and touched her lightly on the cheek. "Go ahead, Ursy," he said gently. "I'm all for it."

"Yes," she cried out, "but you don't believe."

"Never mind. Tell Mr. Alleyn."

"I thought," said Douglas Grace, "that Mr. Alleyn was here to make an expert investigation. I shouldn't think our ideas of Aunt Florence are likely to be of much help. He wants facts."

"But you'll all talk to him about her," said Ursula, "and you won't be fair."

Alleyn stirred a little in his chair in the shadows. "I should be vey glad if you'd tell me about her, Miss Harme," he said. "Please do."

"Yes, Ursy," said Fabian. "We want you to. Please do."

She looked brilliantly from one to another of her companions. "But—it seems so queer. It's months since we spoke of her. I'm not at all good at expressing myself. Are you serious, Fabian? Is it important?"

"I think so."

"Mr. Alleyn?"

"I think so too. I want to start with the right idea of your guardian. Mrs. Rubrick was your guardian, wasn't she?"

"Yes."

"So you must have known her very well."

"I think I did. Though we didn't meet until I was thirteen."

"I should like to hear how that came about."

Ursula leant forward, resting her bare arms on her knees and clasping her hands. She moved into the region of fire-light.

"You see—" she began.

CHAPTER II

ACCORDING TO URSULA

Ursula began haltingly with many pauses but with a certain air of championship. At first, Fabian helped her, making a conversation rather than a solo performance of the business. Douglas Grace, sitting beside Terence Lynne, sometimes spoke to her in a low voice. She had taken up a piece of knitting and the click of her needles lent a domestic note to the scene, a note much at variance with her sleek and burnished appearance. She did not reply to Grace, but once Alleyn saw her mouth flicker in a smile. She had small sharp teeth.

As Ursula grew into her narrative she became less uneasy, less in need of Fabian's support, until presently she could speak strongly, eager to draw her portrait of Florence Rubrick.

A firm picture took shape. A schoolgirl, bewildered and desolated by news of her mother's death, sat in the polished chilliness of a head-mistress's drawing-room. "I'd known ever since the morning. They'd arranged for me to go home by the evening train. They were very kind but they were too tactful, too careful not to say the obvious thing. I didn't want tact and delicacy, I wanted warmth. Literally, I was shivering. I can hear the sound of the horn now. It was the sort that chimes like bells. She brought it out from England. I saw the car slide past the window, and then I heard her voice in the hall asking for me. It's years ago but I can see her as clearly as if it was yesterday. She wore a fur cape and smelt lovely and she hugged me and talked loudly and cheerfully and said she was my guardian and had come for me and that she was my mother's greatest friend and had been with her when it happened. Of course I knew all about her. She was my godmother. But she stayed in England when she married after the last war and when she returned we lived too far away to visit. So I'd never seen her. So I went away with her. My other guardian is an English uncle. He's a soldier and follows the drum, and he was very glad when Aunt Florence (that's what I called her) took hold. I stayed with her until it was time to go back to school. She used to come during term and that was marvellous."

The picture sharpened on a note of adolescent devotion. There had been the year when Auntie Florence returned to England but wrote occasionally and caused sumptuous presents to be sent from London stores. She reappeared when Ursula was sixteen and ready to leave school.

"It was heaven. She took me Home with her. We had a house in London and she brought me out and presented me and everything. It was wizard. She gave a dance for me." Ursula hesitated. "I met Fabian at that dance, didn't I, Fabian?"

"It was a great night," said Fabian. He had settled on the floor; his back was propped against the side of her chair and his thin knees were drawn up to his chin. He had lit a pipe.

"And then," said Ursula, "it was September 1939 and Uncle Arthur began to say we'd better come out to New Zealand. Auntie Florence wanted us to stay and get war jobs but he kept cabling for her to come."

Terence Lynne's composed voice cut across the narrative. "After all," she said, "he was her husband."

"Hear, hear!" said Douglas Grace and patted her knee.

"Yes, but she'd have been wonderful in a war job," said Ursula impatiently. "I always took rather a gloomy view of his insisting like that. I mean, it was a thought selfish. Doing without her would really have been his drop of war work."

"He'd had three months in a nursing home," said Miss Lynne without emphasis.

"I know, Terry, but all the same—Well, anyway, soon after Dunkirk he cabled again and out we came. I had rather thought of joining something but she was so depressed about leaving. She said I was too young to be alone and she'd be lost without me, so I came. I loved coming, of course."

"Of course," Fabian murmured.

"And there was you to be looked after on the voyage."

"Yes, I'd staged my collapse by that time. Ursula acted,"

Fabian said, turning his head towards Alleyn, "as a kind of buffer between my defencelessness and Flossie's zeal. Flossie had been a V.A.D. in the last war, and the mysteries had lain fallow in her for twenty years. I owe my reason if not my life to Ursula."

"You're not fair," she said, but with a certain softening of her voice. "You're ungrateful, Fab."

"Ungrateful to Flossie for plumping herself down in your affections like an amiable—no, not even an amiable— cuttlefish? But, go on, Ursy."

"I don't know how much time Mr. Alleyn has to spare for our reminiscences," began Douglas Grace, "but I must say I feel deeply sorry for him."

"I've any amount of time," said Alleyn, "and I'm extremely interested. So you all three arrived in New Zealand in 1940? Is that it, Miss Harme?"

"Yes. We came straight here. After London," said Ursula gaily, "it did seem rather hearty and primitive but, quite soon after we got here, the member for the district died and they asked her to stand and everything got exciting. That's when you came in, Terry, isn't it?"

"Yes," said Miss Lynne, clicking her needles. "That's where I came in."

"Auntie Floss was marvellous to me," Ursula continued. "You see, she had no children of her own, so I suppose I was rather special. Anyway she used to say so. You should have seen her at meetings, Mr. Alleyn. She loved being heckled. She was as quick as lightning and absolutely fearless, wasn't she, Douglas?"

"She certainly could handle them," agreed Grace. "She was up to her neck in it when I got back. I remember one meeting some woman shouted out: 'Do you think it's right for you to have cocktails and champagne when I can't afford to give my kiddies eggs?' Aunt Floss came back at her in a flash: 'I'll give you a dozen eggs for every alcoholic drink I've consumed.'"

"Because," Ursula explained, "she didn't drink, ever, and most of the people knew and clapped, and Aunt Florence said at once: 'That wasn't fair, was it? You didn't know about my humdrum habits.' And she said: 'If things are as bad as that you should apply to my Relief Supply Service. We send plenty of eggs in from Mount Moon.'" Ursula's voice ran down on a note of uncertainty. Douglas Grace cut in with his loud laugh. "And that woman shouted, 'I'd rather be without eggs,' and Aunt Floss said: 'Just as well perhaps while I'm on my soap-box.' And they roared with laughter."

"Parry and riposte," muttered Fabian. "Parry and riposte!"

"It was damned quick of her, Fabian," said Douglas Grace.

"And the kids continued eggless."

"That wasn't Aunt Florence's fault," said Ursula.

"All right, darling. My sympathies are with the woman but let it pass. I must say," Fabian added, "that in a sort of a way I rather enjoyed Floss's electioneering campaign."

"You don't understand the people in this country," said Grace. "We like it straight from the shoulder and Aunt Floss gave it to us that way. She had them eating out of her hand, didn't she, Terry?"

"She was very popular," said Terence Lynne.

"Did her husband take an active part in her public life?" asked Alleyn.

"It practically killed him," said Miss Lynne, clicking her needles.

ii

There was a flabbergasted silence and she continued sedately: "He went for long drives and sat on platforms and fagged about from one meeting to another. This house was never quiet. What with Red Cross and Women's Institute and E.P.S. and political parties, it was never quiet. Even this room, which was supposed to be his, was invaded."

"She was always looking after him," Ursula protested. "That's unfair, Terry. She looked after him marvellously."

"It was like being minded by a hurricane."

Fabian and Douglas laughed. "You're disloyal and cruel,"

Ursula flashed out at them. "I'm ashamed of you. To make her into a figure of fun! How you can when you, each of you, owed her so much."

Douglas Grace at one began to protest that this was unfair, that nobody could have been fonder of his aunt than he was, that he used to pull her leg when she was alive and that she liked it. He was flustered and affronted, and the others listened to him in an uncomfortable silence. "If we've got to talk about her," Douglas said hotly, "for God's sake let's be honest. We were all fond of her, weren't we?" Fabian hunched up his shoulders but said nothing. "We all took a pretty solid knock when she was murdered, didn't we? We all agreed that Fabian should ask Mr. Alleyn to come? All right. If we've got to hold a post-mortem on her character, which, personally, seems to me to be a waste of time, I suppose we're meant to say what we think."

"Certainly," said Fabian. "Unburden the bosom, work off the inhibitions. But it's Ursy's innings at the moment, isn't it?"

"You interrupted her, Fab."

"Did I? I'm sorry, Ursy," said Fabian gently. He slewed round, put his chin on the arm of her chair and looked up comically at her.

"I'm ashamed of you," she said uncertainly.

"Please go on. You'd got roughly to 1941 with Flossie in the full flush of her parliamentary career, you know. Here we were, Mr. Alleyn. Douglas, recovered from his wound but passed unfit for further service, going the rounds of a kind of superior Shepherd's Calendar. Terry, building up Flossie's prestige with copious shorthand notes and cross-references. Ursula—" He broke off for a moment. "Ursula provided enchantment," he said lightly, "and I comedy. I fell off horses and collapsed at high altitudes, and fainted into sheep-dips. Perhaps these antics brought me *en rapport* with my unfortunate uncle, who, at the same time, was fighting his own endocarditic battle. Carry on, Ursy."

"Carry on with what? What's the good of my trying to give my picture of her when you all—when you all—" Her voice wavered for a moment. "All right," she said more firmly. "The idea is that we each give our own account of the whole thing, isn't it? The same account that I've bleated out at dictation speed to that monumental bore from the detective's office. All right."

"One moment," said Alleyn's voice out of the shadows. He saw the four heads turn to him in the fire-light.

"There's this difference," he said. "If I know anything of police routine you were continually stopped by questions. At the moment I don't want to nail you down to an interrogation. I want you, if you can manage to do so, to talk about this tragedy as if you spoke of it for the first time. You realize, don't you, that I've not come here, primarily, to arrest a murderer. I've been sent to try and discover if this particular crime has anything to do with unlawful behaviour in time of war."

"Exactly," said Douglas Grace. "Exactly, sir. And in my humble opinion," he added, stroking the back of his hand, "it most undoubtedly has. However!"

"All in good time," said Alleyn. "Now, Miss Harme, you've given us a clear picture of a rather isolated little community up to, let us say, something over a year ago. At the close of 1941 Mrs. Rubrick is much occupied by her public duties with Miss Lynne as her secretary. Captain Grace is a cadet on this sheep station. Mr. Losse is recuperating and has begun, with Captain Grace's help, to do some very specialized work. Mr. Rubrick is a confirmed invalid. You are all fed by Mrs. Duck, the cook, and attended by Markins, the house-man. What are you doing?"

"Me?" Ursula shook her head impatiently. "I'm nothing in particular. Auntie Florence called me her A.D.C. I helped wherever I could and did my V.A.D. training in between. It was fun—something going to happen all the time. I adore that," cried Ursula. "To have events waiting for me like little presents in a treasure hunt. She made everything exciting, all her events were tied up in gala wrappings with red ribbon. It was heaven."

"Like the party that was to be held in the wool-shed?" asked Fabian dryly.

"Oh dear!" said Ursula, catching her breath. "Yes. Like that one. I remember—"

iii

The picture of that warm summer evening of fifteen months ago grew as she spoke of it. Alleyn, remembering his view through the dining-room window of a darkling garden, saw the shadowy company move along a lavender path and assemble on the lawn. The light dresses of the women glimmered in the dusk. Lance-like flames burned steadily as they lit cigarettes. They drew deck-chairs together. One of the women threw a coat of some thin texture over the back of her chair. A tall personable young man leant over the back in an attitude of somewhat studied gallantry. The smell of tobacco mingled with that of night-scented stocks and of earth and tussock that had not yet lost all warmth of the sun. It was the hour when sounds take on a significant clearness and the senses are sharpened to receive them. The voices of the party drifted vaguely yet profoundly across the dusk. Ursula could remember it very clearly.

"You must be tired, Aunt Florence," she had said.

"I don't let myself be tired," answered that brave voice. "One mustn't think about fatigue, Ursy, one must nurse a secret store of energy." And she spoke of Indian ascetics and their mastery of fatigue and of munition workers in England and of air wardens. "If they can do so much surely I, with my humdrum old routine, can jog along at a decent trot." She stretched out her bare arms and strong hands to the girls on each side of her. "And with my Second Brain and my kind little A.D.C. to back me up," she cried cheerfully, "what can I not do?"

Ursula slipped down to the warm dry grass and leant her cheek against her guardian's knee. Her guardian's vigorous fingers caressed rather thoroughly the hair which Ursula had been at some expense to have set on a three days' visit down-country.

"Let's make a plan," said Aunt Florence.

It was a phrase Ursula loved. It was the prelude to

adventure. It didn't matter that the plan was concerned with
nothing more exciting than a party in the wool-shed which
would be attended by back-countrymen and their women-
kind dressed unhappily in co-operative store clothes and by a
sprinkling of such run holders as had enough enthusiasm and
petrol to bring them many miles to Mount Moon. Aunt
Florence invested it all in a pink cloud of anticipation. Even
Douglas became enthusiastic and, leaning over the back of
Flossie's chair, began to make suggestions. Why not a dance?
he asked, looking at Terence Lynne. Florence agreed. There
would be a dance. Old Jimmy Wyke and his brothers, who
played accordions, must practise together and take turn
about with the radio-gramophone.

"You ought to take that old piano over from the annex,"
said Arthur Rubrick in his tired breathless voice, "and get
young Cliff Johns to join forces with the others. He's
extraordinarily good. Play anything. Listen to him, now."

It was an unfortunate suggestion, and Ursula felt the
caressing fingers stiffen. As she recalled this moment, fifteen
months later, for Alleyn, he heard her story recede
backwards, into the past, and this quality, he realized, would
be characteristic of all the stories he was to hear. They would
dive backwards from the moment on the lawn into the events
that foreshadowed it.

Ursula said she knew that Aunt Florence had been too
thoughtful to worry Uncle Arthur with the downfall of young
Cliff Johns. It was a story of the basest sort of ingratitude.
Young Cliff, son of the manager, Tommy Johns, had been an
unusual child. He had thrown his parents into a state of
confusion and dubiousness by his early manifestations of
aesthetic preferences, screaming and plugging his ears with
his fists when his mother sang, yet listening with complacency for long periods to certain instrumental programs on the
wireless. He had taken a similar line over pictures and books.
When he grew older and was collected in a lorry every
morning and taken to a minute pink-painted state school out
on the plateau, he developed a talent for writing florid
compositions, which changed their style with each new book
he read, and much too fast for the comprehension of his
teacher. His passion for music grew precociously and the
schoolmistress wrote to his parents saying that his talent was
exceptional. Her letter had an air of nervous enthusiasm. The

boy, she said bravely, was phenomenal. He was, on the other hand, bad at arithmetic and games and made no attempt to conceal his indifference to both.

Aunt Florence, hearing of this, took an interest in young Cliff, explaining to his reluctant parents that they were face to face with The Artistic Temperament.

"Now, Mrs. Johns," she said cheerfully, "you mustn't bully that boy of yours simply because he's different. He wants special handling and lots of sympathy. I've got my eye on him."

Soon after that she began to ask Cliff to the big house. She gave him books and a gramophone with carefully chosen records and she won him completely. When he was thirteen years old she told his bewildered parents that she wanted to send him to the nearest equivalent in this country of an English Public School. Tommy Johns raised passionate objections. He was an ardent trades-unionist, a working manager and a bit of a communist. But his wife, persuaded by Flossie, overruled him, and Cliff went off to boarding-school with sons of the six run holders scattered over the plateau.

His devotion to Florence, Ursula said, appeared to continue. In the holidays he spent a great deal of them with her and, having taken music lessons at her expense, played to her on the Bechstein in the drawing-room. At this point in Ursula's narrative, Fabian gave a short laugh.

"He plays very well," Ursula said. "Or does he?"

"Astonishingly well," Fabian agreed, and she said quickly: "She was very fond of music, Fab."

"Like Douglas," Fabian murmured, "she knew what she liked, but unlike Douglas she wouldn't own up to it."

"I don't know what you mean by that," said Ursula grandly and went on with her narrative.

Young Cliff continued at school when Florence went to England. He had full use of the Bechstein in the drawing-room during the holidays. She returned to find him a big boy but otherwise, it seemed, still docile under her patronage. But when he came home for his summer holidays at the end of 1941, he was changed, not, Ursula said emphatically, for the better. He had had trouble with his eyes and the school oculist had told him that he would never be accepted for active service. He had immediately broken bounds and attempted to enlist. On being turned down he wrote to

Florence saying that he wanted to leave school and, if possible, do a job of war work on the sheep run until he was old enough to get into the army, if only in a C3 capacity. He was now sixteen. This letter was a bomb-shell for Flossie. She planned a university career, followed, if the war ended soon enough, by a move to London and the Royal College of Music. She went to the manager's cottage with the letter in her hand, only to find that Tommy Johns also had heard from his son and was delighted. "We're going to need men on the land as we've never needed them before, Mrs. Rubrick. I'm very very pleased young Cliff looks at it that way. If you'll excuse me for saying so, I thought this posh education he's been getting would make a class-conscious snob of the boy, but, from what he tells me of his ideas, I see it's worked out different." For young Cliff, it appeared, was now a communist. Nothing could have been further removed from Flossie's plans.

When he appeared she could make no impression on him. He seemed to think that she alone would sympathize with his change of heart and plans and would support him. He couldn't understand her disappointment or, as he continued in his attitude, her mounting anger. He grew dogmatic and stubborn. The woman of forty-seven and the boy of sixteen quarrelled bitterly and strangely. It was a cruel thing for him to do, Ursula said, cruel and stupid. Aunt Florence was the most patriotic soul alive. Look at her war work. It wasn't as though he were old enough or fit for the army. The least he could do was to complete the education she had so generously planned and, in part, given him.

After their quarrel they no longer met. Cliff went out with the high-country musterers and continued in their company when they came in from the mountains behind droning mobs of sheep. He became very friendly with Albie Black, the roustabout. There was a rickety old piano in the bunk-house annex and in the evenings Cliff played it for the men. Their voices, singing "Waltzing Matilda" and strangely Victorian ballads, would drift across the yards and paddocks and reach the lawn where Flossie sat with her assembled forces every night after dinner. But on the night she disappeared his mate had gone to the dance and Cliff played, alone in the annex, strange music for that inarticulate old instrument.

"Listen to him, now," said Arthur Rubrick. "Remarkable

chap, that boy. You wouldn't believe that old hurdy-gurdy over there had as much music in it. Extraordinary. Sounds like a professional."

"Yes," Fabian agreed after a pause. "It's remarkable."

Ursula wished they wouldn't talk about Cliff. It would have been better to have told Uncle Arthur about the episode of the previous night, she thought, and let him deal with Cliff. Aunt Florence shouldn't have to cope with everything and this had hurt her so deeply.

For the previous night, Markins the man-servant, hearing furtive noises in the old dairy that now served as a cellar, and imagining them to be made by a rat, had crept up and flashed his torch in at the window. Its beam darted moth-like about dusty surfaces of bottles. There was a brief sound of movement. Markins sought it out with his light. Cliff Johns's face sprang out of the dark. His eyes were screwed up blindly and his mouth was open. Markins had described this very vividly. He had dipped the torch-beam until it discovered Cliff's hands. They were long and flexible hands and they grasped a bottle of Arthur's twenty-year-old whisky. As the light found them they opened and the bottle crashed on the stone floor. Markins, a taciturn man, darted into the dairy, grasped Cliff by his wrist and, without a word, lugged him unresisting into the kitchen. Mrs. Duck, outraged beyond measure, had instantly bustled off and fetched Mrs. Rubrick. The interview took place in the kitchen. It nearly broke Florence's heart, Ursula said. Cliff, who of course reeked of priceless whisky, said repeatedly that he had not been stealing, but would give no further explanation. In the meantime Markins had discovered four more bottles in a sugar bag, dumped round the corner of the dairy. Florence, naturally, did not believe Cliff, and in a mounting scene called him a sneak-thief and accused him of depravity and ingratitude. He broke into a white rage and stammered out an extraordinary arraignment of Florence, saying that she had tried to buy him and that he would never rest until he had returned every penny she had spent on his schooling. At this stage Florence sent Markins and Mrs. Duck out of the kitchen. The scene ended by Cliff rushing away, while Florence, weeping and shaking, sought out Ursula and poured out the whole story. Arthur Rubrick had been very unwell and they decided to tell him nothing of this incident.

Next morning—the day of her disappearance—Florence went to the manager's cottage only to be told that Cliff's bed had not been slept in and his town clothes were missing. His father had gone off in their car down the road to the Pass. At midday he returned with Cliff, whom he had overtaken at the cross-roads, dead-beat, having covered sixteen miles on the first stage down-country to the nearest army depot. Florence would tell Ursula nothing of her subsequent interview with Tommy Johns.

"So Uncle Arthur's suggestion on that same evening that Cliff should play at the dance came at rather a grim moment," said Ursula.

"The boy's a damned conceited pup if he's nothing worse," said Douglas Grace.

"And he's still here?" said Alleyn. Fabian looked round at him.

"Oh, yes. They won't have him in the army. He has something wrong with his eyes and anyway is ranked as doing an essential job on the place. The police got the whole story out of Markins, of course," said Fabian, "and, for want of a better suspect, concentrated on the boy. I expect he looms large in the files, doesn't he?"

"He peters out about half-way through."

"That's because he's the only member of the household who's got a sort of alibi. We all heard him playing the piano until just before the diamond clip was found, which was at five to nine. When he'd just started, at eight o'clock it was, Markins saw him in the annex, playing, and he never stopped for longer than half a minute or less. Incidentally, to the best of my belief, that's the last time young Cliff played on the piano in the annex, or on any other piano, for a matter of that. His mother, who was worried about him, went over to the annex and persuaded him to return with her to the cottage. There he heard the nine-o'clock news bulletin and listened to a program of classical music.

"You may think that was a bit thick," said Fabian. "I mean a bit too much in character with the sensitive young plant, but it's what he did. The previous night, you must remember, he'd had a snorting row with Flossie, and followed it up with a sixteen-mile hike and no sleep. He was physically and emotionally exhausted and dropped off to sleep in his chair. His mother got him to bed, and she and his father sat up until after midnight, talking about him. Before she turned in, Mrs. Johns looked at young Cliff and found him fathoms deep. Even the Detective-Sergeant saw that Flossie would have returned by midnight if she'd been alive. Sorry, Ursy dear, I interrupt continually. We are back on the lawn. Cliff's playing Bach on a piano that misses on six notes and Flossie's talking about the party in the shearing shed. Carry on."

Ursula and Florence had steered Arthur Rubrick away from Cliff, though the piano in the annex continued to remind them of him. Flossie began to plan her speech on post-war land settlement for soldiers. "There'll be no blunders this time," she declared. "The bill we're planning will see to that. A committee of experts." The phrases drifted out over the darkling garden. "Good country, properly stocked ... adequate equipment ... Soldiers Rehabilitation Fund ... I shall speak for twenty minutes before supper ..." But from what part of the wool-shed should she speak? Why not from the press itself? There would be a touch of symbolism in that, Flossie cried, taking fire. It would be from the press itself with an improvised platform across the top. She would be a dominant figure there. Perhaps, some extra lighting? "We must go and look!" she cried, jumping to her feet. That had always been her way with everything—no sooner said than done. She had tremendous driving power and enthusiasm. "I'm going to try my voice there—now. Give me my coat, Douglas darling." Douglas helped her into the diaphanous coat.

It was then that he discovered the loss of the diamond clip.

It had been a silver wedding present from Arthur, one of a pair. Its mate still twinkled on the left lapel of the coat. Flossie announced simply that it must be found, and Douglas organized her search party. "You'll see it quite easily," she told them, "by the glitter. I shall walk slowly to the shearing shed, looking as I go. I want to try my voice. Please don't interrupt me, any of you. I shan't get another chance and I must be in bed before ten. An early start in the morning. Look carefully, and mind you don't tread on it. Off you go."

To Ursula's lot had fallen a long path running down the right-hand side of the tennis lawn between hedges of clipped

poplars dense with summer foliage. This path divided the
tennis lawn from a farther lawn which extended from the
front along the south side of the house. This, also, was
bordered by a hedged walk where Terence Lynne hunted,
and beyond her again lay the kitchen gardens, allotted to
Fabian. To the left of the tennis lawn Douglas Grace moved
parallel with Ursula. Beyond him, Arthur Rubrick explored
a lavender path that led off at right angles through a flower
garden to a farther fence beyond which lay a cart track
leading to the manager's hut, the bunk-houses and the
shearing shed.

"No gossiping, now," said Flossie. "Be thorough."

She turned down the lavender path, moving slowly.
Ursula watched her go. The hills beyond her had now
darkened to a purple that was almost black, and, by the
blotting out of nearer forms, Flossie seemed to walk directly
into these hills until, reaching the end of the path, she turned
to the left and suddenly vanished.

Ursula walked round the top of the tennis-court, past the
front of the house, to her allotted beat between the two lawns.
The path was flanked by scrubby borders of parched annuals
amongst which she hunted assiduously. Cliff Johns now
played noisily but she was farther away and only heard
disjointed passages, strident and angry. She thought it was a
polonaise. *Tum*, te-tum. Te tum-te-tum-te *tum*, te-tum.
Tiddlytumtum. She didn't know how he could proclaim
himself like that after what had happened. Across the lawn,
on her right, Fabian, making for the kitchen garden, whistled
sweetly. Between them Terence Lynne hunted along the
companion path to Ursula's. The poplar fences completely
hid them from each other but every now and then they would
call out: "Any luck?" "Not so far." It was now almost dark.
Ursula had worked her way to the bottom of her beat and
turned into the connecting path that ran right along the lower
end of the garden. Here she found Terence Lynne. "It's no
good looking along here," Terence had said. "We didn't come
here with Mrs. Rubrick. We crossed the lawn to the kitchen
garden." But Ursula reminded her that earlier in the evening,
while Douglas and Fabian played an after-dinner singles, the
girls had come this way with Florence. "But I'm sure she had
the clip then," Terence objected. "We should have noticed if

one was missing. And in any case, I've looked along here. We'd better not be together. You know what she said." They argued in a desultory way and then Ursula returned to her beat. She saw a light flash beyond the fence on the right side of the tennis lawn and heard Douglas call out: "Here's a torch, Uncle Arthur." It was not long after this that Arthur Rubrick found the clip in a clump of zinnias along the lavender walk.

"He said the beam from the torch caught it and it sent out sparks of blue light. They shouted: 'Got it. We've found it!' and we all met on the tennis lawn. I ran out to a place on the drive where you can see the shearing shed, but there was no light there so we all went indoors." As they did this the music in the annex stopped abruptly.

They had trailed rather wearily into the dining-room just as the nine-o'clock bulletin was beginning on the radio. Fabian had turned it off. Arthur Rubrick had sat at the table, breathing short, his face more congested than usual. Terence Lynne, without consulting him, poured out a stiff nip of whisky. This instantly reminded Ursula of Cliff's performance on the previous night. Arthur thanked Terence in his breathless voice and pushed the diamond clip across the table to Ursula.

"I'll just run up with it. Auntie Floss will like to know it's found."

It struck her that the house was extraordinarily quiet. This impression deepened as she climbed the stairs. She stood for a moment on the top landing, listening. In all moments of quietude, undercurrents of sound, generally unheard, became disconcertingly audible. The day had been hot and the old wooden house relaxed with stealthy sighs or sudden cracks. Flossie's room was opposite the stair-head. Ursula, stock-still on the landing, listened intently for any movement in the room. There was none. She moved nearer to the door and, stooping down, could just see the printed legend. Flossie was adamant about obedience to this notice, but Ursula paused while the inane couplet which she couldn't read jigged through her memory:—

Please don't knock upon my door,
The only answer is a snore.

Auntie Flossie, she confessed, was a formidable snorer.
Indeed it was mainly on this score that Uncle Arthur, an
uneasy sleeper, had removed to an adjoining room. But on
this night no energetic counterpoint of intake and expulsion
sounded from behind the closed door. Ursula waited in vain
and a small trickle of apprehension dropped down her spine.
She stole away to her own room and wrote a little note: "It's
found. Happy trip, darling. We'll listen to you."

When she came back and slid it under Flossie's door the
room beyond was still quite silent.

Ursula returned to the dining-room. She said the light
dazzled her eyes after the dark landing and she stood in the
doorway and peered at the group round the table. "It's odd,
isn't it, how, for no particular reason, something you see will
stick in your memory? I mean there was no particular
significance about my going back to the dining-room. I didn't
know, then. Terry stood behind Uncle Arthur's chair. Fabian
was lighting a cigarette and I remember feeling worried about
him—" Ursula paused unaccountably. "I thought he'd been
overdoing things a bit," she said. "Douglas was sitting on the
table with his back towards me. They all turned their heads as
I came in. Of course they were just wondering if I'd given her
the diamond clip, but it seems to me now that they asked me
where she was. And, really, I answered as if they had done so.
I said: 'She's in her room. She's asleep!'"

"Did it strike you as odd that she'd made no inquiries
about the clip?" Alleyn asked.

"Not very odd. It was her way to organize things and then
leave them, knowing they'd be done. She was rather
wonderful like that. She never nagged."

"There's no need to nag if you're an efficient dictator,"
Fabian pointed out. "I'll admit her efficiency."

"Masculine jealousy," said Ursula without malice and he
grinned and said: "Perhaps."

Ursula waited for a moment and then continued her
narrative.

"We were all rather quiet. I suppose we were tired. We had
a drink each and then we parted for the night. We keep early
hours on the plateau, Mr. Alleyn. Can you face breakfast at a
quarter to six?"

"With gusto."

"Good.... We all went quietly upstairs and said good-night in whispers on the landing. My room is at the end of the landing and overlooks the side lawn. Terry's is opposite Auntie Florence's, and there's a bathroom next door to her that is opposite Uncle Arthur's dressing-room where he was sleeping. He'd once had a bad attack in the night and Auntie always left the communicating door open so that he could call to her. He remembered afterwards that this door was shut and that he'd opened it a crack and listened, thinking, as I had thought, how still she was. The boys' rooms are down the corridor and the servants' quarters at the back. When I came out in my dressing-gown to go to the bathroom, I met Terry. We could hear Uncle Arthur moving about quietly in his room. I glanced down the corridor and saw Douglas there and, farther along, Fabian in the door of his room. We all had candles, of course. We didn't speak. It seemed to me that we were all listening. We've agreed, since, that we felt, not exactly uneasy, but not quite comfortable. Restless. I didn't go to sleep for some time and when I did it was to dream that I was searching in rather terrifying places for the diamond clip. It was somewhere in the wool-shed but I couldn't find it because the party had started and Auntie Florence was making a speech on the edge of a precipice. I was late for an appointment and hunted in that horribly thwarted way one does in nightmares. I wouldn't have bored you with my dream if it hadn't turned into the dark staircase with me feeling on the treads for the brooch. The stairs creaked, like they do at night, but I knew somebody was crossing the landing and I was terrified and woke up. The point is," said Ursula, leaning forward and looking directly at Alleyn, "somebody really was crossing the landing."

The others stirred. Fabian reached over to the wood box and flung a log on the fire. Douglas muttered impatiently. Terence Lynne put down her knitting and folded her elegant hands together in her lap.

"In what direction?" Alleyn asked.

"I'm not sure. You know how it is. Dream and waking overlap, and by the time you are really alert the sound that came into your dream and woke you has stopped. I simply know that it was real."

"Mrs. Duck returning from the party," said Terence.

"But it was three o'clock, Terry. I heard the grandfather strike about five minutes later and Duckie says they got back at quarter to two."

"They'd hung about, cackling," said Douglas.

"For an hour and a quarter? And anyway Duckie would come up the back stair. I don't suppose it amounts to anything, Mr. Alleyn, because we know now that—that it hadn't—that it happened away from the house. It must have. But I don't care what anyone says," Ursula said, lifting her chin, "somebody was about on the landing at five minutes to three that morning."

"And we don't know definitely and positively," said Fabian, "that it wasn't Flossie herself."

CHAPTER III

ACCORDING TO DOUGLAS

Fabian's suggestion raised a storm of protest. The two girls and Douglas Grace began at once to combat it. It seemed to Alleyn that they thrust it from them as an idea that shocked and horrified their emotions rather than offended their reason. In the blaze of fire-light that sprang from the fresh log he saw Terence Lynne's hands weave together.

She said sharply: "That's a beastly thing to suggest, Fabian."

Alleyn saw Douglas Grace slide his arm along the sofa behind Terence. "I agree," Douglas said. "Not only beastly but idiotic. Why in God's name should Flossie stay out until three in the morning, return to her room, go out again and get murdered?"

"I didn't say it was likely. I said it wasn't impossible. We can't prove it wasn't Flossie."

"But what possible reason—"

"A rendezvous?" Fabian suggested and looked out of the corner of his eyes at Terence.

"I consider that's a remark in abominable taste, Fab," said Ursula.

"Do you, Ursy? I'm sorry. Must we never laugh a little at people after they are dead? But I'm very sorry. Let's go back to our story."

"I've finished," said Ursula shortly, and there was an uncomfortable silence.

"As far as we're concerned," said Douglas at last, "that's the end of the story. Ursula went into Aunt Floss's room the next morning to do it out, and she noticed nothing wrong.

The bed was made but that meant nothing because we all do our own beds and Ursy simply thought Flossie had tidied up before she left."

"But it was odd all the same," said Terence. "Mrs. Rubrick's sheets were always taken off when she went away and the bed made up again the day she returned. She always left it unmade, for that reason."

"It didn't strike me at the time," said Ursula. "I ran the carpet-sweeper over the floor and dusted and came away. It was all very tidy. She was a tremendously orderly person."

"There was another thing that didn't strike you, Ursula," said Terence Lynne. "You may remember that you took the carpet-sweeper from me and that I came for it when you'd finished. It wanted emptying and I took it down to the rubbish bin. I noticed there was something twisted around one of the axles, between the wheel and the box. I unwound it." Terence paused, looking at her hands. "It was a lock of wool," she said tranquilly. "Natural wool, I mean, from the fleece."

"You never told us that," said Fabian sharply.

"I told the detective. He didn't seem to think it important. He said that was the sort of thing you'd expect to find in the house at shearing time. He was a town-bred man."

"It might have been there for ages, Terry," said Ursula.

"Oh, no. It wasn't there when you borrowed the sweeper from me. I'm very observant of details," said Terence, "and I know. And if Mrs. Rubrick had seen it she'd have picked it up. She hated bits on the carpet. She had a 'thing' about them and always picked them up. I'll swear it wasn't there when she was in the room."

"How big was it?" Fabian demanded.

"Quite small. Not a lock really. Just a twist."

"A teeny-weeny twist," said Ursula in a ridiculous voice, suddenly gay again. She had a chancy way with her, one moment nervously intent on her memories, the next full of mockery.

"I suppose," said Alleyn, "one might pick up a bit of wool in the shed and, being greasy, it might hang about on one's clothes?"

"It might," said Fabian lightly.

"And being greasy," Douglas added, "it might also hang about in one's room."

"Not in Auntie Floss's room," Ursula said. "I always did her room, Douglas, you shan't dare to say I left greasy wool lying squalidly about for days on the carpet. Pig!" she mocked at him.

He turned his head lazily and looked at her. Alleyn saw his arm slip down the back of the sofa to Terence Lynne's shoulders. Ursula laughed and pulled a face at him. "It's all nonsense," she said, "this talk of locks of wool. Moonshine!"

"Personally," said Terence Lynne, "I can't think it very amusing. For me, and I'd have thought for all of us, the idea of sheep's wool in her room that morning is perfectly horrible."

"You're hateful, Terry," Ursula flashed at her. "It's bad enough to have to talk about it. I mind more than any of you. You all know that. It's because I mind so much that I can't be too solemn. You know I'm the only one of us that loved her. You're cold as ice, Terry, and I hate you."

"Now then, Ursy," Fabian protested. He knelt up and put his hands over hers. "Behave!" he said. "Be your age, woman. You astonish me."

"She was a darling and I loved her. If it hadn't been for her—"

"All right, all right."

"You would never even have seen me if it hadn't been for her."

"Who was it," Fabian murmured, "who held the grapes above Tantalus' lips? Could it have been Aunt Florence?"

"All the same," said Ursula with that curious air, half-rueful, half-obstinate, that seemed to characterize her relationship with Fabian, "you're beastly to me. I'm sorry, Terry."

"May we go on?" asked Douglas.

Alleyn, in his chair beyond the fire-light, stirred slightly and at once they were attentive and still.

"Captain Grace," Alleyn said. "During the hunt for the diamond brooch, you went up to the house for a torch, didn't you?"

"For two torches, sir. I gave one to Uncle Arthur."

"Did you see anyone in the house?"

"No. There was only Markins. Markins says he was in his room. There's no proof of that. The torches are kept on the hall table. The telephone rang while I was there and I answered it. But that only took a few seconds. Somebody wanting to know if Aunt Florence was going north in the morning."

"From the terrace in front of the house you look down on the fenced paths, don't you? Could you see the other seachers from there?"

"Not Uncle Arthur or Fabian, but I could just see the two girls. It was almost dark. I went straight to my uncle with the torch; he was there all right."

"Were you with him when he found the brooch?"

"No. I simply gave him the torch and returned to my own beat with mine. I heard him call out a few moments later. He left the brooch where it was for me to see. It looked like a cluster of blue and red sparks in the torchlight. It was half hidden by zinnia leaves. He said he'd looked there before. It wasn't too good for him to stoop much and his sight wasn't so marvellous. I suppose he'd just missed it."

"Did you go into the end path, the one that runs parallel with the others and links them?"

"No. He did."

"Mr. Rubrick?"

"Yes. Earlier. Just as I was going to the house and before you went down there, Ursy, and talked to Terry."

"Then you and Mr. Rubrick must have been there together, Miss Lynne," said Alleyn.

"No," said Terence Lynne quickly.

"I understood Miss Harme to say that when she met you in the bottom path you told her you had been searching there."

"I looked about there for a moment. I don't remember seeing Mr. Rubrick. I wasn't with him."

"But—" Douglas broke off. "I suppose I made a mistake," he said. "I had it in my head that as I was going up to the house for the torches he came out of the lavender walk into my path and then moved on into the bottom path. And then I had the impression that as I returned with the torches he came back from the bottom path. It was just then that I heard you two arguing about whether you'd stop in the bottom path or not. You were there, then."

"I may have seen him," said Terence. "I was only there a short time. I don't remember positively but we didn't speak— I mean we were not together. It was getting dark."

"Well, but Terry," said Ursula, "when I went into the bottom path you came towards me from the far end, the end nearest the lavender walk. If he was there at all it would have been at that end."

"I don't remember, Ursula. If he was there we didn't speak and I've simply forgotten."

"Perhaps I was mistaken," said Douglas uncertainly. "But it doesn't matter much, does it? Arthur was somewhere down there and so were both of you. I don't mind admitting that the gentleman whose movements that evening I've always been anxious to trace is our friend Mr. Markins."

"And away we go," said Fabian cheerfully. "We're on your territory now, sir."

"Good," said Alleyn, "what about Markins, Captain Grace? Let's have it."

"It goes back some way," said Douglas. "It goes back, to be exact, to the last wool sale held in this country, which was early in 1939."

ii

" ... So Aunt Floss jockeyed poor old Arthur into scraping acquaintance with this Jap. Kurata Kan his name was. They brought him up here for the week-end. I've heard that he took a great interest in everything, grinning like a monkey and asking questions. He'd got a wizard of a camera, a German one, and told them photography was his hobby. Landscape mostly, he said, but he liked doing groups of objects too. He took a photograph in the Pass. He was keen on flying. Uncle Arthur told me he must have spent a whole heap of money on private trips while he was here, taking his camera with him. He bought photographs too, particularly infra-red aerial affairs. He got the names of the photographers from the newspaper offices. We found that out afterwards, though apparently he didn't make any secret of it at the time. It seems he was bloody quaint in his ways and talked liked something out of the movies. Flossie fell for it like an avalanche. 'My dear little Mr. Kan.' She was frightfully bucked because he gave top price for her wool clip. The Japs always bought second-rate stuff and anyway it's very unusual for merino wool to fetch top price. I consider the whole thing was damn' fishy. When she went to England they kept up a correspondence. Flossie had always said the Japs would weigh in on our side when war came. 'Mr. Kurata Kan tells me all sorts of things.' By God, there's this to say for the totalitarian countries—they wouldn't have had gentlemen like Mr. Kurata Kan hanging about for long. I'll hand that to them. They know how to keep the rats out of their houses." Douglas laughed shortly.

"But not the bats out of their belfries," said Fabian. "Please don't deviate into *Herrenvolk*-lore, Douglas."

"This Kan lived for half the year in Australia," Douglas continued. "Remember that. Flossie got back here in '40 bringing Ursy and Fabian with her. Before she went Home she used to run this place on a cook and two housemaids, but the maids had gone and this time she couldn't raise the sight of a help. Mrs. Duck was looking after Uncle Arthur single-handed. She said she couldn't carry on like that. Ursy did what she could but she wasn't used to housework, and anyway it didn't suit Flossie."

"Ursy seemed to me to wield a very pretty mop," said Fabian.

"Of course she did, but it was damned hard work scrubbing and so on and Auntie Floss knew it."

"I didn't mind," said Ursy.

"Anyway, when I got back after Greece I found the marvellous Markins running the show. And where d'you think he'd blown in from? From Sydney with a letter from Mr. Kurata Kan. Can you beat that?"

"A reference, do you mean?"

"Yes. He hadn't actually been with these precious Kans. He says he was valet to an English artillery officer who'd picked him up in America. He says he was friendly with the Kans' servants. He says that when his employer left Australia he applied to Kan for a job. But the Kans were winging their way to Japan. Markins said he'd like to try his luck in New Zealand, and Kan remembered Flossie moaning about the servant problem in this country. Hence, the letter. That's Kan's story. The whole thing looks damned fishy to me. Markins, an efficient well-trained servant, could have taken a job anywhere. Beyond the fact that he was born British but has an American passport we know nothing about him. He gave the name of his American employers but doesn't know their present address."

"I think I should tell you," said Alleyn, "that the American employers have been traced for us and verify the story."

This produced an impression. Fabian said: "Not Understood, or the Modest Detective! I take back some of my remarks about him. Only some," he added. "I still maintain that, taking him by and large, our Mr. Jackson is almost certifiable."

"It makes no difference," Douglas said. "It proves nothing. My case rests on pretty firm ground as I think you'll agree, sir, when you've heard it."

"Do remember, Douglas," Fabian murmured, "that Mr. Alleyn has seen the files."

"I realize that, but God knows what sort of a hash they've made of it. Now I don't want to be unnecessarily hard on the dead," said Douglas loudly. Fabian grimaced and muttered to himself. "But I look at it this way. It's my duty to give an honest opinion and I wouldn't be honest if I didn't say that Aunt Floss liked to know about things. Not to mince matters, she was a very inquisitive woman, and what's more she enjoyed showing people that she was in on everything."

"I know what you're going to say next," said Ursula brightly, "and I disagree with every word of it."

"My dear girl, you're talking through your hat. Look here, sir. When I got back from Greece and was marched out of the army and came here, I found Fabian doing a certain type of work. I needn't be more explicit than that," said Douglas portentously and raised his eyebrows.

"You're superb, Douglas," said Fabian. "Of course you needn't. Do remember that Mr. Alleyn is the man who knows all."

"Be quiet, Losse," said Alleyn unexpectedly. Fabian opened his mouth and shut it again. "You're a mosquito," Alleyn added mildly.

"I really am sorry," said Fabian. "I know."

"Shall I go on?" asked Douglas huffily.

"Please do."

"Fabian told me about his work. He called it, for security reasons, the egg-beater. Fabian's idea. I prefer simply the X Adjustment."

"I see," said Alleyn. "The X Adjustment." Fabian grinned.

"And he asked me if I'd like to have a look at his notes and drawings and so on. As a gunner I was, of course, interested. I satisfied myself there was something in it. I'd taken my electrical engineering degree before I joined up and was rather keen on the magnetic-fuse idea. I need go no further at the moment," said Douglas with another significant glance.

Alleyn thought, "He really is superb," and nodded solemnly.

"Of course," Douglas continued, "Auntie Floss had to be told something. I mean we wanted a room and certain facilities and so on. She advanced us the cash for our gear. There's no electrical supply this side of the plateau. We built a windmill and got a small dynamo. Later on she was going to have the house wired, but at the moment we've only got the juice in the workroom. She paid for all that. We began to spend more and more time on it. And later on, when we were ready to show something to somebody in the right quarter, she was damned useful. She'd talk anybody into anything, would Flossie, and she got hold of a Certain Authority at Army Headquarters and arranged for us to go up north and see him. He sent a report Home and things began to look up. We've now had a very encouraging answer from— However! I need not go into that."

"Quite," said Alleyn. Fabian suddenly offered him a cigar which he refused.

"Well, as I say, she was very helpful in many ways but she did *gimlet* rather and she used to talk jolly indiscreetly at meal times."

"You should have heard her," said Fabian. "'Now what do my two inventors think?' And then, you know, she'd pull an arch face and, for all the world like one of the weird sisters in *Macbeth*, she'd lay her rather choppy finger on her lips and say: 'But we mustn't be indiscreet, must we?'"

Alleyn glanced up at the picture. The spare, wiry woman stared down at him with the blank inscrutability of all Academy portraits. He was visited by a strange notion. If the painted finger should be raised to those lips that seemed to be strained with such difficulty over projecting teeth! If she could give him a secret signal: "Speak now. Ask this question. Be silent here, they are approaching a matter of importance."

"That's how she carried on," Douglas agreed. "It was damned difficult and of course everybody in the house knew we were doing something hush-hush. Fabian always said: 'What of it? We keep our stuff locked up and even if we didn't nobody could understand it.' But I didn't like the way Flossie talked. Later on her attitude changed."

"That was after questions had been asked in the House about leakage of information to the enemy," said Ursula. "She took that very much to heart, Douglas, you know she did. And then that ship was torpedoed off the North Island. She was terribly upset."

"Personally," said Fabian, "I found her caution much more alarming than her curiosity. You'd have thought we had the Secret Death Key of fiction on the stocks. She papered the walls with cautionary posters. Go on, Douglas."

"It was twenty-one days before she was killed that it happened," said Douglas. "And if you don't find a parallel between my experience and Ursy's, I shall be very much surprised. Fabian and I had worked late on a certain improvement to a crucial part of our gadget—a safety device, let us call it."

"Why not," said Fabian, "since it is one?"

"I absolutely fail to understand your attitude, Fabian, and I'm sure Mr. Alleyn does. Your bloody English facetiousness—"

"All right. You're perfectly right, old thing, only it's just that all these portentous hints seem to me to be so many touches. You know as well as I do that the idea of a sort of aerial magnetic mine must have occurred to countless schoolboys. The only thing that could possibly be of use to the most sanguine dirty dog would be either the drawings, or the dummy model."

"Exactly!" Douglas shouted and then immediately lowered his voice. "The drawings and the model."

"And it's all right about Markins. He's spending the evening with the Johns family."

"So he says," Douglas retorted. "Well now, sir, on this night, a fortnight before Aunt Floss was killed, I was worrying about the alteration in the safety device—"

His story did bear a curious resemblance to Ursula's.

On this particular evening, at about nine o'clock, Douglas and Fabian had stood outside their workroom door, having locked it for the night. They were excited by the proposed alteration to the safety device which Fabian now thought could be improved still further. "We'd talked ourselves silly and decided to chuck it up for the night," said Douglas. He usually kept the keys of the workroom door and safe, but on this occasion each of them said that he might feel inclined to return to the calculations later on that night. It was agreed that Douglas should leave the keys in a box on his dressing-table where Fabian, if he so desired, could get them without disturbing him. It was at this point that they noticed Markins, who had come quietly along the passage from the backstairs. He asked them if they knew where Mrs. Rubrick was as a long-distance call had come through for her. He almost certainly overheard the arrangement about the keys. "And, by God," said Douglas, "he tried to make use of it."

They parted company and Douglas went to bed. But he was over-stimulated and slept restlessly. At last, finding himself broad awake and obsessed with their experiment, he had decided to get up and look through the calculations they had been working on that evening. He had stretched out his hand to his bedside table when he heard a sound in the passage beyond his door. It was no more than the impression of stealthy pressure, as though someone advanced with exaggerated caution and in slow motion. Douglas listened spell-bound, his hand still outstretched. The steps paused outside his door. At that moment he made some involuntary movement of his hand and knocked his candlestick to the floor. The noise seemed to him to be shocking. It was followed by a series of creaks fading in a rapid diminuendo down the passage. He leapt out of bed and pulled open his door.

The passage was almost pitch-dark. At the far end it met a shorter passage that ran across it like the head of a T. Here, there was a faint glow that faded while Douglas watched it as if, he said, somebody with a torch was moving away to the left. The only inhabited room to the left was Markins'. The backstairs were to the right.

At this point in his narrative, Douglas tipped himself back on the sofa and glanced complacently about him. Why, he demanded, was Markins abroad in the passage at a quarter to three in the morning (Douglas had noted the time) unless it was upon some exceedingly dubious errand? And why did he pause outside his, Douglas', door? There was one explanation which, in the light of subsequent events, could scarcely be refuted. Markins had intended to enter Douglas' room and attempt to steal the keys to the workshop.

"Well, well," said Fabian, "let's have the subsequent events."

They were, Alleyn thought, at least suggestive.

After the incident of the night Douglas had taken his keys to bed with him and lay fuming until daylight, when he woke Fabian and told him of his suspicions. Fabian was sceptical. "A purely gastronomic episode, I bet you anything you like." But he agreed that they should be more careful with the keys, and he himself contrived a heavy shutter which padlocked over the window when the room was not in use. "There was no satisfying Douglas," Fabian said plaintively. "He jeered at my lovely shutter and didn't believe I went to bed with the keys on a bootlace round my neck. I did though."

"I wasn't satisfied to let it go like that," said Douglas. "I was damned worried and next day I kept the tag on Master Markins. Once or twice I caught him watching me with a very funny look in his eye. That was on the Thursday. Flossie had given him the Saturday off and he went down to the Pass with the mail car. He's friendly with the pub keeper there. I thought things over and decided to do a little investigation, and I think you'll agree I was justified, sir. I went to his room. It was locked, but I'd seen a bunch of old keys hanging up in the store-room and after filing one of them I got it to function all right." Douglas paused, half-smiling. His arm still rested along the back of the sofa behind Terence Lynne. She turned and, clicking her knitting needles, looked thoughtfully at him.

"I don't know how you could, Douglas," said Ursula. "Honestly!"

"My dear child, I had every reason to believe I was up against a very nasty bit of work—a spy, an enemy. Don't you understand?"

"Of course I understand, but I just don't believe Markins is a spy. I rather like him."

Douglas raised his eyebrows and addressed himself pointedly to Alleyn.

"At first I thought I'd drawn a blank. Every blinking box and case in his room, and there were five all told, was locked. I looked in the cupboard and there, on the floor, I did discover something."

Douglas cleared his throat, took a wallet from his breast pocket and an envelope from the wallet. This he handed to Alleyn. "Take a look at it, sir. It's not the original. I handed that over to the police. But it's an exact replica."

"Yes," said Alleyn, raising an eyebrow at it. "A fragment of the covering used on a film package for a Leica or similar camera."

"That's right, sir. I thought I wasn't mistaken. A bloke in our mess had used those films and I remembered the look of them. Now it seemed pretty funny to me that a man in Markins' position should be able to afford a Leica camera. They cost anything from £25 to £100 out here when you could get them. Of course, I said to myself, it mightn't be his. But there was a suit hanging up in the cupboard and in one of the pockets I found a sales docket from a photographic supply firm. Markins had spent five pounds there, and amongst the stuff he'd bought were twelve films for a Leica. I suppose he was afraid he'd run out. I shifted one of his locked cases and it rattled and clinked. I bet it had his developing plant in it. When I left his room I was satisfied I'd hit on something pretty startling. Markins was probably going to photograph everything he could lay his hands on in our workroom and send it on to his principals."

"I see," said Alleyn. "So what did you do?"

"Told Fabian," said Douglas. "Right away."

Alleyn looked at Fabian.

"Oh yes. He told me and we disagreed completely over the whole thing. In fact," said Fabian, "we had one hell of a flaming row over it, didn't we, Doug?"

iii

"There's no need to exaggerate," said Douglas. "We merely took up different attitudes."

"Wildly different," Fabian agreed. "You see, Mr. Alleyn, my idea, for what it's worth, was this. Suppose Markins was a dirty dog. If questioned about his nightly prowl he had only to say: (a) That his tummy was upset and he didn't feel up to going to the downstairs Usual Offices so had visited ours, or (b) that it wasn't him at all. As for his photographic zeal, if it existed, he might have been given a Leica camera by a grateful employer or saved up his little dimes and dollars and bought one second-hand in America. Every photographic zealot is not a fifth columnist. If he kept his developing stuff locked up it might be because he was innately tidy or because he didn't trust us, and I must say that with Douglas on the premises he wasn't far wrong."

"So you were for doing nothing about it?"

"No. I thought we should keep our stuff well stowed away and our eyes open. I suggested that if, on consideration, we thought Markins was a bit dubious, we should report the whole story to the people who are dealing with espionage in this country."

"And did you agree with this plan, Grace?"

Douglas had disagreed most vigorously. He had, he said with a short laugh, the poorest opinion of the official counter-espionage system and would greatly perfer to tackle the matter himself. "That's what we're like out here, sir," he told Alleyn. "We like to go to it on our own and get things done." He added that he felt, personally, so angry with Markins that he had to do something about it. Fabian's suggestion he dismissed as unrealistic. Why wait? Report the matter certainly, but satisfy themselves first and then go direct to the Authority they had seen at Army Headquarters and get rid of the fellow. They argued for some time and separated without having come to any conclusion. Douglas on parting from Fabian encountered his aunt, who as luck would have it launched out on an encomium upon her man-servant. "What should I do without my Markins? Thank heaven he comes back this evening. I touch wood," Flossie had said, tapping a gnarled finger playfully on her forehead, "every time he says he's happy here. It'd be so unspeakably dreadful if he were lost to us."

This, Douglas said, was too much for him. He followed his aunt into the study and, as he said, gave her the works. "I stood no nonsense from Flossie," said Douglas, brushing up his moustache. "We understood each other pretty well. I used to pull her leg a bit and she liked it. She was a good scout, taking her all round, only you didn't want to let her ride roughshod over you. I talked pretty straight to her. I told her she'd have to get rid of Markins and I told her why."

Terence Lynne said under her breath: "I never realized you did that."

Flossie had been very much upset. She was caught. On the one hand there was her extreme reluctance to part with her jewel, as she had so often called Markins; on the other her noted zeal, backed up by public utterance, in the matter of counter-espionage. Douglas said he reminded her of a speech she had made in open debate in which she had wound up with a particularly stately peroration: "I say now, and I say it solemnly and advisedly," Flossie had urged, "that, with our very life-blood at stake, it is the duty of us all not only to get a guard upon our own tongue but to make a public example of anyone, be he stranger or dearest friend, who, by the slightest deviation from that discretion which is his duty, endangers in the least degree the safety of our realm. Make no doubt about it," she had finally shouted, "there is an enemy in our midst, and let each of us beware lest, unknowingly, we give him shelter." This piece of rhetoric had a wry flavour in regurgitation, and for a moment Flossie stared miserably at her nephew. Then she rallied.

"You've been working too hard, Douglas," she said. "You're suffering from nervous strain, dear."

But Douglas made short work of this objection and indignantly put before her the link with Mr. Kurata Kan, at which Flossie winced, the vagueness of Markins' antecedents, the importance of their work, the impossibility of taking the smallest risk and their clear duty in the matter. It would be better, he said, if, after further investigation on Douglas' part, Markins still looked suspicious, for Flossie and not Douglas or Fabian to report the matter to the highest possible authority.

Poor Flossie wrung her hands. "Think of what he does," she wailed. "And he's so good with Arthur. He's marvellous with Arthur. And he's so obliging, Douglas. Single-handed butler in a house of this size! Everything so nice, always. And there's no help to be got. None."

"The girls will have to manage."

"I don't believe it!" she cried, rallying. "I'm always right in my judgment of people. I never go wrong. I won't believe it."

But, as Ursula had said, Flossie was an honest woman and it seemed as if Douglas had done his work effectively. She tramped up and down the room hitting her top teeth with a pencil, a sure sign that she was upset. He waited.

"You're right," Flossie said at last. "I can't let it go." She lowered her chin and looked at Douglas over the tops of her *pince-nez*. "You were quite right to tell me, dear," she said. "I'll handle it."

This was disturbing. "What will you do?" he asked.

"Consider," said Florence magnificently. "And act."

"How?"

"Never you mind." She patted him rather too vigorously on the cheek. "Leave it all to your old Floosie," she said. This was the abominable pet name she had for herself.

"But, Auntie," he protested, "we've a right to know. After all—"

"So you shall. At the right moment." She dumped herself down at her desk. She was a tiny creature but all her movements were heavy and noisy. "Away with you," she said. Douglas hung about. She began to write scratchily and in a moment or two tossed another remark at him. "I'm going to tackle him," she said.

Douglas was horrified. "Oh, no, Aunt Floss. Honestly, you mustn't. It'll give the whole show away. Look here, Aunt Floss—"

But she told him sharply that he had chosen to come to her with his story and must allow her to deal with her own servants in the way that seemed best to her. Her pen scratched busily. When in his distress he roared at her, she, too, lost her temper and told him to be quiet. Douglas, unable to make up his mind to leave her, stared despondently through the window and saw Markins, neatly dressed, walk past it mopping his brow. He had tramped up from the front gate.

"Auntie Floss, please listen to me!"

"I thought I told you—"

Appalled at his own handiwork, he left her.

At this point in his narrative Douglas rose and straddled the hearth-rug.

"I don't mind telling you," he said, "that we weren't the same after it. She got the huff and treated me like a kid."

"We noticed," Fabian said, "that your popularity had waned a little. Poor Flossie! You'd hoist her with the petard of her own conscience. A maddening and unforgivable thing to do, of course. Obviously she would hate your guts for it."

"There's no need to put it like that," said Douglas grandly.

"With a little enlargement," Fabian grinned, "it might work up into quite a pretty motive against you."

"That's a damned silly thing to say, Fabian," Douglas shouted.

"Shut up, Fab," said Ursula. "You're impossible."

"Sorry, darling."

"I still don't see," Douglas abjectly fumed, "that I could

have taken any other line. After all, as she pointed out, it was her house and he was her servant."

"You didn't think of that when you picked his door lock," Fabian pointed out.

"I didn't pick the lock, Fabian, and anyhow that was entirely different."

"Did Mrs. Rubrick tackle him?" Alleyn asked.

"I presume so. She said nothing to me, and I wasn't going to ask and be ticked off again."

Douglas lit a cigarette and inhaled deeply. "Obviously," Alleyn thought, "he still has something up his sleeve."

"As a matter of fact," said Douglas lightly, "I'm quite positive she did tackle him, and I believe it's because of what she said that Markins killed her."

iv

"And there," said Fabian cheerfully, "you have it. Flossie says to Markins: 'I understand from my nephew that you're an enemy agent. Take a week's wages in lieu of notice and expect to be arrested and shot when you get to the railway station!' 'No you don't,' says Markins to himself. He serves up the soup with murder in his heart, takes a stroll past the wool-shed, hears Flossie in the full spate of her experimental oratory, nips in and—does it. To me it just doesn't make sense."

"You deliberately make it sound silly," said Douglas hotly.

"It is silly. Moreover it's not in her character, as I read it, to accuse Markins. It would have been the action of a fool and, bless my soul, Flossie was no fool."

"It was her deliberately expressed intention."

"To 'tackle Markins.' That was her phrase, wasn't it? That is, to tackle *l'affaire Markins*. She wanted to get rid of you and think. And, upon my soul, I don't blame her."

"But how would she tackle Markins," Terence objected,

"except by questioning him?" She spoke so seldom that the sound of her voice, cool and incisive, came as a little shock.

"She was a bit of a Polonius, was Flossie. I think she went round to work. She may even," said Fabian, giving a curious inflection to the phrase, "she may even have consulted Uncle Arthur."

"No," said Douglas.

"How on earth can you tell?" asked Ursula.

There was a moment's silence.

"It would not have been in her character," said Douglas.

"Her character, you see," Fabian said to Alleyn. "Always her character."

"Ever since fifth-column trouble started in this country," said Douglas, "Flossie had been asking questions about it in the house. Markins knew that as well as we did. If she gave him so much as an inkling that she suspected him, how d'you suppose he'd feel?"

"And even if she decided not to accuse him straight out," Ursula said, "don't you think he'd notice some change in her manner?"

"Of course he would, Ursy," Douglas agreed. "How could she help herself?"

"Quite easily," said Fabian. "She was as clever as a bagful of monkeys."

"I agree," said Terence.

"Well, now," said Alleyn, "did any of you, in fact, notice any change in her manner towards Markins?"

"To be quite honest," said Fabian slowly, "we did. But I think we all put it down to her row with Cliff Johns. She was extremely cantankerous with all hands and the cook during that last week, was poor Flossie."

"She was unhappy," Ursula declared. "She was wretchedly unhappy about Cliff. She used to tell me everything. I'm sure if she'd had a row with Markins she'd have told me about it. She used to call me her Safety Valve."

"Mrs. Arthur Rubrick," said Fabian, "accompanied by Miss U. Harme, S.V., A.D.C., etc., etc.!"

"She may have waited to talk to him until that night," said Douglas. "The night she disappeared, I mean. She may have written for advice to a certain Higher Authority, and waited for the reply before she tackled Markins. Good Lord, that might have been the very letter she started writing while I was there!"

"I think," said Alleyn, "that I should have heard if she'd done that."

"Yes," agreed Fabian. "Yes. After all you are the Higher Authority, aren't you?"

Again there was a silence, an awkward one. Alleyn thought: Damn that boy, he's said precisely the wrong thing. He's made them self-conscious again.

"Well, there's my case against Markins," said Douglas grandly. "I don't pretend it's complete or anything like that, but I'll swear there's something in it, and you can't deny that after she disappeared his behaviour was suspicious."

"I can deny it," said Fabian, "and what's more I jolly well do. Categorically, whatever that may mean. He was worried and so were all of us."

"He was jumpy."

"We were all as jumpy as cats. Why shouldn't he jump with us? It'd have been much more suspicious if he'd remained all suave and imperturbable. You're reasoning backwards, Douglas."

"I couldn't stand the sight of the chap about the house," said Douglas. "I can't now. It's monstrous that he should still be here."

"Yes," Alleyn said. "Why is he still here?"

"You might well ask," Douglas rejoined. "You'll scarcely credit it, sir, but he's here because the police asked Uncle Arthur to keep him on. It was like this . . ."

The story moved forward. Out of the narrative grew a theme of mounting dissonance, anxiety and fear. Five days after Florence had walked down the lavender path and turned to the left, the overture opened on the sharp note of a telephone bell. The Post Office at the Pass had a wire for Mrs. Rubrick. Should they read it? Terence took it down. TRUST YOU ARE NOT INDISPOSED YOUR PRESENCE URGENTLY REQUESTED AT THURSDAY'S MEETING. It was signed by a brother M.P. There followed a confused and hurried passage. Florence had not gone north! Where was she? Inquiries, tentative at first but growing hourly less guarded and more frantic; long-distance calls, calls to her lawyers with whom she was known to have made an appointment, to hospitals and police stations; the abandonment of privacy following a dominion-wide SOS on the air; search-parties radiating from Mount Moon and culminating in the sudden collapse of Arthur Rubrick; his refusal to have a trained nurse or indeed anyone but Terence and Markins to look after him—all these abnormalities followed each other in an ominous crescendo that reached its peak in the dreadful finality of discovery.

As this phase unfolded, Alleyn thought he could trace a change of mood in the little company assembled in the study. At first Douglas alone stated the theme. Then one by one, at first reluctantly, then with increasing freedom, the other voices joined in, and it seemed to Alleyn that after their long avoidance of their subject they now found ease in speaking of it. After the impact of the discovery, there followed the slow assembly of official themes: the inquest adjourned, the constant appearance of the police, and the tremendous complications of the public funeral. These events mingled like phrases of a movement till interrupted emphatically by Fabian. When Douglas, who had evidently been impressed by it, described Flossie's *cortège*—"there were three bands"—Fabian shocked them all by breaking into laughter. Laughter bubbled out of him. He stammered: "It was so horrible...disgusting...I'm terribly sorry, but when you think of what had happened to her...and then to have three brass bands...Oh God, it's so electrically comic!" He drew in his breath in a shuddering gasp.

"Fabian!" Ursula murmured and put her arm about him, pressing him against her knees. "Darling Fabian, don't."

Douglas stared at Fabian and then looked away in embarrassment. "You don't want to think of it like that," he said. "It was a tribute. She was enormously popular. We had to let them do it. Personally—"

"Go on with the story, Douglas," said Terence.

"Wait," said Fabian. "I've got to explain. It's my turn. I want to explain."

"No," cried Ursula. "Please not."

"We agreed to tell him everything. I've got to explain why

I can't join in this *nil nisi* stuff. It crops up at every turn. Let's clear it up and then get on with the job."

"No!"

"I've got to, Ursy. Please don't interrupt, it's so deadly important. And after all one can't make a fool of oneself without some sort of apology."

"Mr. Alleyn will understand." Ursula appealed urgently to Alleyn, her hands still pressed down on Fabian's shoulders. "It's the war," she said. "He was dreadfully ill after Dunkirk. You mustn't mind."

"For pity's sake shut up, darling, and let me tell him," said Fabian violently.

"But it's crazy. I won't let you, Fabian. I won't let you."

"You can't stop me," he said.

"What the hell is this about?" Douglas asked angrily.

"It's about me," said Fabian. "It's about whether or not I killed your Aunt Florence. Now for God's sake hold your tongue and listen."

CHAPTER IV

ACCORDING TO FABIAN

Sitting on the floor and hugging his knees, Fabian began his narrative. At first he stammered. The phrases tumbled over each other and his lips trembled. As often as this happened he paused, frowning, and, in a level voice, repeated the sentence he had bungled, so that presently he was master of himself and spoke composedly.

"I think I told you," he said, "that I got a crack on the head at Dunkirk. I also told you, didn't I, that for some weeks after I was supposed to be more or less patched up they put me on a specialized job in England? It was then I got the notion of a magnetic fuse for anti-aircraft shells, which is, to make no bones about it, the general idea behind our precious X Adjustment. I suppose, if things had gone normally, I'd have muddled away at it there in England, but they didn't.

"I went to my job one morning with a splitting headache. What an admirably chosen expression that is—'a splitting headache.' My head really felt like that. I'd had bad bouts of it before and tried not to pay any attention. I was sitting at my desk looking at a memorandum from my senior officer and thinking I must collect myself and do something about it. I remember pulling a sheet of paper towards me. An age of nothingness followed this and then I came up in horrible waves out of dark into light. I was hanging over a gate in a road a few minutes away from my own billet. It was a very high gate, an eight-barred affair with wire on top and padlocked. The place beyond was army property. I must have climbed up. I was very sick. After a bit I looked at my watch. It'd missed an hour. It was as if it had been cut out of my mind. I looked at my right hand and saw there was ink on my fingers. Then I went home, feeling filthily ill. I rang up the office and I suppose I sounded peculiar because the army

71

quack came in the next morning and had a look at me. He said it was the crack on my skull. I've got the report he gave me to bring out here. You can see it if you like.

"While he was with me the letter came.

"It was addressed to me by me. That gives one an unpleasant feeling at any time. When I opened it six sheets of office paper fell out. They were covered in my writing and figures. Nonsense they were, disjointed bits and pieces from my notes and calculations hopelessly jumbled together. I showed them to the doctor. He found it all enthralling and had me marched out of the army. That was when Flossie turned up."

Fabian paused for a moment, his chin on his knees.

"I only had two other goes of it," he said at last, rousing himself. "One was in the ship. I was supposed to be resting in my deck-chair. Ursy says she found me climbing. This time it was up the companion-way to the boat deck. I don't know if I told you that when I caught my packet at Dunkirk I was climbing up a rope ladder into a rescue ship. I've sometimes wondered if there's a connection. Ursy couldn't get me to come down so she stayed with me. I wandered about, it seems, and generally made a nuisance of myself. I got very angry about something and said I was going to knock hell out of Flossie. A point to remember, Mr. Alleyn. I think I've mentioned before that Flossie's ministrations in the ship were very agitating and tiresome. Ursy seems to have kept me quiet. When I came up to the surface she was there, and she helped me get back to my cabin. I made her promise not to tell Flossie. The ship's doctor was generally tight so we didn't trouble him either.

"Then the last go. The last go. I suppose you've guessed. It was on what your friend in the force calls the Night in Question. It was, in point of fact, while I was among the vegetable marrows hunting for Flossie's brooch. Unhappily, this time Ursy was not there."

"I suppose," Fabian said, shifting his position and looking at his hands, "that I'd walked about, with my nose to the ground, for so long that I'd upset my equilibrium or something. I don't know. All I do know is that I heard the two girls having their argument in the bottom path and then, without the slightest warning, there was the blackout, and, after the usual age of nothingness, that abominable, that disgusting sense of coming up to the surface. There I was at the opposite end of the vegetable garden, under a poplar tree, feeling like death and bruised all over. I heard Uncle Arthur call out: 'Here it is. I've found it.' I heard the others exclaim and shout to each other and then to me. So I pulled myself together and trotted round to meet them. It was almost dark by then. They couldn't see my face which I daresay was bright green. Anyway they were all congratulating themselves over the blasted brooch. I trailed indoors after them and genteelly sipped soda-water while they drank hock and Uncle Arthur's whisky. He was pretty well knocked up himself, poor old thing. So I escaped notice, except—"

He moved away a little from Ursula and looked up at her with a singularly sweet smile. "Except by Ursula," he said. "She appeared to have noted the resemblance to a dead groper and she tackled me about it the next morning. So I told her that I'd had another of my 'turns,' as poor Flossie called them."

"It's so silly," Ursula whispered. "The whole thing's so silly. Mr. Alleyn is going to laugh at you."

"Is he? I hope he is. I must say it'd be a great relief to me if Mr. Alleyn began to rock with professional laughter, but at the moment I see no signs of it. Of course you know where all this is leading, sir, don't you?"

"I think so," said Alleyn. "You wonder, don't you, if in a condition of amnesia or automatism or unconscious behaviour or whatever it should be called, you could have gone to the wool-shed and committed this crime?"

"That's it."

"You say you heard Miss Harme and Miss Lynne talking in the bottom path?"

"Yes. I heard Terry say, 'Why not just do what we're asked? It would be so much simpler.'"

"Did you say that, Miss Lynne?"

"Something like it, I believe."

"Yes," said Ursula. "She said that. I remember."

"And then I blacked-out," said Fabian.

"Soon after you came to yourself again you heard Mr. Rubrick call out that he had found the diamond clip?"

"Yes. It's the first thing I was fully aware of. His voice."

"And how long," Alleyn asked Terence Lynne, "was the interval between your remark and the discovery of the brooch?"

"Perhaps ten minutes. No longer."

"I see. Mr. Losse," said Alleyn, "you seem to me to be a more than usually intelligent young man."

"Thank you," said Fabian, "for those few unsolicited orchids."

"So why on earth, I wonder, have you produced this ridiculous taradiddle?"

ii

"There!" cried Ursula. "There! What did I tell you?"

"All I can say," said Fabian stiffly, "is that I am extremely relieved that Mr. Alleyn considers pure taradiddle a statement upon which I found it difficult to embark and which was, in effect, a confession."

"My dear chap," said Alleyn. "I don't doubt for a moment that you've had these beastly experiences. I spoke carelessly and I apologize. What I do suggest is that the inference you have drawn is quite preposterous. I don't say that, pathologically speaking, you were incapable of committing this crime, but I do say that, physically speaking, on the evidence we've got, you couldn't possibly have done so."

"Ten minutes," said Fabian.

"Exactly. Ten minutes. Ten minutes in which to travel about a fifth of a mile, strike a blow, and—I'm sorry to be specific over unpleasant details but it's as well to clear this up—suffocate your victim, remove a great deal of wool from the press, bind up the body, dispose of it, and refill the press. You couldn't have done it during the short time you were unconscious, and I don't imagine you are going to tell me you returned later, master of yourself, to tidy up a crime you didn't remember committing. As you know, these must have been the circumstances. You wore white flannels, I understand? Very well, what sort of state were they in when you came to yourself?"

"Loamy," said Fabian. "Don't forget the vegetable marrows. Evidently I'd collapsed into them."

"But not woolly? Not stained in any other way?"

Ursula got up quickly and walked over to the window.

"Need we?" asked Fabian, watching her.

"Certainly not. It can wait."

"No," said Ursula. "We asked for it; let's get on with it. I'm all right. I'm only getting a cigarette."

Her back was towards them. Her voice sounded remote and it was impossible to glean from it the colour of her thoughts. "Let's get on with it," she repeated.

"You may remember," said Fabian, "that the murderer was supposed to have used a suit of overalls belonging to Tommy Johns and a pair of working gloves out of one of the pockets. The overalls hung on a nail near the press. Next morning when Tommy put them on he found a seam had split and he noticed—other details."

"If that theory is correct," said Alleyn, "and I think that very probably it is, another minute or two is added to the time-table. You know you must have thought all this out for yourself. You must have thrashed it out a great many times. To reach the wool-shed and escape the notice of the rest of the party in the garden, you would have had to go round about, either through the house or by way of the side lawn and the yards at the back. You couldn't have used the bottom path because Miss Lynne or Miss Harme would have seen you. Now, before dinner I ran by the most direct route from the vegetable garden to the wool-shed and it took me two minutes. In your case the direct route is impossible. By the indirect routes it took three and four minutes respectively. That leaves a margin, at the best, of about four minutes in which to commit the crime. Can you wonder that I described your theory, inaccurately perhaps but with some justification, as a taradiddle?"

"In England," Fabian said, "after I'd had my first lapse, I went rather thoroughly into the whole business of unconscious behaviour following injuries to the head. I was—" his mouth twisted—"rather interested. The condition is quite well-known and apparently not even fantastically unusual.

Oddly enough it's sometimes accompanied by an increase in physical strength."

"But not," Alleyn pointed out mildly, "by the speed of a scalded cat going off madly in all directions."

"All right, all right," said Fabian with a jerk of his head. "I'm immensely relieved. Naturally."

"I still don't see—" Alleyn began, but Fabian, with a spurt of nervous irritation, cut him short: "Can you see, at least, that a man in my condition might become morbidly apprehensive about his own actions? To have even one minute cut out of your life, leaving an unknown black lane down which you must have wandered, horribly busy! It's a disgusting, an intolerable thing to happen to you. You feel that nothing was impossible during the lost time, nothing!"

"I see," said Alleyn's voice quietly in the shadow.

"I assure you I'm not burning to persuade you. You say I couldn't have done it. All right. Grand. And now, for God's sake let's get on with it."

Ursula came back from the window and sat on the arm of the sofa. Fabian got to his feet, and moved restlessly about the room. There was a brief silence.

"I've always thought," Fabian said abruptly, "that the Buchmanite habit of public confession was one of the few really indecent practices of modern times, but I must say it has its horrid fascination. Once you start on it, it's very difficult to leave off. It's like taking the cap off a steam whistle. I'm afraid there's still a squeak left in me."

"Well, I don't pretend to understand—" Douglas began.

"Of course not," Fabian rejoined. "How should you? You're not the neurotic sort like me, Douglas, are you? I wasn't that sort before, you know. Before Dunkirk, I mean. You were wounded in the bottom, I was cracked on the head. That's the difference between us."

"To accuse yourself of murder—"

"War neurosis, my dear Doug. Typical case: 'Losse, F., First Lieut. Subject to attacks of depression. Refusal to discuss condition. Treatment: Murder in the family followed by psychotherapy (police brand) and Buchmanism. Patient evinced marked desire to talk about himself. Sense of guilt strongly manifested. Cure, doubtful.'"

"I don't know what the hell you're talking about."

"Of course not. Sense of guilt aggravated by history of violent antagonism to victim. In fact," said Fabian, coming to a halt before Alleyn's chair, "three weeks before she was killed, Flossie and I had one hell of a row!"

Alleyn looked up at Fabian and saw his lips tremble into a sneer. He made a small breathy sound something like laughter. He wore the conceited, defiant air of the neurotic who bitterly despises his own weakness. Difficult, Alleyn thought, and damned tiresome. He's going to treat me like an alienist. Blast! "And," he said, "so you had a row?"

Ursula bent forward and put her hand in Fabian's. For a moment his fingers closed tightly about hers and then, with an impatient movement, he jerked away from her.

"Oh, yes," he said loudly. "I'm afraid, since I've started on my course of indecent exposure, I've got to tell you about that too. I'm sorry I can't wait until we're alone together. Very boring for the others. Especially Douglas. Douggy always pays. And I apologize to Ursula because she comes into it. Sorry, Ursy, very bad form."

"If you mean what I think you mean," said Douglas, "I most certainly agree. Surely Ursy can be left out of this."

"Don't be an idiot, Douglas," Ursula said impatiently. "It's what he's doing to himself that matters."

"And to Douglas, of course," Fabian cut in loudly. "Don't forget what I'm doing to poor old Douglas. He becomes the traditional figure of fun. Upon my word it's like a *fin de siècle* farce. Flossie was the duenna of course, and you, Douglas, her candidate for the *mariage de convenance*. Ursy is the wayward heroine who shakes her curls and looks elsewhere. I, at least, should have the sympathy of the audience if only because I didn't get it from anybody else. There is no hero, I go sour in the part. You ought to be the confidante, Terry, but I've an idea you ran a little sub-plot of your own."

"I told you," said Terence Lynne, clearly, "that if we started to talk like this, one, if not all of us, would regret it."

Fabian turned on her with extraordinary venom. "But that one won't be you, will it, Terry? At least, not yet."

She put her work down in her lap. A thread of scarlet wool trickled over her black dress and fell in a little pool on the floor. "No," she said easily, "it won't be me. Except that I find all this talk rather embarrassing. And I don't know what you mean by your 'not yet,' Fabian."

"You will please keep Terry's name..." Douglas began.

"Poor Douglas!" said Fabian. "Popping up all over the place as the little pattern of chivalry. But it's no good you know. I'm hell-bent on my Buchmanism. And, really, Ursy, you needn't mind. I may have a crack in my skull and seem to be a bit crazy, but I did pay you the dubious compliment of asking you to marry me."

iii

"It's a further sidelight on Flossie," Fabian said, "that the story is really significant," and as he listened to it Alleyn was inclined to agree with him. It was also a sidelight, he thought, on the character of Ursula Harme, who, when she found there was no stopping Fabian, took the surprising and admirable line of discussing their extraordinary courtship objectively and with an air of judicial impartiality.

Fabian, it appeared, had fallen in love with her during the voyage out. He said, jeering at himself, that he had made up his mind to keep his feelings to himself: "Because, taking me by and large, I was not a suitable claimant for the hand of Mrs. Rubrick's ward." On his arrival in New Zealand he had consulted a specialist and had shown him the official report on his injury and subsequent condition. By that time Fabian was feeling very much better. His headaches were less frequent and there had been no recrudescence of the blackouts. The specialist took fresh X-ray photographs of his head, and, comparing them with the English ones, found an improvement at the site of injury. He told Fabian to go slow and said there was no reason why he should not make a complete recovery. Fabian, greatly cheered, returned to Mount Moon. He attempted to take part in the normal activities of a sheep station but found that undue exertion still upset him, and he finally settled down to work seriously on his magnetic fuse.

"All this time," he said, "I did not change either in my feeling for Ursy or in my decision to say nothing about it. She was heavenly kind to me, which perhaps made things a little more difficult, but I had no idea, none at all, that she was in the least fond of me. I avoided anything like a declaration, not only because I thought it would be dishonest, but because I believed it would be useless and embarrassing."

Fabian made this statement with simplicity and firmness, and Alleyn thought: He's working his way out of this. Evidently it was necessary for him to speak.

One afternoon some months after his arrival at Mount Moon, Flossie had plunged upstairs and beat excitedly on the workroom door. Fabian opened it and she shook a piece of paper in his face. "Read that," she shouted. "My Favourite Nephew! Isn't it perfectly splendid!"

It was a cable taken down by Markins over the telephone, and it announced the imminent return of Douglas Grace. Flossie was delighted. He was, she repeated emphatically, her Favourite Nephew. "So sweet always to his old aunt. We had such high old times together in London before the war." Douglas was to come straight to Mount Moon. As a schoolboy he had spent all his holidays there. "It's his home," said Flossie emphatically. His father had been killed in 1918, and his mother had died some three years ago when Douglas was taking a post-graduate engineering course at Heidelberg. "So he's only got his old auntie," said Flossie. "Your uncle says that if he's demobilized he shall stay here as a salaried cadet. We don't know how badly he's been hurt, of course." Fabian asked where Douglas had been wounded. "A muscular wound," said Flossie evasively, and then added, "the *glutoeus maximus,*" and was deeply offended when Fabian laughed. But she was too excited to remain long in a huff, and Fabian saw that she hovered on the edge of a confidence. "Isn't it fun," she exclaimed, letting her lips fly apart over her prominent teeth, "that Ursy and Douglas should meet! My little A.D.C. and my Favourite Nephew. And you, of course, Fab. I've told Ursy so much about Douglas that she feels she knows him already." Here Flossie gave Fabian a very sharp, gimlet-like glance. He came out, shut the workroom door and locked it. He felt a cold jolt of apprehension in the pit of his stomach, a dreadful turning-

over. Flossie took his arm and walked him along the passage.
"You'll call me a silly, romantic old thing," she began, and
even in his distress he found time to reflect how irritating she
was when she playfully assumed octogenarian whimsies. "It's
only a little dream of course," she continued, "but it would
make me so happy if they should come together. It's always
been a little plot of poor old Floosie's. Now, if I was a French
guardian and aunt..." She gave Fabian's arm a little
squeeze. "Ah, well," she said, "we'll see." He received another
gimlet-like glance. "He'll be very good for you, Fab," she said
firmly. "He's so sane and vigorous. Take you out of yourself.
Ha!"

So Douglas arrived at Mount Moon, and presently the
two young men began their partnership in the workroom.
Fabian said, wryly, that from the beginning he had watched
for an attraction to spring up between Ursula and Douglas.
"Certainly Flossie made every possible effort to promote it.
She left no stone unturned. The trips *à deux* to the Pass! The
elaborate sortings-out. She displayed the virtuosity of
Tommy Johns in the drafting yards. Ursy and Douglas to the
right. Terry, Uncle Arthur and me to the left. It was masterly
and quite shameless. One evening when, on the eve of one of
her trips north, her machinations had been particularly
blatant, Uncle Arthur called her 'Pandora,' but she missed
the allusion and thought he was making a joke about her
luggage."

For a time Fabian had thought her plot was going to work
and tried to accustom himself to the notion. He watched, sick
with uncertainty, for intimate glances, private jokes, the
small change of courtship, to develop between Ursula and
Douglas and thought he saw them where they didn't exist. "I
was even glad to keep Douglas in the workshop because then,
at least, I knew they were not together. I was mean and subtle
but I tried not to be, and I don't think anyone noticed."

"I merely thought he was fed-up with me," Ursula said to
Alleyn. "He treated me with deathly courtesy."

And then on a day when Fabian had one of his now very
rare headaches, there had been a scene between them. "A
ridiculous scene," he said, looking gently at Ursula. "I
needn't describe it. We talked at cross-purposes like people in
a Victorian novel."

"And I bawled and wept and said if I irritated him he needn't talk to me at all, and then," said Ursula, "we had a magic scene in which everything was sorted out and it all looked as if it was going to be heaven."

"But it didn't work out that way," Fabian said. "I came to earth and remembered I'd no business making love to anybody and, ten minutes too late, did the little hero number and told Ursy to forget me. She said no. We had the sort of argument that you might imagine from the context. I weakened, of course. I never was much good at heroics and—well, we agreed I should see the quack again and stand by what he told me. But we'd reckoned without our Floss."

Fabian turned back to the fire-place and, thrusting his hands in his pockets, looked up at the portrait of his aunt.

"I told you she was as clever as a bagful of monkeys, didn't I? That's what this thing doesn't convey. She was sharp. For example she was wise enough to avoid tackling Ursy about me, and, still more remarkable, she had denied herself, too, many heart-to-heart talks with Ursy about Douglas. I imagine what she did say was indirect, a building-up of allusive romantics. She was by no means incapable of subtlety. Just a spot or two of the Beatrice and Benedict stuff, and the merest hint that she'd be so so happy if ever—and then a change of topic.... Like that, wasn't it, Ursy?"

"But she would have liked it," said Ursula unhappily. "She was so fond of Douglas."

"And not so proud of me. From what you've heard already, Mr. Alleyn, you'll have gathered that my popularity had waned. I wasn't a good enough yes-man for Flossie. I hadn't responded too well to her terrifying ministrations when she nursed me, and she didn't really like my friendship with Uncle Arthur."

"That's nonsense," Ursula said. "Honestly, darling, it's the purest bilge. She told me it was so nice for Uncle Arthur having you to talk to."

"You old innocent," he said, "of course she did. She disliked it intensely. It was something outside the Flossie System, something she wasn't in on. I was very fond of my Uncle Arthur," Fabian said thoughtfully, "he was a good vintage, dry, with a nice bouquet. Wasn't he, Terry?"

"You're straying from the point," said Terence.

"Right. After Ursy and I had come to our decision I tried to be very non-committal and unexalted, but I suppose I made a poor fist at it. I was—translated. I'm afraid," said Fabian abruptly, "that all this is intolerably egotistical but I don't see how that can be avoided. At any rate, Flossie spotted something was up. That eye of hers! You do get a hint of it in the portrait. It was sort of blank and yet the pupils had the look of drills. Ursy managed better than I did. She rather made up to you, Douglas, didn't she, during lunch?"

The fire had burned low and the glowing ball of the kerosene lamp was behind Douglas, but Alleyn thought that he had turned redder in the face. His hand went to his moustache and he said in an easy, jocular voice: "I think Ursy and I understood each other pretty well, didn't we, Ursy? We both knew our Flossie, what?"

Ursy moved uncomfortably. "No, Douglas," she said. "I won't quite take that. I mean—oh, well, it doesn't matter."

"Come on, Douglas," said Fabian with something of his former impishness, "be a little gent and take your medicine."

"I've said a dozen times already that I fail to see what we gain by parading matters that are merely personal before Mr. Alleyn. Talk about dirty linen!"

"But, my God, isn't it better to wash it, however publicly, than to hide it away, still dirty, in our cupboards? I'm persuaded," said Fabian vigorously, "that only by getting the whole story, the whole complicated mix-up of emotions and circumstances sorted out and related shall we ever get at the truth. And, after all, this particular bit of linen is perfectly clean. Only rather comic, like Mr. Robertson Hare's underpants."

"Honestly!" said Ursula and giggled.

"Come on now, Douglas. Egged on by Flossie you did make a formal pass at Ursy that very afternoon. Didn't you, now?"

"I only want to spare Ursy—"

"No you don't," said Fabian. "Come off it, Doug. You want to spare yourself, old cock. This is how it went, I fancy: Flossie, observing my exaltation, told you that it was high time you made a move. Encouraged by Ursy's carryings-on at lunch—you overdid it a bit, Ursy—and gingered up by Flossie, you proposed and were refused."

"You didn't really mind, though, did you, Douglas?" asked Ursula gently. "I mean, it was all rather spur-of-the-momentish, wasn't it?"

"Well, yes," said Douglas. "Yes, it was. But I don't mean..."

"Give it up," Fabian advised him kindly. "Or were you by any chance in love with Ursy?"

"Naturally. I wouldn't have asked Ursy to be my wife..." Douglas began and then swore softly to himself.

"And with the wealthy aunt's blessing why shouldn't the good little heir speak up like a man? We'll let it go at that," said Fabian. "Ursy said her piece, Mr. Alleyn, and Douglas took it like a hero, and the next thing that happened was me on the mat before Flossie."

The scene had been formidable and had taken place there, in the study. Flossie, Fabian explained, had contrived to give the whole thing an air of the grossest impropriety. She had spoken in a cold hushed voice. "Fabian, I'm afraid what I'm going to say to you is very serious and most unpleasant. I am bitterly disappointed and dreadfully grieved. I think you know what it is that has hurt me so much, don't you?"

"I'm afraid I haven't an inkling so far, Aunt Flossie," Fabian had answered brightly and with profound inward misgivings.

"If you think for a minute, Fabian, I'm sure your conscience will tell you."

But Fabian refused to play this uncomfortable game and remained obstinately unhelpful. Flossie extended her long upper lip and the corners of her mouth turned down dolorously. "Oh, Fabian, Fabian!" she said in a wounded voice, and after an unfruitful pause she added: "And I put such trust in you. Such trust!" She bit her lip and shielded her eyes wearily. "You refuse to help me, then. I had hoped it would be easier than this. What have you been saying to Ursula? What have you done, Fabian?"

This persistent repetition of his name had jarred intolerably on his nerves, Fabian said, but he had replied without emphasis. "I'm afraid I've told Ursula that I'm fond of her."

"Do you realize how dreadfully wrong that was? What right had you to speak to Ursy?"

There was only one answer to this. "None," said Fabian.

"None," Flossie repeated. "None! You see? Oh, Fabian."

"Ursula returns my love," said Fabian, taking some pleasure in the old-fashioned phrase.

Two brick-red patches appeared over Flossie's cheekbones. She abandoned her martyrdom. "Nonsense," she said sharply.

"I know it's incredible, but I have her word for it."

"She's a child. You've taken advantage of her youth."

"That's ridiculous, Aunt Florence," said Fabian.

"She's sorry for you," said Flossie cruelly. "It's pity she feels. You've played on her sympathy for your bad health. That's what it is. Pity," she added with an air of originality, "may be akin to love, but it's not love and you've behaved most unscrupulously in appealing to it."

"I made no appeal. I agree that I've no business to ask Ursula to marry me and I said as much to her."

"That was very astute of you," she said.

"I said there must be no engagement between us unless my doctor could give me a clean bill of health. I assure you, Aunt Florence, I've no intention of asking her to marry a crock."

"If you were bursting with health," Flossie shouted, "you'd still be entirely unsuited to each other." She elaborated her theme, pointing out to Fabian the weaknesses in his character—his conceit, his cynicism, his absence of ideals. She emphasized the difference in their circumstances. No doubt, she said, Fabian knew very well that Ursula had an income of her own and, on her uncle's death, would be extremely well provided for. Fabian said that he agreed with everything Flossie said but that after all it was for Ursula to decide. He added that if the X Adjustment came up to their expectations he would be in a better position financially and could hope for regular employment in specialized and experimental jobs. Flossie stared at him. Almost, Fabian said, you could see her lay back her ears.

"I shall speak to Ursula," she said.

This announcement filled him with dismay. He lost his head and implored her to wait until he had seen the doctor. "You see," he told Alleyn, "I knew so well what would happen. Ursy, of course, doesn't agree with me, but the truth is that for her Flossie was a purely symbolic figure. You've heard what Flossie did for Ursy. When Ursy was thirteen years old, and completely desolate, Flossie came along like a plain but comforting goddess and snatched her up into a system of pink clouds. She still sees her as the beneficent super-mother. Flossie had a complete success with Ursula. She caught her young. She loaded her down with a sense of gratitude and gingered her up with inoculations of heroine-worship. Flossie was, as people say, everything to Ursula. She combined the roles of adored form-mistress, queen-mother and lover."

"I never heard such utter tripe," said Ursula, quite undisconcerted by this analysis. "All this talk of queen-mothers! Do pipe down, darling."

"I mean it," Fabian persisted. "Instead of having a good healthy giggle about some frightful youth or mooning over a talkie idol or turning violently Anglo-Catholic, which is the correct behaviour in female adolescence, you converted all these normal impulses into a blind devotion to Flossie.

"Shut up, do. We've had it all out a dozen times."

"It wouldn't have mattered if it had passed off in the normal way, but it became a fixation."

"She was marvellous to me. I owed everything to her. I was decently grateful. And I loved her. I'd have been a monster if I didn't. You and your fixations!"

"Would you believe it," said Fabian, angrily addressing himself to Alleyn, "this silly girl, although she says she loves me, won't marry me, not because I'm a bad bargain physically, which I admit, but simply because Flossie, who's dead, screwed some sort of undertaking out of her that she'd give me up."

"I promised to wait two years and I'm going to keep my promise."

"There!" cried Fabian triumphantly. "A promise under duress if ever there was one. Imagine the interview. All the emotional jiggery-pokery that she'd tried on me and then some. 'Darling little Ursy, if I'd had a baby of my own she couldn't have been dearer. Poor old Floosie knows best. You're making me so unhappy.' Faugh!" said Fabian violently. "It's enough to make you sick."

"I didn't think anybody ever said 'Faugh' in real life," Ursula observed. "Only Hamlet: 'And smelt so. Faugh!'"

"That was 'Puh!'" said Alleyn mildly.

iv

"Well, there you have it," said Fabian after a pause. "Ursy went off the day after our respective scenes with Flossie. The Red Cross people rang up to know if she could do her sixty-hours hospital duty. I've always considered that Flossie arranged it. Ursula wrote to me from the hospital and that was the first I knew about this outrageous promise. And, by the way, Flossie didn't commute the sentence into two years' probation until afterwards. At first she exacted a straight-out pledge that Ursy would give me up altogether. The alteration was due, I fancy, to my uncle."

"You confided in him?" Alleyn asked.

"He found out for himself. He was extraordinarily perceptive. He seemed to me," said Fabian, "to resemble some instrument. He would catch and echo in himself, delicately, the coarser sounds made by other people. I suppose his ill health made for a contemplative habit of mind. At all events he achieved it. He was very quiet always. One would sometimes almost forget he was in the room, and then one would look up and meet his eye and know that he had been with one all the time; perhaps critically, perhaps sympathetically. That didn't matter. He was a good companion. It was like that over this affair with Ursy. Apparently he had known all the time that I was in love with her. He asked me to come and see him while he was having his afternoon rest. It was the first time, I believe, that he'd ever asked me a direct question. He said: 'Has it reached a climax, then, between you and that child?' You know, he was fond of you, Ursy. He said, once, that since Flossie was not transparent he could hardly expect that you would notice him."

"I liked him very much," said Ursula defensively, "he was just so quiet that somehow one didn't notice him."

"I told him the whole story. It was one of his bad days. He was breathing short and I was afraid I'd tire him but he made me go on. When I'd finished he asked me what we were going to do if the doctor didn't give me a clean bill. I said I didn't know, but it didn't matter much because Flossie was going to take a stand about it and I was afraid of her influence over Ursy. He said he believed that might be overcome. I thought then that perhaps he meant to tackle Flossie. I still think that he may have been responsible for her suddenly commuting the life sentence into a mere two years, but of course her row with Douglas over Markins may have had something to do with it. You were never quite the same hot favourite after that, were you, Douglas?"

"Not quite," Douglas agreed sadly.

"Perhaps it was a bit of both," Fabian continued. "But I fancy Uncle Arthur did tackle her. Before I left him he said with that wheezy little laugh of his: 'It takes a strong man to be a weak husband. Matrimonially speaking a condition of perpetual apology is difficult to sustain. I've failed signally in the role.' I think I know what he meant, don't you, Terry?"

"I?" said Terence. "Why do you ask me?"

"Because, unlike Ursy, you were not blinded by Flossie's splendours. You must have been able to look at them both objectively."

"I don't think so," she said, but so quietly that perhaps only Alleyn heard her.

"And he must have been attached to you, you know, because when he became so ill you were the one he wanted to see."

As if answering some implied criticism in this Douglas said: "I don't know what we'd have done without Terry all through that time. She was marvellous."

"I know," said Fabian, still looking at her. "You see, Terry, I've often thought that of all of us you're best equipped to look at the whole thing in perspective. Or are you?"

"I wasn't a relation," said Terence, "if that's what you mean. I was an outsider, a paid employee."

"Put it that way if you like. What I meant was that in your case there were no emotional complications." He waited, and then, with a precise repetition of his former inflection, he added: "Or were there?"

"How could there be? I don't know what you want me to say. I'm no good at this kind of thing."

"Not much in our line, is it, Terry?" said Douglas, instantly forming an alliance. "When it comes to all this messing about and holding post-mortems and wondering what everybody was thinking about everybody else, you and I are out of the picture, aren't we?"

"All right," said Fabian, "let's put it to the authority. What do you say, Mr. Alleyn? Is this admittedly ragged discussion a complete waste of time? Does it leave you precisely where you were with the police files? Or has it, if only in the remotest degree, helped you along the path towards a solution?"

"It's of interest," Alleyn replied. "It's given me something that no amount of poring over the files could have produced."

"And my third question?" Fabian persisted.

"I can't answer it," Alleyn rejoined gravely. "But I do hope, very much, that you'll carry on with the discussion."

"There you are, Terry," said Fabian, "it's up to you, you see."

"To do what?"

"To carry forward the theme to be sure. To tell us where we were wrong and why. To give us, without prejudice, your portrait of Flossie Rubrick."

Again Fabian looked up at the painting. "You said you thought that blank affair up there was like her. Why?"

Without glancing at the portrait, Miss Lynne said: "It's a stupid-looking face in the picture. In my opinion that's what she was. A stupid woman."

CHAPTER V

ACCORDING TO TERENCE

The aspect of Terence Lynne that struck Alleyn most forcibly was her composure. He felt quite sure that, more than any of them, she disliked and resented these interminable discussions. Yet she answered his questions composedly. Unlike her companions, she showed no sign of launching into a continuous narrative, and the sense of release which had encouraged them to talk was, he felt certain, absent in Miss Lynne. He had a feeling that unless he was careful he would find himself engaged in something very like a routine police interrogation. This, above all things, he was anxious to avoid. He wanted to retain his position as an onlooker before whom the spoil of an indiscriminate rummage was displayed, leaving him free to sort, reject and set aside. Terence Lynne waited for a specific demand, yet her one contribution up to date had been, in its way, sufficiently startling.

"Here at least," Alleyn said, "are two completely opposed views. Losse, if I remember him, said Mrs. Rubrick was as clever as a bagful of monkeys. You disagree, Miss Lynne?"

"She had a few tricks," said Terence. "She could talk."

"To her electors?"

"Yes, to them. She had the knack. Her speeches sounded rather effective. They didn't read well."

"I always thought you wrote them for her, Terry," said Fabian with a grin.

"If I'd done that they would have read well and sounded dull. I haven't the knack."

"But wasn't it pretty hot to know what they'd like?" asked Douglas.

"She used to listen to people on the wireless and then adapt the phrases."

"By golly, so she did!" cried Fabian delightedly. "Do you

remember, Ursy, the clarion call in the speech on rehabilitation? 'We shall settle them on the good ground, in the fallow fields, in the workshops and in the hills. We shall never abandon them!' Good Lord, she had got a nerve."

"It was utterly unconscious!" Ursy declared. "An instinctive echo."

"Was it!" said Terence Lynne quietly.

"You're unfair, Terry."

"I don't think so. She had a very good memory for other people's ideas. But she couldn't reason very well and she used to make the most painful floaters over finance. She hadn't got the dimmest notion of how her rehabilitation scheme would work out financially."

"Uncle Arthur helped in that department," said Fabian. "Of course he did."

"He played an active part in her public life?" asked Alleyn.

"I told you," she said, "I think it killed him. People talked about the shock of her death but he was worn-out before she died. I tried to stop it happening but it was no good. Night after night we would sit up working on the notes she handed over to him. She gave him no credit for that."

She spoke rapidly and with more colour in her voice. Hullo, Alleyn thought, she's off!

"His own work died of it, too," she said.

"What on earth do you mean, Terry?" asked Fabian. "What work?"

"His essays. He'd started a group of six essays on the pastoral element in Elizabethan poetry. Before that, he wrote a descriptive poem treating the plateau in the Elizabethan mode. That was the best thing he did, we thought. He wrote very lucidly."

"Terry," said Fabian, "you bewilder me with these revelations. I knew his taste in reading of course. It was surprisingly austere. But—essays? I wonder why he never told me."

"He was sensitive about them. He didn't want to talk about them until they were complete. They were really very good."

"I should have liked to know," said Fabian gently. "I wish he had felt he could tell me."

"I suppose he had to have a hobby," said Douglas. "He

couldn't play games of course. There's nothing much in that, just doing a bit of writing, I mean."

"'Scribble, scribble, scribble, Mr. Gibbon.'" Alleyn muttered. Terence and Fabian looked quickly at him and Fabian grinned.

"They were never finished," said Terence. "I tried to help by taking down at his dictation and then by typing, but he got so tired and there were always other things."

"Terry," said Fabian suddenly, "have I by any chance done you rather a bloody injustice?"

Alleyn saw the oval shape of Terence's face lift attentively. It was the colour of a Staffordshire shepherdess, a cool cream. The brows and eyes were dark accents, the mouth a firm red brush stroke. It was an enigmatic face, a mask framed neatly in its sleek cap of black hair.

She said: "I tried very hard not to complicate things."

"I'm sorry," said Fabian. She raised her hands a little way and let them fall into her lap.

"It doesn't matter," she said, "in the very least. It's all over. I didn't altogether succeed."

"You people!" Fabian said, bending a look of tenderness and pain upon Ursula. "You rather make for complications."

"We people?" she said. "Terry and me?"

"Both of you, it seems," he agreed.

Douglas suddenly, raised his cry of: "I don't know what all this is about."

"It doesn't matter," Terence repeated. "It's over."

"Poor Terry," said Fabian, but it seemed that Miss Lynne did not respond easily to sympathy. She took up her work again and the needles clicked.

"Poor Terry," Douglas echoed playfully, obtusely, and sat beside her again, laying his big muscular hand on her knee.

"Where are the essays?" Fabian asked.

"I've got them."

"I'd like to read them, Terry. May I?"

"No," she said coldly.

"Isn't that rather churlish?"

"I'm sorry. He gave them to me."

"I always thought," said Douglas out of a clear sky, "that they were an ideal couple. Awfully fond of each other. Uncle

Arthur thought she was the cat's whiskers. Always telling people how marvellous she was." He slapped Terence's knee. "Wasn't he?" he persisted.

"Yes."

"Yes," said Ursula. "He was. He admired her tremendously. You can't deny that, Fabian."

"I don't deny it. It's incredible but true. He thought a great deal of her."

"For the things he hadn't got," said Terence. "Vitality. Initiative. Drive. Popularity. Nerve."

"You're prejudiced," Ursy said fiercely, "you and Fabian. It's not fair. She was kind, kind and warm and generous. She was never petty or spiteful and how you, both of you, who owed her so much—"

"I owed her nothing whatever," said Terence. "I did my job well. She was lucky to have me. I admit she was kind in the way that vain people are kind. She knew how kind she was. She was quite kind."

"And generous?"

"Yes. Quite."

"And unsuspicious?"

"Yes," Terence agreed after a pause. "I suppose so."

"Then I think it's poor Florence Rubrick," said Ursula stoutly. "I do indeed, Terry."

"I won't take that," Terence said, and for the first time Alleyn heard a note of anger in her voice. "She was too stupid to know, to notice how fortunate she was . . . might have been . . . She didn't even look after her proprietary rights. She was like an absentee landlord."

"But she didn't ask you to poach on the estates."

"What are you two arguing about?" demanded the punctual Douglas. "What's it all in aid of?"

"Nothing," said Fabian. "There's no argument. Let it go."

"But it was you who organized this strip-tease act, Fabian," Ursula pointed out. "The rest of us have had to do our stuff. Why should Terry get off?"

She looked at Terence and frowned. She was a lovely creature, Alleyn thought. Her hair shone in copper tendrils along the nape of her neck. Her eyes were wide and lively, her mouth vivid. She had something of the quality of a Victorian portrait in crayons, a resemblance that was heightened by the extreme delicacy and freshness of her complexion and by the slender grace of her long neck and her elegant hands. She displayed, too, something of the waywardness and conscious poise of such a type. These qualities lent her a dignity that was at variance with her modern habit of speech. She looked, Alleyn thought, as though she knew she would inevitably command attention and that much would be forgiven her. She was obstinate he thought, but he doubted if obstinacy alone was responsible for her persistent defence of Florence Rubrick. He had been watching her closely and, as though she felt his gaze upon her and even caught the tenor of his thoughts, she threw him a brilliant glance and ran impulsively to Terence.

"Terry," she said, "am I unfair? I don't want to be unfair but there's no one else but me to speak for her."

Without looking at him she held out her hand to Fabian and immediately he was beside her, holding it.

"You're not allowed to snub me, Fabian, or talk over my head or go intellectual at me. I loved her. She was my friend. I can't stand off and look at her and analyze her faults. And when all of you do this, I have to fight for her."

"I know," said Fabian, holding her by the hand. "It's all right. I know."

"But I don't want to fight with Terry. Terry, I don't want to fight with you, do you hear? I'd rather after all that you didn't tell us. I'd rather go on liking you."

"You won't get me to believe," said Douglas, "that Terry's done anything wrong and I tell you straight, Fabian, that I don't much like the way you're handling this. If you're suggesting that Terry's got anything to be ashamed about..."

"Be quiet!"

Terence was on her feet. She had spoken violently as if prompted by some intolerable sense of irritation. "You're talking like a fool, Douglas. 'Ashamed' or 'not ashamed,' what has that got to do with it? I don't want your companionship and, Ursula, I promise you I don't give a damn whether you think you're being fair or unfair or whether, as you put it, you're prepared to 'go on liking me.' You make too many assumptions. To have dragooned me into going so far and then to talk magnanimously about

letting me off! You've all made up your minds, haven't you,
that I loved him. Very well, then, it's perfectly true. If Mr.
Alleyn is to hear the whole story, at least let me tell it, plainly
and, if it's not too fantastic a notion, with a little dignity."

ii

It was strange, Alleyn thought, that Terence Lynne, who
from the beginning had resented the discussion and all that it
implied, should suddenly yield, as the others had yielded, to
this intolerable urge for self-revelation. As she developed her
story, speaking steadily and with a kind of ruthlessness, he
regretted more and more that he could form no clear picture
in his mind of Florence Rubrick's husband—of how he
looked, of how wide a physical disparity there had been
between Arthur Rubrick and this girl who must have been
twenty years his junior.

Terence had been five years in New Zealand. Equipped
with a knowledge of shorthand and typing and six letters of
recommendation, including one from the High Commission-
er in London to Flossie herself, she had sought her fortune in
the Antipodes. Flossie immediately engaged her, and she
settled down to life at Mount Moon interspersed with
frequent visits to Flossie's *pied-à-terre* near Parliament
Buildings in Wellington. She must, Alleyn thought, have
been lonely in her quiet, contained way; separated by half the
world from her own country, her lot fallen among strangers.
Fabian and Ursula, he supposed, had already formed an
alliance in the ship, Douglas Grace had not yet returned from
the Middle East, and she had obviously felt little respect or
liking for her employer. Yes, she must have been lonely. And
then Flossie began to send her on errands to her husband.
"Those statistics on revaluation, Miss Lynne, I want
something I can quote. Something comparative. You might
just go over the notes with my husband. Nothing elaborate,
tell him. Something that will score a point." And Arthur

Rubrick and Terence Lynne would work together in the study. She found she could lighten his task by fetching books from the shelves and by taking notes at his dictation. Alleyn formed a picture of this exquisitely neat girl moving quietly about the room or sitting at the desk while the figure in the armchair dictated, a little breathlessly, the verbal bullets that Flossie was to fire at her political opponents. As they grew to know each other well, she found that, with a pointer or two from Arthur Rubrick, she was able to build up most of the statistical ammunition required by her employer. She had a respect for the right phrase and for the just fall of good words, each in its true place, and so, she found, had he. They had a little sober fun together, concocting paragraphs for Flossie, but they never heard themselves quoted. "She used to peck over the notes like a magpie," Terence said, "and then rehash them with lots of repetition so that she would be provided with opportunities to thump with her right fist on the palm of her left hand. 'In 1938,' she would shout, beating time with her fist, 'in 1938, mark you, in 1938 the revenue from such properties amounted to three and a quarter million. To three and a quarter million. Three and a quarter million pounds, Mr. Speaker, was the sum realized . . .' And she was quite right. It went down much better than our austerely balanced phrases would have done if ever she'd been fool enough to use them. *They* only appeared when she handed in notes of her speeches for publication. She kept them specially for that purpose. They looked well in print."

It had been through this turning of phrases that Flossie's husband and her secretary came to understand each other more thoroughly. Flossie was asked by a weekly journal to contribute an article on the theme of women workers in the back-country. She was flattered, said Terence, but a bit uneasy. She came into the study and talked a good deal about the beauty of women's work in the home. She said she thought the cocky-farmer's wife led a supremely beautiful existence because it was devoted to the basic fundamentals (she occasionally coined such phrases) of life. "A noble life," Flossie said, ringing for Markins, "they also serve—" But the quotation faltered before the picture of any cocky-farmer's wife whose working-day is fourteen hours long and comparable only to that of a man under a sentence of hard

labour. "Look up something appropriate, Miss Lynne.
Arthur darling, you'll help her. I want to stress the sanctity of
women's work in the high country. Unaided, alone. You
might say matriarchal," she threw at them as Markins came
in with the cup of patent food she took at eleven o'clock.
Flossie sipped it and walked up and down the room throwing
out unrelated words: "True sphere...splendour...heri-
tage...fitting mate." She was called to the telephone but
found time to pause in the door and say: "Away you go, both
of you. Quotations, remember, but not too highbrow, Arthur
darling. Something sweet and natural and telling." She
waved her hand and was gone.

The article they wrote was frankly heretical. They had
stood side by side in the window and looked over the plateau
to the ranges, now a clean thin blue in the mid-morning
sunshine.

"When I look out there," Arthur Rubrick had said, "it
always strikes me as being faintly comic that we should talk
of 'settling' on the plateau and of 'bringing in new country.'
All we do is to move over the surface of a few hills. There is
nothing new about them. Primal, yes, and almost unblotted
by such new things as men and sheep. Essentially back
among the earlier un-human ages." He had added that
perhaps this was the reason why no one had been able to
write very well about this country. It had been possible, he
said, to write of the human beings moving about parasitically
over the skin of the country, but the edge of modern idiom
was turned when it was tried against the implacable surface
of the plateau. He said that some older and therefore fresher
idiom was needed, "something that has the hard edge of a
spring wind in it, something comparable to the Elizabethan
mode." From this conversation was born his idea of writing
about the plateau in a prose that smacked of Hakluyt's
Voyages. "It sounds affected," said Terence, "but he only did
it as a kind of game. I thought it really did give one the
sensation of this country. But it was only a game."

"A fascinating game," said Alleyn. "What else did he
write?"

Five more essays, she said, that were redrafted many times
and never really completed. Very often he wasn't up to
working on them, and Flossie's odd jobs absorbed his energy

when he was well. There were many occasions when he fagged over her speeches and reports, or dragged himself to meetings and parties when he should have been resting. He had a morbid dread of admitting to his wife that he was unwell. "It's so tiresome for her," he used to say. "She's too good about it, too kind."

"And she was kind," Ursula declared. "She took endless trouble."

"It was the wrong kind of trouble," Fabian said. "She oozed long-suffering patronage."

"I didn't think so. Nor did he."

"Did he, Terry?" asked Fabian.

"He was extraordinarily loyal. That's all he ever said: 'It's too good of her, too kind.' But, of course it wasn't much fun being the object of that sort of compassion. And then—" Terence paused.

"Then what, Terry?" said Fabian.

"Nothing. That's all."

"But it isn't quite all, is it? Something happened, didn't it? There was some crisis, wasn't there? What was he worrying about that last fortnight before she died? He was worried, you know. What was it?"

"He was feeling ill. He had an idea things were going wrong in the background. Mrs. Rubrick obviously was upset. I see now that it was the trouble with Cliff Johns and Markins that had put her in a difficult mood. She didn't tell him about Cliff and Markins, I'm sure, but she dropped dark hints about ingratitude and disappointment. She was always doing it. She kept saying that she stood alone, that other women in her position had somebody to whom they could turn and that she had nobody. He sat over there in the window, listening, with his hand shading his eyes, just taking it. I could have murdered her."

This statement was met by a scandalized hush.

"A commonplace exaggeration," said Fabian at last. "I've used it repeatedly myself in speaking of Flossie. 'I could have murdered her.' I suppose she got home with her cracks at Uncle Arthur, didn't she? Every time a coconut?"

"Yes," said Terence. "She got home."

A longer silence followed. Alleyn felt certain that Terence had reached a point in her story where something was to be withheld from her listeners. The suggestion of antagonism, never long absent from her manner, now deepened. She set her lips and, after a quick look into the shadow where he sat, took up her work again with an air of finality.

"Funny," said Fabian suddenly. "I thought she seemed to be rather come-hither-ish with Uncle Arthur during that last week. There was a hint of skittishness which I found extremely awe-inspring. And, I may say, extremely unusual. You must have noticed it, all of you. What was she up to?"

"Honestly, Fabian darling," said Ursula, "you are too difficult. At one moment you find fault with Aunt Floss for neglecting Uncle Arthur and at the next you complain because she was nice to him. What should she have done, poor darling, to please you and Terry?"

"How old was she?" Douglas blurted out. "Forty-seven, wasn't it? Well, I mean to say she was jolly spry for her age, wasn't she? I mean to say . . . well, I mean, there it was . . . I suppose . . ."

"Let it pass, Douglas," Fabian said kindly. "We know what you mean. But I can't think that Florence's sudden access of playfulness was entirely due to natural or even pathological causes. There seemed to me to be a distinct suggestion of proprietary rights. What I have I hold. The bitch, if you will excuse the usage, Douglas, in the marital manger."

"It's entirely inexcusable," said Ursula, "and so are you, Fab."

"I don't mean to show off and be tiresome, darling, I promise you I don't. You can't deny that she was different during that last week. As sour as a lemon with all of us and suddenly so, so keen on Uncle Arthur. She watched him too. Indeed she looked at him as if he was some *objet d'art* that she'd forgotten she possessed until someone else came along and saw that it was—well, rare, and in its way rather beautiful. Wasn't it like that, Terry?"

"I don't know. I thought she was horrible, baiting him about his illness. That's what it amounted to and that's what I saw."

"But don't you agree," Fabian persisted, "that along with that there was a definite—what shall I call it?—why damn it, she made advances. She was kittenish. She shook her curls and did the little-devil number. Didn't she, now?"

"I didn't watch her antics," said Terence coldly.

"But you did, Terry. You watched. Listen to me, Terry," said Fabian very earnestly, "don't get it into your head that I'm an enemy. I'm not. I'm sorry for you and I realize now that I've misjudged you. You see I thought you were merely doing your line of oomph with Uncle Arthur out of boredom. I thought you just sat round being a cryptic woman at him to keep your hand in. I know this sounds insufferable but he was so very much older and, well, as I thought, so definitely not your cup of tea. It was perfectly obvious that he was losing his heart to you and I resented what I imagined was merely a bit of practice technique on your part. I don't suppose you give two tuppenny damns for what I thought, Terry, but I am sorry. All right. Now, when I suggested that we should ask Mr. Alleyn to come, we all agreed that rather than carry on as we were, with this unspeakable business festering in our minds, we would, each of us, risk becoming an object of suspicion. We agreed that none of us suspected any of the other three and, even with the terrifying example of the local detective force to daunt us, we said we didn't believe that the truth, the whole truth, although it might be unpalatable, could do us any harm. Were we right in that, Mr. Alleyn?"

Alleyn stirred a little in his armchair and joined his long fingers. "It's a truism to say that if the whole facts of a case are known there can be no miscarriage of justice. It's very seldom indeed, in homicide investigations, that the police arrive at the whole truth. Sometimes they get enough of the truth to enable them to build up a case and make an arrest. Most often they get a smattering of essential facts, a plethora of inessential facts and a maddening accumulation of lies. If you really do stick to your original plan of thrashing out the whole story here to-night, in this room, you will, I think, bring off a remarkable, indeed a unique performance."

He saw that they were young enough to be flattered and stimulated by this assurance. "There, now!" said Fabian triumphantly.

"But," said Alleyn, "I don't believe for a moment that you will succeed. How long does it take a psychoanalyst to complete his terrifying course of treatment? Months, isn't it? His aim, as I understand it, is to get to the bottom, to spring-clean completely, to arrive, in fact, at the clinical truths. Aren't you, Losse, attempting something of that sort? If so, I'm sure you cannot succeed, nor, as a policeman, would I want you to do so. As a policeman, I am not concerned with the whole clinical truth. Faced with it, I should probably find myself unable to make any arrest, ever. I am required only to produce facts. If your discussion of Mrs. Rubrick's character and that of her husband can throw the smallest ray of light along the path that leads to an unknown murderer who struck her from behind, suffocated her, bound up her body, and concealed it in a wool press, then from the official point of view it will have been valuable. If, at the same time, somewhere along that path there is the trace of an enemy agent, then again from my point of view, as an investigator of espionage in this country, it will have been valuable. If, finally, it relieves the burden of secrecy under which you have all suffered, you, also, may profit by it, though, as you have already seen, the process is painful and may be dangerous."

"We realize that," Fabian said.

"Do you fully realize it? You told me at first that there was a complete absence of motive among you. Would you still say so? Look what has come out. Captain Grace was Mrs. Rubrick's heir. That circumstance, which suggests the most common of all motives, has of course always been recognized by the police and must have occurred to all of you. You, Losse, advanced a theory that you yourself in a condition of amnesia attacked Mrs. Rubrick and killed her. What's more, as you developed this theme you also revealed a motive, Mrs. Rubrick's opposition to your engagement to Miss Harme. Now, under this same process of self-revelation, Miss Lynne must also be said to have a motive. Most courageously she has told us that she had formed a deep attachment for the murdered woman's husband and you, Losse, say that this attachment obviously was returned. The second most common motive appeares in both your case and hers. You have said, bravely, that none of you has anything to fear from this discussion. Are you sure you have the right to make this statement? You are using this room as a sort of confessional but I am bound by no priestly rule. What you tell me I shall consider from the practical point of view and may afterwards use in the report I send to your police. I should neglect my duty if, before she goes any further, I didn't remind Miss Lynne of all the circumstances." Alleyn paused and rubbed his nose. "That all sounds pompous," he said. "But there it is. The whole thing's a departure from the usual procedure. I doubt if any collection of possible suspects had ever before decided to have what Miss Harme has aptly described as a verbal strip-tease, before an investigating officer." He looked at Terence. "Well, now, Miss Lynne," he said, "if you don't want to go on—"

"It's not because I'm afraid," she said. "I didn't do it and any attempt to prove I did would fail. I suppose I ought to be afraid but I'm not. I don't feel in the least anxious for myself."

"Very well. Losse has suggested that there is some significance in the change, during the last week of Mrs. Rubrick's life, in her manner towards her husband. He has suggested that you can explain this change. Is he right?"

She did not answer. Slowly and, as it seemed, reluctantly, she raised her eyes and looked at the portrait of Florence Rubrick.

"Terry!" said Ursula suddenly. "Did she know? Did she find out?"

Fabian gave a sharp ejaculation and Terence turned, not upon Ursula but upon him.

"You idiot, Fabian," she said. "You unutterable fool."

iii

The fire had burnt low, and the room was colder and stale with tobacco smoke.

"I give it up," said Douglas loudly. "I never was any good at riddles and I'm damned if I know half the time what you're all getting at. For God's sake let's have some air in this room."

He went to the far end of the study, jerked back the curtains, and pushed open a French window. The night air came in, not as a wind, but stilly, with a tang of extreme cleanliness. The moon was up and, across the plateau, fifty miles away, it shone on the Cloud Piercer and his attendant peaks. Alleyn joined Douglas at the window. "If I spoke," he thought, "my voice would go out towards those mountains and between my moving lips and that distant snow there would be only clear darkness." He had noticed, on the drive up to Mount Moon, that the flats in front of the homestead were swampy and studded with a few desultory willows. Now, in the moonlight, he caught a glint of water and he heard the cry of wild duck and the beat of wings. Behind him in the room, someone threw wood upon the fire and Alleyn's shadow flickered across the terrace.

"Need we freeze?" Ursula asked fretfully. Douglas reached out his hand to the French window but before he shut it or drew the curtain a footfall sounded briskly and a man walked along the terrace towards the north side of the house. As he reached the part of the terrace that was lit from the room he was seen to be wearing a neat black suit and a felt hat. It was Markins, returning from his visit to the manager's cottage. Douglas slammed the French window and pulled the curtain across it.

"And there goes the expert," he said, "who runs about the place, scot-free, while we sit yammering a lot of highfalutin bilge about the character of the woman he may have killed. I'm going to bed."

"He'll bring the drinks in a minute," said Fabian. "Why not wait and have one?"

"If he's got wind of this I wouldn't put it past him to monkey with the decanter."

"Honestly, Douglas!" Fabian and Ursula said together. "You are—"

"All right, all right," Douglas said angrily. "I'm a fool. Say no more." He flung himself down on the sofa again but this time he did not rest his arm along the back behind Terence. Instead he eyed her with an air of discomfort and curiosity.

"So you prefer to leave Miss Harme's question unanswered," Alleyn said to Terence.

She had picked up her knitting as if hoping by that gesture to recapture something of her composure. But her hands turned her work over, rolling the scarlet mesh round the white needles and, as aimlessly, spreading it out again across her knees.

"You force me to speak of it," she said. "All of you. You talk about us all agreeing to this discussion, Fabian. When you and Ursula and Douglas planned it how could I not agree? It's not my business to refuse. I'm an outsider. I was paid to work for Mrs. Rubrick and now you, Fabian, pay me to work for you in your garden. It's not my business to refuse."

"Nonsense, Terry," said Fabian.

"You've never been in my position. You don't understand. You're all very kind and informal and treat me, as we say in my class, almost like one of yourselves. Almost, not quite."

"My dear girl, that's an insult to me, at least. You know quite enough about my views to realize that any such attitude is revolting to me. 'Your class.' How dare you go class-conscious at me, Terry?"

"You're my boss. You were not too much of a communist to accept Mount Moon when he left it to you."

"I think," said Alleyn crisply, "that we might come back to the question which, believe me, Miss Lynne, you are under no compulsion to answer. This is it. Did Mrs. Rubrick, during the last week of her life, become aware of the attachment between you and her husband?"

"And if I don't answer what will you think? What will you do? Go to Mrs. Aceworthy, who dislikes me intensely, and get some monstrously distorted story that she's concocted. When he was ill he wanted me to look after him and wouldn't see her or have her here. She's never forgiven me. Better you should hear the truth, from me."

"Very much better," Alleyn agreed cheerfully. "Let's have it."

It would have come as something of an anticlimax if it had not made a little clearer the still nebulous picture of that strange companionship. They had been working together over one of Flossie's articles, he at the table near the windows and Terence moving between him and the bookcases. She had returned to him with a volume of Hansard and had laid it on the table before him, standing behind him and pressing it open with her hand at the passage he had asked for. He leant forward and the rough tweed of his coat sleeve brushed her forearm. They were motionless. She looked down at him but his face was hidden from her. He stooped. Her free hand moved and rested on his shoulder. She described the scene carefully, with precision, as if these details were important, as if, having undertaken her story, she was resolved to leave nothing unsaid. She was, Alleyn thought, a remarkable young woman. She said it was the first passage of its kind between them and she supposed they were both too much moved by it to hear the door open. Her right hand was still upon him when she turned and saw her employer. He was even slower to move and her left hand remained, weighed down by his, upon the open pages of the book. It was only when she pulled it away that he too turned, and saw his wife.

Florence remained in the doorway. She had a sheaf of papers in her hand and they crackled as her grip tightened on them. "Hers was an expressionless face," Terence said and Alleyn glanced up at the portrait. "Her teeth showed a little, as usual. Her eyes always looked rather startled, they looked no more so, then. She just stared at us."

Neither Rubrick nor Terence spoke. Florence said loudly: "I'm in a hurry for those reports," and turned on her heel. The door slammed behind her. Rubrick said to Terence: "My dear, I hope you can forgive me," and Terence, sure now that he loved her, and feeling nothing but pleasure in her heart, kissed him lightly and moved away. They returned tranquilly to Flossie's interminable reports. It was strange, Terence said, how little troubled they both were at that time by Flossie's entrance. It seemed then to be quite irrelevant, something to be dismissed impatiently, before the certainty of their attachment. They continued with their employment, Terence said, and Alleyn had a picture of the two of them at work there, sometimes exchanging a brief smile, more often turning the pages of Hansard, or making notes of suitable platitudes for Flossie. An odd affair, he thought.

This mood of acceptance sustained them through their morning's work. At luncheon when the party of six assembled, Terence noticed that her employer was less talkative than usual and she realized that she herself was being closely watched by Flossie. This did not greatly disturb her. She thought vaguely: "I suppose she merely said to herself that it's not much like me to put my hand on anyone's shoulder. I suppose she thinks it was a bit of presumption on my part. She's noticing me as a human being."

At the end of lunch Flossie suddenly announced that she wanted Terence to work with her all the afternoon. She kept Terence hard at it, taking down letters and typing them. It was a perfectly normal routine and at first Terence noticed nothing unusual in Flossie's manner. Presently, however, she became conscious that Flossie, from behind the table, across the room, or by the fireplace, was watching her closely. She would deny herself the uncomfortable experience of meeting this scrutiny but sooner or later she would find herself unable to resist and would look up and there, sure enough, would be that gimlet-like stare that contrived to be at once so penetrating and so expressionless. Terence began to feel that she could not support this behaviour and to wish, in acute discomfort, that Florence would speak to, or even upbraid, her. The flood of contentment that had come upon her when she knew that Rubrick loved her now receded and left in its wake a sensation of shame. She began to see herself with Flossie's eyes as a second-rate little typist who flirted with her employer's husband. She felt sick and humiliated and was filled with a kind of impatience for the worst to happen. There must be a climax, she thought, or she would never recover from the self-disgust that Flossie's stare had put upon her. But there was no climax. They plodded on with their work. When at last they had finished and Terence was gathering together her papers, Flossie, as she walked to the door, said over her shoulder: "I don't think Mr. Rubrick's at all well." Calling him "Mr. Rubrick," Terence felt, put her very neatly in her place. "I don't consider," Florence added, "that we should bother him just now with our silly old statistics. I am rather worried about him. We'll just leave him quietly to himself, Miss Lynne. Will you remember that?" And she went out, leaving Terence to draw what conclusions she chose from this pronouncement.

"And it was after that," Terence said, "almost immediately after—it was the same night, at dinner—when the change you all noticed appeared in her manner towards him. To me it was horrible."

"She decided, in fact," said Fabian, "to meet you on your

own ground, Terry, and give battle." He added awkwardly: "That doesn't seem horrible to me; pitiful, rather, and intensely embarrassing. How like her and how futile."

"But he was devoted to her," Ursula protested. And as if she had made a discovery that astonished and shocked her, she cried out: "You cheated, Terry. It happened because you were young. You shouldn't cheat in that way when you're young. They're all alike—men of his age. If you'd gone away he'd have forgotten."

"No!" said Terence strongly.

To Alleyn's discomfiture they both turned to him.

"He'd have forgotten," Ursula repeated. "Wouldn't he?"

"My dear child," Alleyn said, intensely conscious of his age, "how can I possibly tell?" But when he thought of Arthur Rubrick, ill, and exhausted by his wife's public activities, he was inclined to believe that Ursula was partly right. With Terence gone, might not the emotion that Rubrick had felt for her have faded soon into an only half-regretful memory?

"You're all the same," Ursula muttered, and Alleyn felt himself classed, disagreeably, with Arthur Rubrick, among the senile romantics. "You go queer."

"Well, but damn it all," Fabian protested. "If it comes to that, Flossie's behaviour was pretty queer too. To flirt with your husband after twenty-five years of married life—"

"That was entirely different," Ursula flashed at him, "and anyway, Terry, if she did, it was your fault."

"I didn't do it," Terence said, for the first time defending herself. "It happened. And until she came into the room it was right. I knew it was right. I knew it completely with my reason as well as with my emotion. It was as if I had suddenly been brought into focus, as if I was, for the first time, completely Me. It couldn't possibly be wrong."

She appealed to Ursula and perhaps, Alleyn thought, to the two young men. She asked them for understanding and succeeded in faintly embarrassing them.

"Yes," said Ursula uncomfortably, "but how you could! With Uncle Arthur! He was nearly fifty."

Silence followed this statement. Alleyn, who was forty-seven, realized with amusement that Douglas and Fabian found Ursula's argument unanswerable.

"I didn't hurt him, Fabian," Terence said at last. "I'm certain I didn't. If he was hurt it was by her. She was atrociously possessive."

"Because of you," said Ursula.

"But we couldn't help it. You talk as if I planned what happened. It came out of a clear sky. It wasn't of my doing. And there wasn't a sequel, Ursula. You needn't think we had surreptitious scenes. We didn't. We were both of us, I believe, a little happier in our knowledge of each other. That was all."

"When he was ill," said Fabian, "did you talk about it, Terry?"

"A little. Just to say we were glad we knew."

"If he had lived," said Ursula harshly, "would you have married him?"

"How can I tell?"

"Why shouldn't you have married? Auntie Florence, who was such a bore to both of you, was out of the way. Wasn't she?"

"That's an extraordinary cruel thing to say, Ursula."

"I agree," said Douglas and Fabian muttered: "Pipe down, Ursy."

"No," said Ursula. "We undertook to finish our thoughts in this discussion. You're all cruel to her memory. Why should any of us get off? Why not say what you all must have thought: with her death they were free to marry."

A footfall sounded outside in the hall, accompanied by a faint jingle of glasses. It was Markins with the drinks.

CHAPTER VI

ACCORDING TO THE FILES

With Markins' arrival the discussion ended. It was as if he had opened the door to a wave of self-consciousness. Douglas fussed over the drinks, urging Alleyn to have whisky. Alleyn, who considered himself to be on duty, refused it and wondered regretfully if it was from the same matchless company as the bottle that Cliff Johns had smashed on the diary floor. Any suggestion that the discussion might be taken up again was dispelled by the entrance of Mrs. Aceworthy, who, with the two girls, drank tea, and who had many playful remarks to make about the lateness of the hour. It was high time, she said, that all her chickens were in their nests. And she asked Alleyn pointedly if he had brought a hot-water bottle. Upon this hint he bade them all good-night. Fabian brought in candles and offered to see him to his room.

They went upstairs together, their shadows mounting gigantically beside them. On the landing Fabian said: "You will realize now, of course, that you're in Flossie's room. It's the best one, really, but we all preferred to stay where we were."

"Ah, yes."

"It's got no associations for you, of course."

"None."

Fabian led the way through Florence's door. He lit candles on the dressing-table and the room came into being, a large white room with gay curtains, a pretty desk, a fine bed and a number of flower prints on the walls. Alleyn's pyjamas were laid out on the bed, by Markins, he supposed, and his locked dispatch and investigation cases were displayed prominently on the desk. He grinned to himself.

"Got everything you want?" Fabian asked.

"Everything, thanks. Before we say good-night, though, I wonder if I might take a look at your workroom."

"Why not? Come on."

It was the second door on the left along the passage. Fabian detached the key from about his neck. "On a bootlace, you see," he said. "No deception practised. Here we go."

The strong electric lamp over their working bench dazzled eyes that had become accustomed to candlelight. It shone down on a rack of tools and an orderly collection of drawing materials. A small precision lathe was established on a side bench which was littered with a heterogeneous collection of pieces of metal. A large padlocked cupboard was built into the right-hand wall and beside it Alleyn saw a good modern safe with a combination lock. Three capacious drawers under the bench also were locked.

"The crucial drawings and formulas have always been kept in the safe," Fabian explained. "As you can see, everything is stowed away under lock and key. And pray spare a kind thought for my window shutter, so witheringly dismissed by dear old Douglas."

It was, Alleyn thought, an extremely workmanlike job. "And, I can assure you," Fabian added, "it has not been fiddled with." He sat on the bench and began to talk about their work. "It's a magnetic fuse for anti-aircraft shells," he said. "The shell is made of non-ferrous metal and contains a magnetically operated fuse which will explode the shell when it approaches an aircraft engine, or other metallic object. It will, we hope, be extremly useful at high altitudes where a direct hit is almost impossible. Originally I got the idea from a magnetic mine which, as of course you know, explodes in the magnetic field surrounding steel ships. Now, even though it contains a good deal of alloy, an aeroplane engine must, of necessity, also contain an appreciable amount of steel and, in addition, there's a magnetic field from ignition coils. Our fuse is very different from the fuse in a magnetic mine but it's a kind of second cousin in that it's designed to explode a shell in the aeroplane's magnetic field. As a matter of fact," said Fabian with a glint in his eye, "if it comes off, and it will come off, I believe, it'll be a pretty big show."

"Of course it will. Very big indeed. There's one question I'd like to ask. What about 'prematures' by attraction to the gun itself, or explosion in transit?"

"There's a safety device incorporated in the doings and it sees to it that the fuse won't do its stuff until the shell starts to rotate and after it leaves the gun barrel. The result, in effect, is an aerial magnetic mine. I'll show you the blueprints on presentation of your official card," Fabian ended with a grin.

"I should be enormously interested. But not to-night if you don't mind. I've still a job of work to do."

"In that case, I'll escort you back to your room, first making sure that no adventuresses lurk under the benches. Shall we go?"

Back in Alleyn's room Fabian lit a cigarette at a candle, and gave his guest one of his sidelong glances. "Any good," he asked, "or rotten?"

"The discussion?"

"Yes. Post-mortem. Inquest. Was it hopelessly stupid to do it?"

"I don't think so."

"To-morrow, I suppose, you'll talk to the Johns family and the men and so on."

"If I may."

"We're crutching. You'll be able to see the set-up. It's pretty much the same. All except—"

"Yes?" asked Alleyn as he paused.

"The press is new. I couldn't stomach that. It's the same kind, though."

"I'll just turn up there if I may."

"Yes. O.K. I don't know if you're going to keep our unearthly hours. Please don't if you'd rather not. Breakfast at a quarter to six."

"Of course."

"Then I'll take you over to the shed. You'll ask me for anything you want?"

"I just want a free hand to fossick. I'd be grateful if I could be disregarded."

"Not very easy, I'm afraid. But of course you'll have a free hand. I've told the men and Ducky and everybody that you'll be talking to them."

"How did they like that?"

"Quite keen. It's given a fillip to the ever-popular murder story. Damned ghouls! There'll be one or two snags, though. Wilson, the wool sorter, and Jack Merrywether, the presser, are not at all keen. Your friend Sub-Inspector Jackson got badly offside with both of them. And there's Tommy Johns."

"The boy's father?"

"Yes. He's a difficult chap, Tommy. I get on with him all right. He thinks for himself, does Tommy, and what's more," said Fabian with a grin, "he thinks much like me, politically, so I consider him a grand guy. But he's difficult. He resented Flossie's handling of young Cliff and small blame to him. And what he thinks of police methods! You won't find him precisely come-to-ish."

"And the boy himself?"

"He's all right, really. He's a likely lad, and he thinks for himself, too. We're good friends, young Cliff and I. I lend him the *New Statesman* and he rebuilds the government, social customs and moral standards of mankind on a strictly non-economic basis two or three times a week. His music is really good, I believe, though I'm afraid it's not getting much of a run these days. I've tried to induce him to practise on the Bechstein over here but he's an obstinate young dog and won't."

"Why?"

"It was Flossie's."

"So the quarrel went deep?"

"Yes. It's lucky for young Cliff that he spent the crucial time screwing Bach out of that haggard old mass of wreckage in the annex. Everybody knew about the row and his bolt down-country afterwards. Your boy-friend, the Sub-Inspector, fastened on it like a limpet but fortunately we could all swear to the continuous piano playing. Cliff's all right."

"What's the explanation of the whisky incident?"

"I've not the slightest idea but I'm perfectly certain he wasn't pinching it. I've tried to get the story out of him but he won't come clean, blast him."

"Does he get on well with the other men?"

"Not too badly. They were inclined at one time to look

upon him as a freak. His schooling and tastes aroused their
deepest suspicions, of course. In this country, young men are
judged almost entirely on their ability to play games and do
manual labour. However, Cliff set about his holiday jobs on
the station with such energy that they overlooked his other
unfortunate interests and even grew to encourage him in
playing the piano in the evening. When he came home a good
whole-hog Leftist, they were delighted, of course. They're a
good lot—most of them."

"Not all?"

"The shearers' cook is not much use. He only comes at
shearing time. Mrs. Johns looks after the regular hands at
other times. Lots of the shearers wait until they've knocked
up a good fat cheque and then go down-country and blue it
all at the pub. That's the usual routine and you won't change
it until you change the social condition of the shearer. But
this expert keeps the stuff in his cookhouse and if we get
through the shearing season without a bout of D.T.s we're
lucky. He's a nasty affair is Cookie but he's unavoidable.
They don't dislike him, oddly enough. The roustabout, Albie
Black, is rather thick with him. He used to be quite mately
with young Cliff, too, but they had a break of some sort.
Fortunately, I consider. Albie's a hopeless sort of specimen.
Now, if it'd been Albie who pinched the whisky I shouldn't
have been the least surprised. Or Perce. The cook's name is
Percy Gould, commonly called Perce. All Christian names
are abbreviated in this country."

"How did Mrs. Rubrick get on with the men?"

"She thought she was a riotous success with them. She
adopted a pose of easy jocularity that set my teeth on edge.
They took it, with a private grin, I fancy. She imagined she
had converted them to a sort of antipodean feudal system.
She couldn't have been more mistaken, of course. I heard the
wool sorter, a perfectly splendid old boy, he is, giving a very
spirited imitation of her one evening. I'm glad the men were
fifteen miles away from the wool-shed that night. The Sub-
Inspector is a very class-conscious man. His suspicions
would have gravitated naturally to the lower orders."

"Nonsense," said Alleyn cheerfully.

"It's not. He brightened up no end when Douglas started

off on his Markins legend. Markins, being a servant, might so much more easily be a murderer than any of us gentry. God, it makes you sick!"

"Tell me," said Alleyn, "have you any suspicions?"

"None! I think it's odds on a swagger had strayed up to the wool-shed and decided to doss down for the night. Flossie may have surprised him and had a row with him. In the heat of the argument he may have lost his temper and gone for her. Then when he found what he'd done, he put on Tommy Johns's overalls, disposed of his mistake in the first place that suggested itself to him, and made off down-country. She hated swaggers. Most stations gave them their tucker and a doss-down for the night in exchange for a job of work, but not Flossie. That's my idea. It's the only explanation that seems reasonable. The only type that fits."

"One of the lower orders in fact?"

"Yes," said Fabian after a pause. "You got me there, didn't you?"

"It was a cheap score, I'm afraid. Your theory is reasonable enough but no wandering tramp was seen about the district that day. I understand they stick to the road and usually make themselves known at the homesteads."

"Not at Mount Moon with Flossie at home."

"Perhaps not. Still your swagger remains a figure that as far as the police investigations go, and they seem to have been painstaking and thorough, was seen by nobody, either before or after the night of the disappearance."

"I've no other contribution to offer, I'm afraid, and I'm keeping you up. Good night, sir. I'm still glad you came."

"I hope you'll continue of that mind," said Alleyn. "Before you go, would you tell me how many of you played tennis on the night Mrs. Rubrick disappeared?"

"Now, this," said Fabian with an air of gratification, "is the real stuff. Why should you want to know that, I wonder? Only Douglas and I played tennis."

"You wore rubber-soled shoes during the search, then?"

"Certainly."

"And the others? Can you remember?"

"Pin heels. They always did in the evenings."

"When, actually, did Mrs. Rubrick first say she was going to the wool-shed?"

"Soon after we sat down. Might have been before. She was all arch about it. 'What do you suppose your funny old Floosie's going to do presently?' That kind of thing. Then she developed her theme; the party and what-not."

"I see. Thank you, very much. Good night."

ii

Fabian had gone and Alleyn was alone in the silent room. He stood motionless, a tall thin shape, dark in the candlelight. Presently he moved to the desk and opened one of the locked cases. From this he took a small tuft of cotton wool and dropped it on the carpet. Even by candlelight it was conspicuous, unavoidable, a white accent on a dark green ground. So must the tuft of wool have looked when Ursula, on the morning after Florence disappeared, caught it up in the carpet sweeper. Yet she hadn't noticed it. Or had she merely forgotten it? They were all agreed that Flossie would never have suffered it to lie there. She had been up to her room after dinner and before the walk through the garden. Presumably, there had been no wool on her carpet then. Alleyn heard again Ursula Harme's voice: "I don't care what anybody says. Somebody was about on the landing at five minutes to three that morning."

Alleyn pulled out his pipe, sat down at the desk, and unlocked his dispatch case. Here were the police files. With a sigh he opened them out on the desk. The room grew hazy with tobacco smoke, the pages turned at intervals and the grandfather clock on the landing told twelve, half-past twelve and one o'clock.

...on February 19th, 1942, at 2.45 P.M. I received instructions to proceed to the wool store of Riven Brothers at 68 Jernighan Avenue. I arrived there in company with P.C. Wetherbridge at 2.50 P.M. and was met by the storeman, Alfred Clark, and by Mr. Samuel Joseph, buyer for Riven Brothers. I was shown a certain wool pack and noted a strong

odour resembling decomposition. I was shown a bale hook
which was stained brownish-red. I noted that twisted about
the hook there was a hank of hair, reddish-gold in colour. I
noted that the pack in question had been partly slit. I
instructed P.C. Wetherbridge to extend the slit and open up
the pack. This was done in my presence and that of Alfred
Clark. Samuel Joseph was not present, having taken sick for
the time being, and retired to the outer premises. In the pack
we located a body in an advanced state of decomposition. It
was secured, in a sitting position, with the legs doubled up
and fastened to the trunk with nineteen turns of cord
subsequently identified as binder twine. The arms were
doubled up and secured to the body by twenty-five turns of
twine used for wool bales passing round the arms and legs.
The chin rested on the knees. The body rested upon a layer of
fleece, hard packed and six inches in depth. The body was
packed round with wool. Above the body the bale was
packed hard with fleece up to the top. The bale measured 28
inches in width both ways, and four feet in height. The body
was that of a woman of very slight build. I judged it to be
about five feet three inches in height. I left it as it was and
proceeded to...

The pages turned slowly.

...the injury to the back of the head. According to
medical evidence it might have been caused by a
downward blow from the rear made by a blunt
instrument. Three medical men agreed that the injury
was consistent with such a blow from the branding iron
found in the shearing shed. A microscopic examination
of this iron revealed stains subsequently proved by
analysis to be human blood-stains. Post-mortem
examination revealed that death had been caused by
suffocation. The mouth and nostrils contained quanti-
ties of sheep's wool. The injury to the skull would almost
certainly have brought about unconsciousness. It is
possible that the assailant, after striking the blow,
suffocated the deceased while she was unconscious. The
medical experts are agreed that death cannot be

attributed to accidental causes or to self-inflicted injuries.

Here followed a detailed report from the police surgeon. Alleyn read on steadily:—

...a triangular tear near the hem of the dress, corresponding in position to the outside left ankle bone, the apex of the tear being uppermost... subsequent investigation... nail in wall of wool-shed beside press... thread of material attached... lack of evidence after so long an interval.

"Don't I know it," Alleyn sighed and turned a page.

...John Merryweather, wool presser, deposed that on the evening of January 29th at knocking-off time, the press was full in both halves. It had been tramped but not pressed. He left it in this condition. The following morning it appeared to be in the same state. The two halves were ready for pressing as he had left them, the top in position on the bottom half. He pressed the wool, using the ratchet mechanism in the ordinary way. He noticed nothing that was unusual. The wool in the top half was compressed until it was packed down level with the top of the bottom half. The bale was then sewn up and branded. It was stacked alongside the other bales and the same afternoon was removed with them and trucked down-country....

Sydney Barnes, lorry driver, deposed that on January 30th, 1942 he collected the Mount Moon clip and trucked it down-country.... Alfred Clark, storeman... received the Mount Moon clip on February 3rd and stacked it to await assessment.... James MacBride, government wool-assessor... February 19th... noticed smell but attributed it to dead rat.... Slit all packs and pulled out tuft of wool near top... noticed nothing unusual... assessed with rest of clip... Samuel Joseph, buyer...

● ● ●

"And back we come, full circle," Alleyn sighed and refilled his pipe.

"Subsequent investigations," said the files ominously. In their own language they boiled down, dehumanized and tidied up the long accounts he had listened to that evening. "It seems certain," said the files twenty minutes later, "that the disposal of the body could not have been effected in under forty-five minutes. Tests have been made. The wool must have been removed from the press; the body bound up in the smallest possible compass, placed in the bottom half of the press, and packed round with wool. The fleeces must then have been replaced and tramped down both in the bottom and the top halves of the press, and the top half replaced on the bottom half.... Thomas Johns, working manager, deposed that on the next morning he found that his overalls had been split and were stained. He accused the 'fleecies' of having interfered with his overalls. They denied having done so."

It was getting very cold. Alleyn hunted out a sweater and pulled it on. The house was utterly silent now. So must it have been when Ursula Harme awoke to find her dream continued in the sound of a footfall on the landing, and when Douglas Grace heard retreating steps in the passage outside his room. It would be nice, Alleyn thought wearily, to know if the nocturnal prowler was the same in each instance.

He rose stiffly and moved to the large wardrobe whose doors were flush with the end wall of the room. He opened them and was confronted with his own clothes neatly arranged on hangers. The invaluable Markins again. It was here, at the back of the wardrobe, hidden under three folded rugs, that Flossie Rubrick's suitcase had been found, ready packed for the journey north that she never took. Terence Lynne had discovered it, three days after the night in the garden. The purse with her travelling money and official passes had been in the drawer of the dressing-table. Had this been the errand of Ursula's nocturnal prowler? To conceal the suitcase and the purse? And had the fragment of wool been dropped then? From a shoe that had tramped down the wool over Flossie Rubrick's head?

This, thought Alleyn, had been a neat and expeditious job. Not too fancy. A blow on the head, solid enough to stun, not savage enough to make a great mess. Suffocation, and then the answer to the one great problem, the disposal of the body. Very cool and bold. Risky, but well-conceived and justified by results. The most difficult part had been done by other people.

And the inevitable speculation arose in his mind. What had been the thoughts of his murderer when the shearers went to work the next morning, when the moment came for the wool presser to throw his weight on the ratchet arm and force down the trampled wool from the top half of the press into the pack in the lower half? Could the murderer have been sure that when the pack was sewn up and the press opened there would be no bulges, no stains? And when the time came for a bale hook to be jabbed into the top corner of the pack and for it to be hauled and heaved into the waiting lorry? Its weight? She had been a tiny woman and very thin but how much more did she weigh than her bulk in pressed wool?

He turned back to the files.

The medical experts are of the opinion that the binding of the body was probably effected within six hours of death as the onset of *rigor mortis*, after that period, would probably have rendered such a process impossible. They add, however, that in the circumstances, i.e. warm temperature, lack of violent exercise before death, the onset would be unlikely to be early.

"Cautious, as always," Alleyn thought. "Now then. Supposing he was a man. Did the murderer of Florence Rubrick, believing that he would be undisturbed, finish his appalling job while the members of the household were still up? The men were away, certainly, but what about the Johns family, and Markins and Albert Black? Might their curiosity not have been aroused by a light in the wool-shed windows? Or were they blacked-out in 1942? Probably they were not as Ursula Harme remarked that the shed was in darkness at five to nine, when she went in search of her guardian. This suggests that she expected to see lights." The files, he reflected, made no mention of this point. If the step that Ursula had heard was the murderer's, had he returned,

having finished his work, to hide away the suitcase and purse
and thus preserve the illusion that Florence had gone north?
Were the killing and the trussing-up and the hiding away of
the body done as a continuous operation or was there an
interval? She was killed some time after eight o'clock—
nobody can give the exact time when she walked down the
lavender path and turned left. It had been her intention to try
her voice in the shearing shed and return. She would have
been anxious, surely, to know if the brooch was found.
Would she have stayed longer than ten minutes or a quarter
of an hour giving an imitation of an M.P. talking to herself in
a deserted shed? Surely not. Surely, then, she was killed
before, or quite soon after, the search-party went indoors. It
was five to nine when the brooch was found, and five to nine
when, on his mother's entrance into the annex, Cliff Johns
stopped playing and went home with her. During the period
after the people in the house went to bed and before the party
returned from the dance at a quarter to two, the wool-shed
would be completely deserted. The lorry itself had broken
down at the gate but the revellers would be heard long before
they reached the shed. He would still have time to put out the
lights, and, if necessary, hide. By that time, almost certainly,
the body would have been in the bottom half of the press and
probably the top half would be partially packed.

"It boils down to this then," Alleyn thought. "If any of the
five members of the search-party committed this crime, he or
she probably did so during the actual hunt for the brooch,
since, if she'd been alive after then, Mrs. Rubrick would
almost certainly have returned to the house." But as, in the
case of the searchers, this allowed only a margin of four
minutes or so, the murderer, if one of that party, must have
returned later to complete the arduous task of encasing the
body with firmly packed wool and refilling the press exactly
as it was before the job was begun. The business of packing
round the body would be particularly exacting. The wool
must have been forced down into a layer solid enough, for all
its thinness, to form a kind of wall and prevent the
development of bulges on the surface of the pack.

But suppose it was the murderer whom Ursula heard on
the landing at five minutes to three. If his errand was to hide
the suitcase and purse, whether he was an inmate of the house

or not, he would almost certainly wait until he could be reasonably certain that the household was asleep.

Alleyn himself was sleepy now, and tired. The stale chilliness of extreme exhaustion was creeping about his limbs. "It's been a long day," he thought, "and I'm out of practice." He changed into pyjamas and washed vigorously in cold water. Then, for warmth's sake, he got into bed, wearing his dressing-gown. His candle, now a stump, guttered, spattered in its own wax, and went out. There was another on the desk but Alleyn had a torch at his bedside and he did not stir. It was half-past two on a cold morning.

"Can I allow myself a cat-nap," he muttered, "or shall I write to Troy?" Troy was his wife, thirteen thousand miles away, doing camouflage and pictorial surveys instead of portraits, at Bossicote in England. He said wistfully: "She's very easy to think about." He considered the chilly journey from his bed to the writing desk and had flung back the bed-clothes when, in a moment, he was completely still.

No night wind sighed about the windows of Mount Moon, no mouse scuttled in the wainscoting. From somewhere far outside the house, by the men's quarters, he supposed, a dog barked, once, very desolately. But the sound that had arrested Alleyn came from within the house. It was the measured creak made by the weight of someone moving up the old stairs. Then, very slow but vivid because of their slowness, sensed rather than heard, footfalls sounded on the landing. Alleyn counted eight of them, reached for his torch and waited for the brush of finger tips against his own door, and the decisive unmuffled click of the latch. His eyes had grown accustomed to the dark and he could make out a faint greyness which was the surface of his white-painted door. It shifted towards him, slowly at first, and remained ajar for some seconds. Then, incisively, candidly as it seemed, the door was pushed wide and against the swimming blue of the landing he saw the shape of a man. His back was towards Alleyn. He shut the door delicately and turned. Alleyn switched on his torch. As if by trickery, a face appeared, its eyes screwed up in the unexpected light.

It was Markins.

"You've been the hell of a time," said Alleyn.

iii

As seen when the remaining candle had been lighted, he
was a spare bird-like man. His black hair was brushed
strongly back, like a coarse wig with no parting. He had small
black eyes, a thin nose and a mobile mouth. Above his black
trousers he wore a servant's alpaca working jacket. His habit
of speech was basic cockney with an overlay of American-
isms, but neither of these characteristics was very marked
and he would have been a difficult man to place. He had an
air of naïveté and frankness, almost of innocence, but his
dark eyes never widened and he seemed, behind his manner,
which was pleasing, to be always extremely alert. He carried
the candle he had lit to Alleyn's bedside table and then stood
waiting, his arms at his sides, his hands turned outwards at
the wrists.

"Sorry I couldn't make it before, sir," he murmured.
"They're light sleepers, all of them, more's the pity. All four."

"No more?" Alleyn whispered.

"Five."

"Five's out."

"It used to be six."

"And two from six is four with the odd one out."

They grinned at each other.

"Right," said Alleyn. "I walk in deadly fear of forgetting
these rigmaroles. What would you have done if I'd got it
wrong?"

"Not much chance of that, sir, and I'd have known you
anywhere, Mr. Alleyn."

"I should keep a false beard by me," said Alleyn gloomily.
"Sit down for heaven's sake, and shoot the works. Have a
cigarette? How long is it since we met?"

"Back in '37, wasn't it, sir? I joined the Special Branch in
'36. I saw you before I went over to the States on that pre-war
job."

"So you did. We fixed you up as a steward in a German
liner, didn't we?"

"That's right, sir."

"By the way, is it safe to speak and not whisper?"

"I think so, sir. There's nobody in the dressing-room or on this side of the landing. The two young ladies are over the way. Their doors are shut."

"At least we can risk a mutter. You did very well on that first job, Markins."

"Not so good this time, I'm afraid, sir. I'm properly up against it."

"Oh, well," said Alleyn resignedly, "let's have the whole story."

"From the beginning?"

"I'm afraid so."

"Well, sir," said Markins and pulled his chair closer to the bed. They leant towards each other. They resembled some illustration by Cruikshank from Dickens: Alleyn in his dark gown, his long hands folded on the counterpane; Markins, small, cautious, bent forward attentively. The candle glowed like a nimbus behind his head, and Alleyn's shadow, stooping with theatrical exaggeration on the wall beside him, seemed to menace both of them. They spoke in a barely vocal but pedantically articulate mutter.

"I was kept on in the States," said Markins, "as of course you know. In May, '38, I got instructions from your people, Mr. Alleyn, to get alongside a Japanese wool buyer called Kurata Kan, who was in Chicago. It took a bit of time but I made the grade, finally, through his servant. A half-caste Jap this servant was, and used to go to a sort of night school. I joined up, too, and found that this half-caste was sucking up to another pupil, a janitor at a place where they made hush-hush parts for aeroplane engines. He was on the job, all right, that half-caste. They pay on the nail for information, never mind how small, and he and Kan were in the game together. It took me weeks of geography and American history lessons before I got a lead and then I sold them a little tale about how I'd been sacked for showing too much interest. After that it was money for jam. I sold Mr. Kurata Kan quite a nice little line of bogus information. Then he moved on to Australia. I got instructions from the Special Branch to follow him up. They fixed me up as a gent's valet in Sydney. I was supposed to have been in service with an artillery expert from Home who visited the Governor of New South Wales. He gave me the references himself on Government House notepaper. He was in touch with your people, sir. Well, after a bit I looked up Mr. Kan and made the usual offer. He was quite glad to see me and I handed him a little line of stuff the gentleman was supposed to have let out when under the influence. Your office supplied it."

"I remember."

"He was trying to get on to some stuff about fortifications at Darwin and we strung him along quite nicely for a time. Of course he was away a great deal on his wool-buying job. Nothing much happened, till August 1940, when he put it up to me that it might be worth my while to come over here with a letter from him to a lady friend of his, a Mrs. Arthur Rubrick M.P., who was keen on English servants. He said a nephew of Mr. Rubrick's was doing a job they'd like to get a line on. Very thorough, the Japs, sir."

"Very."

"That's right. I cabled in code to the Special Branch and they told me to go ahead. They were very interested in Mr. Kan. So I came over and it worked out nicely. Mrs. Rubrick took me on, and here I stuck. The first catch in it, though, was what would I tell Kurata Kan? The Special Branch warned me that Mr. Losse's work was important and they gave me some phoney stuff I could send on to Kan when he got discontented. That was O.K. I even rigged up a bit of an affair with some spare radio parts, all pulled to pieces and done up different. I put it in a bad light and took a bad photograph of it and told him I'd done it through a closed window from the top of a ladder. I've often wondered how far it got before some expert took a look at it and said the Japanese for 'Nuts.' Kan was pleased enough. He knew nothing. They pulled him in at last on my information and then there was Pearl Harbor. Finish!"

"Only as far as Kan was concerned."

"True enough, sir. There was the second catch. But you know all about that, Mr. Alleyn."

"I'd like to hear your end of it."

"Would you, sir? O.K., then. My instructions from your end had been that I was on no account to let Mrs. Rubrick or either of the young gentlemen get any idea that I wasn't exactly what I seemed. After a bit your people let me know that there'd been leakage of information—not my phoney dope, but genuine stuff—about this magnetic fuse. Not. through Japanese canals but German ones. Now that *was* a facer. So my next job was to turn round after three years' working the bogus agent and look for the genuine article. And that," said Markins plaintively, "was where I fluttered to pieces. I hadn't got a thing. Not a bloody inkling, if you'll pardon the expression."

"So we gathered," said Alleyn.

"The galling thing, Mr. Alleyn, the aspect of the affair that got under my professional skin, as you might say, was this: somebody in this household had been working under my nose for months. What did I feel like when I heard it? Dirt. Kuh! Thinking myself the fly operator, cooking up little fake photographs and all the time—look, Mr. Alleyn, I handed myself the raspberry in six different positions. I did indeed."

"If it's any satisfaction to you," said Alleyn, "one source of transit was stopped. Two months ago a German supply ship was taken off the Argentine coast. Detailed drawings of the magnetic fuse and instructions in code were found aboard her. The only link we could establish between this ship and New Zealand was the story of a free-lance journalist who was cruising round the world in a tramp steamer. There are lots of these sportsmen about, harmless eccentrics, no doubt, for the most part. This particular specimen, a native of Portugal, visited most of the ports in this country during last year. Our people have tracked him down to a pub in a neutral port where he was seen drinking with the skipper of this German ship, and was suddenly very flush with cash. Intensive probing brought to light an involved story that cast a very murky light on the journalist. All the usual stuff. We're pretty certain of him and he won't be given a shore permit next time the *Wanderlust* drives him this way, romantic little chap."

"I remember when he was about," said Markins. "Señor or Don or Something de Something. He was in town during Easter race week last year. The two young gentlemen and Miss Harme and most of the staff went down for three days, I stayed behind. Mr. Rubrick was very poorly."

"And Miss Lynne?"

"She stayed behind too. Wouldn't leave him." Markins looked quickly at Alleyn. "Very sad, that," he added.

"Very. We've found that this gentleman lived aboard his tramp steamer while he was in port. He showed up at the races wearing a white beret and clad for comfort rather than smartness; a conspicuous figure. We think this stuff about this gadget of Mr. Losse's was passed to him at this time. It had been folded small. The paper was of New Zealand manufacture."

Markins clucked angrily. "Under my very nose, you might say."

"Well, your nose was up here and the transaction probably took place on a race-course two hundred miles away or more."

"All the same."

"So you see, by a stroke of luck, we stopped the hole, and the information, as far as we know, didn't reach the enemy. Mr. Losse was warned by Headquarters that he should take particular care, and at the same time was advised to confide in nobody, not even his partner, about the attempt. Oddly enough he seems to have been sceptical about the danger of espionage while Captain Grace, from the beginning, has taken a very gloomy view of—who do you think?"

"You're asking me, sir," said Markins in an indignant whisper. "Look! If that young man had crawled about after me on his stomach in broad daylight he wouldn't have given himself away more than he did. Look, sir. He got into my room and messed about like a coal heaver. His prints all over everything! Butted his head in among my suits and left them smelling of his hair oil and I'm blest if he didn't pinch a bill out of my pockets. Well, I mean to say, it was awkward. If he went howling up to Headquarters about me being a spy or some such, they'd be annoyed with me for putting myself away. It was comical too. I was there to watch his blinking plant for him and he goes and makes up his mind I'm just what I pretended I was to Kan & Co."

"You must have done something to arouse his suspicions."

"I never!" said Markins indignantly. "Why should I? As far as he knew, I never went near his blinking workroom, but once. That was when I had an urgent telephone call for Mrs. Rubrick. I heard voices up there and went along. He and Mr. Losse were muttering in the doorway and didn't hear me. When he did see me, he looked at me like I was the Demon King."

"He says he heard you prowling about the passage at a quarter to three in the morning, a fortnight before Mrs. Rubrick was killed."

Markins made a faint squeaking noise. "Like hell he did! I never heard such a thing! What'd I be doing outside his workroom? Yes, and what does he do but rush off to Madam and tell her she's got to give me the sack."

"You heard about that, did you?"

"Madam told me. She said she had something very serious to talk to me about. She as good as said I'd been suspected of prying into the workroom. You could have pulled me to pieces with a pin, I was that taken aback. And riled! I reckon my manner was convincing, because she was satisfied. I ought to explain, Mr. Alleyn, that I myself had heard somebody that night. I'm a light sleeper and I heard someone all right and it wasn't either of the young gents. They get spasms of working late but they don't bother to tiptoe into the workroom. I got out of bed, you bet, and had a look, but it was all quiet and after a bit I give up. I told Madam. She was very put about. Naturally. I satisfied her, of course, but it was awkward and what's more I evidently missed a bit of funny business. Who was it, anyway, in the passage? I'm a sweet little agent, and that's a fact. But before we parted she says: 'Markins,' she says, 'there's something I don't like about this business and next time I go up to Wellington,' she says, 'I'm going to speak about it to the authorities. I'm going to suggest that the young gentlemen work under proper protection,' she says, 'in their own interest, and I shall tell the Captain what I've decided.' What I can not understand," said Markins, pulling at his thin underlip, "is why the Captain got it into his head I was an agent."

"Perhaps you look like one, Markins."

"I begin to think I must, Mr. Alleyn, but I'd prefer it was the British variety."

"Actually, you know, the circumstances were a bit suspicious. He opened his bedroom door and saw a light disappear in the direction of your room. That afternoon, as you yourself admit, you'd come upon Captain Grace and Mr. Losse arranging where they'd leave the key of the workroom. I think he had some cause for alarm."

Markins darted a very sharp glance at Alleyn. "She never

said a word about that," he said.

"She didn't?"

"Not a word. Only that the Captain was upset because he thought I'd been poking about the passage late at night. I didn't hear what they were saying that afternoon. They spoke too low and stopped as soon as they saw me." He gave a thoughtful hiss. "That's different. It's a whole lot different. Saw something did he?"

"A light," said Alleyn and repeated Douglas' account of the night prowler.

"The only tangible bit of evidence and I miss it," said Markins. "That's the way to get promotion. I'm disgusted."

Alleyn pointed out that, whoever the night prowler might have been, he didn't gain access to the room that night. But Markins instantly objected that this failure must have been followed by success as copies for designs had been handed over to the Portugese journalist at Easter. "You're disappointed in my work, sir," he whispered dolorously. "You're disgusted and I'm sure I don't blame you. Put it bluntly, this expert's been one too many for me. He's got into that room and he's got away with the stuff and I don't know who he is or how he did it. It's disgraceful. I'd be better in the Middle East."

"Well," said Alleyn, "it's a poor show, certainly, but I shan't do any good by rubbing it in and you won't do any good by calling yourself names. I'll look at the room. Losse has rigged a home-made but effective shutter that's padlocked over the window every night. There's a Yale lock on the door and after the scare he wore the key on a bootlace round his neck. You can gain entrance by boring a hole in the door-post and using wire. That might have been the prowler's errand on the night Grace heard him. He failed then but brought it off some time before Easter. How about that?"

"No, sir. I kept an eye on that lock. There'd been no interference. While they were away at the races that Easter I took a good look round. The room was sealed all right, Mr. Alleyn."

"Very well, then, the entrance was effected before the scare when they were not so careful and the interloper was returning for another look when Grace heard him. Any objections?"

"No," said Markins slowly. "No. He'd got enough to work on for the stuff he handed to the Portuguese, and he kept it until the man got to this country. That'll work."

"All right," said Alleyn. "Any suspicions?"

"It might have been the old girl herself," said Markins, "for anything I know to the contrary. There!"

"Mrs. Rubrick?"

"Well, she was in and out of the room often enough. Always tapping at the door and saying: 'Can my busy bees spare me a moment?'"

Alleyn stirred and his shadow moved on the wall. It might be difficult to interview Markins at great length during the day and he himself had a formidable program to face. Four versions of Flossie already and it must now be half-past two at least. Must he listen to a fifth? He reached out his hand for his cigarettes.

"What did you think of her?" he asked.

"Peculiar," said Markins.

iv

"Ambitious," Markins added, after reflection. "The ambitious type. You see them everywhere. Very often they're childless women. She was successful, too, but I wouldn't say she was satisfied. Capable. Knew how to get her own way, but once she'd got it liked everybody else to be comfortable when she remembered them. When women get to her age," said Markins, "they're one of three kinds. They may be O.K. They may go jealous of younger women and peculiar about men, particularly young men, or they may take it out in work. She took it out in work. She thrashed herself and everybody round her. She wanted to be the big boss, and round here she certainly was. Now, you ask me, sir, would she be an enemy agent? Not for money, she wouldn't. She'd got plenty of that. For an idea? Now, what idea in the Nazi book of words would appeal to Madam? The *Herrenvolk* spiel? I'd say, yes, if she was to be one of the *Herrenvolk*. But was she the type of lady who'd work against her own folk and her own country? Now, was she? She was great on talking Imperialism. You know. The brand that's not taken for granted quite so much, these days. She talked a lot about patriotism. I don't know how things are at Home, sir, having been away so long, but it seems to me we are getting round to thinking more about how we can improve our country and bragging about it less than we used to. From what I read and hear, it strikes me that the people who criticize are the ones that work and are most set on winning the war. Take some of the English people who got away to the States when the war began. Believe me, a lot of them talked that big and that optimistically you'd wonder how the others got on in the blitz without them. And when there was hints about muddle or hints that before the war we'd got slack and a bit too keen on easy money and a bit too pleased with ourselves—Lord, how they'd perform. Wouldn't have it at any price! I've heard these people say that what was wanted at Home was concentration camps for the critics and that a bit of Gestapo technique wouldn't do any harm. Now Mrs. Rubrick was a little in that line of business herself."

"Miss Harme says she wanted to stay in England and do a job of work."

"Yes? Is that so? But she'd have had to be the boss or nothing, I'll be bound. My point is this, Mr. Alleyn. Suppose she was offered something pretty big in the way of a position, a Reich-something-or-other ship, when the enemy had beaten us, would she have fallen for the notion? That's what I asked myself."

"And how did you answer yourself?"

"Doubtful. Not impossible. You see with her as the only member of the house who had a chance of getting into this workroom I thought quite a lot about Madam. She might have got a key for herself when she had the Yale lock put on the door for the young gentlemen. It wasn't impossible. She had to be considered. And the more she talked about getting rid of enemy agents in this country the more I wondered if she might be one herself. She used to say that we oughtn't to be afraid to use what was good in Nazi methods, their youth-training schemes and fostering of nationalistic ideas, and she used to come down very hard on anything like independent critical thinking. It was all right, of course. Lots of people think that way, all the die-hards, you might say. She read a lot of their pre-war books, too. And she didn't like Jews. She used to say they were parasites. I'd get to thinking about her this way and then I'd kind of come down with a bump and call myself crazy."

Alleyn asked him if he had anything more tangible to go on and he shook his head mournfully. Nothing. Beyond her curiosity about the young men's work, and she was by nature curious, there had been nothing. There was, he said, another view to take, and in many ways a more reasonable one. Mrs. Rubrick had been appointed to a counter-espionage committee and, in that capacity, may have threatened the success of an agent. She may even have formed suspicions of a member of her household and have given herself away. She was not a discreet woman. This, pushed a little further, might produce a motive for her murder.

"Yes," said Alleyn dryly. "That's why Captain Grace thinks you killed her, you know."

Markins said with venom that Captain Grace was not immune from suspicion himself. "He's silly enough to do anything," he whispered angrily. "And what about his background, anyway? Heidelberg. He doesn't look so hot. And what about him being a Nazi sympathizer? I may be dumb but I haven't overlooked that little point."

"You don't really believe it, though, do you?" Alleyn asked with a smile.

Markins muttered disconsolately: "No brains."

"There's one other point," Alleyn said. "We've got to consider whether this attempt to forward documentary information was the be-all and end-all of the agent's mission. If, having achieved this object, no more was expected of him, or if he was to forward other information as regards, for instance, Mrs. Rubrick's counter-espionage activities, which is the sort of stuff that needs no documentary evidence. That perennial nuisance, the hidden radio transmitter, would meet the case."

"Don't I know it," Markins grumbled. "And there's a sizable range of mountains where it could be cached."

"It'd have to be accessible, though. He would be under

instruction to transmit his stuff every so often when an enemy craft would edge far enough into these waters to pick it up. The files say that under cover of the hunt for Mrs. Rubrick, an extensive search was made. They even brought up a radio-locator in a car and bumped up the river-bed with it. But of course you were in that party."

"Yes," said Markins, "I was in with the boys. They expected me to show them the works and what could I do? Tag on and look silly. Me, supposed to be the expert! It's a hard world."

"It's a weary world," said Alleyn, swallowing a yawn. "We're both supposed to appear in less than four hours, with shining morning faces. I'm out of training, Markins, and you're a working man. I think we'll call it a night."

Markins at once got up and, by standing attentively, his head inclined forward, seemed to reassume the character of a man-servant. "Shall I open the window, sir?" he asked.

"Do, there's a good chap, and pull back the curtains. You've got a torch, haven't you? I'll put out the candle."

"We're not as fussy as that about the blackout, Mr. Alleyn. Not in these parts."

The curtain rings jingled. A square, faintly luminous, appeared in the wall. Now the air of the plateau gained entry. Alleyn felt it cold on his face and in his eyes. He pinched out the candle and heard Markins tiptoe to the door.

"Markins," said Alleyn's voice, quiet in the dark.

"Sir?"

"There's another solution. You've thought of it, of course?"

Quite a long silence followed this.

"He may talk highbrow," Markins whispered, "but when you get to know him, he's a nice young gentleman."

The door creaked and Alleyn was alone. He composed himself for sleep.

CHAPTER VII

ACCORDING TO BEN WILSON

Having left instructions with himself to wake at five, Alleyn did so and was aware of distant stirrings in the house. Outside in the dark a cock crew and the clamour of his voice echoed into nothingness. Beneath Alleyn's window someone walked firmly along the terrace path and round the corner of the house. He carried a tin bucket that clanked with his stride and he whistled shrilly. From over in the direction of the men's quarters all the Mount Moon sheep-dogs broke into a chorus, their voices sounding hollow and cold in the dawn air. There followed the ring of an axe, an abrupt burst of conversation and, presently, the smell of wood smoke, aromatic and pleasing. Beyond the still nighted windows there was only a faint promise of light, a vague thinning, but, as he watched, there appeared in the darkness a rosy horn, unearthly clear. It was the Cloud Piercer, far beyond the plateau, receiving the dawn.

Alleyn bathed and shaved by candlelight and, when he returned to his room, found visible outside his window the vague shapes of trees, patches of blanket mist above the swamp, and the road, lonely and bleached, reaching out across the plateau. Beneath his window the garden waited, straw-coloured, frosty and rigid. As he dressed, the sky grew clear behind the mountains and though the plateau was still dusky, they became articulate in remote sunlight.

Breakfast began in artificial light, but before it was over the lamp had grown wan and ineffectual. It was now full morning. The character of the house had changed. There was an air of preparation for the working day. Douglas and Fabian wore farm clothes—shapeless flannel trousers, faded sweaters pulled over dark shirts, old tweed jackets and heavy boots. Ursula was briskly smocked. Terence Lynne ap-

133

peared, composed as ever, in a drill coat, woollen stockings and breeches—an English touch, this, Alleyn felt: alone of the four she seemed to be dressed deliberately for a high-country role. Mrs. Aceworthy, alternately dubious and arch, presided.

Douglas finished before the rest and, with a word to Fabian, went out, passing in front of the dining-room windows. Presently he appeared, far beyond the lawn in the ram paddock, a dog at his heels. Five merino rams at the far end of the paddock jerked up their heads and stared at him. Alleyn watched Douglas walk to a gate, open it, and wait. After a minute or two the rams began to cross the paddock towards him, heavily, not hurrying. He let them through the gate and they disappeared together, a portentous company.

"When you're ready," said Fabian, "shall we go over to the wool-shed?"

"If there's anything you would like—" Mrs. Aceworthy said. "I mean, I'm sure we all want to be helpful—so dreadful—so many inquiries. One might almost feel—but of course this is quite different, I'm sure." She drifted unhappily away.

"The Ace-pot's a bit scattered this morning," Ursula said. "You'll tell us, won't you, Mr. Alleyn, if there's anything we can do?"

Alleyn thanked her and said there was nothing. He and Fabian went out of doors.

The sun had not yet reached Mount Moon. The air was cold and the ground crisp under their feet. From the direction of the yards came the authentic voice of the high-country, a dreamlike and conglomerate drone, the voice of a mob of sheep. Fabian led the way along the left-hand walk between clipped poplar hedges, already flame-coloured. They turned down the lavender path and through a gate, making a long stride over an icy little water race, and then walked uphill in the direction of the wool-shed and cottages.

The sound increased in volume. Individual bleatings, persistent and almost human, separated out from the multiple drone. A long galvanized-iron shed appeared, flanked with drafting yards beyond which lay a paddock so full of sheep that at a distance it looked like a shifting greyish lake. The sheep were driven up to the yards by men and dogs: the men yelled and the dogs barked remorselessly and without rhythm. A continual flood of sheep poured through a series of yards, each smaller than the last, into a narrow runway or race and was forced and harried towards a two-way gate which a short, monkey-faced man shoved now this way, now that, drafting them into separate pens. This progress was assisted by a youth outside the rails who continually ran towards the sheep waving his hat and crying out in a falsetto voice. At each of these sallies the sheep, harried from the rear by dogs, would dart past the youth towards the drafting gate. The acrid smell of greasy wool was strong on the cold air.

"That's Tommy Johns," said Fabian, jerking his head at the man at the drafting gate. "The boy's young Cliff."

He was rather a nice-looking lad, Alleyn thought. He had a well-shaped head and a thatch of light brown hair that overhung his forehead. His face was thin. There was an agreeable sharpness and delicacy in the bony structures of the eyes and cheek-bones. The mouth was obstinate. He still had a lean, gangling air about him, the last characteristic of adolescence. His hands were broad and nervous. His grey sweater and dirty flannel trousers had a schoolboyish look that contrasted strongly with the clothes of the other men. When he saw Fabian he gave him a sidelong grin and then with a whoop and a flourish ran again at the oncoming sheep. They streamed past him to the drafting gate and huddled together, clambering on each other's backs.

Now that he had drawn closer Alleyn could resolve the babel into its component parts: the complaint of the sheep, the patter of their feet on frozen earth and their human-like coughing and breathing; the yelp of dogs and men and, within the shed, the burr of an engine and intermittent bumping and thuds.

"There'll be a smoke-oh in ten minutes," said Fabian. "Would you like to see inside?"

"Right," said Alleyn.

Tommy Johns didn't raise his eyes as they passed him. The gate bumped to and fro against worn posts and the sheep darted through. "He's counting," Fabian said.

ii

The wool-shed seemed dark when they first went in and the reek of sheep was almost tangible. The greatest area of light fell where the shearers were at work. It came through a doorless opening from which a sacking curtain had been pulled back and through the open port-holes that were exits for the sheep. From where Alleyn stood the shearers themselves were outlined with light and each sheep's woolly coat had a bright nimbus. This strangely dramatic illumination focused attention on the shearing board. The rest of the interior seemed at first to be lost in a swimming dusk. But presently a wool sorter's bench, ranked packs, and pens filled with waiting sheep, took shape in the shadows and Alleyn was able to form a comprehensive picture of the whole scene.

For a time he watched only the shearers. He saw them lug sheep out of the pens by their hind legs and handle them with dexterity so that they became quiescent, voluptuously quiescent almost, lolling back against the shearers' legs, in a ridiculous sitting posture, or suffering their necks to be held between the shearers' knees while the mechanically propelled blades, hanging from long arms with flexible joints, rolled away their wool.

"Is this crutching?" he asked.

"That's it. De-bagging, you might call it."

Alleyn saw the dirty wool turn back in a wave that was cream inside and watched the quarter-denuded sheep shoved away through the port-holes. He saw the broomies, two silent boys, sweep the dirty crutchings up to the sorter and fling them out on his rack. He saw the wool sorted and tossed into bins and finally he followed it to the press.

The press was in a central position, some distance from the shearing board. It faced the main portion of the shed and actually looked, Alleyn thought, a little like an improvised rostrum. Here Flossie Rubrick was to have stood on the night of her wool-shed party. From here she was to harangue a mob of friends, voters, and fellow high-countrymen, almost as quiescent as the shorn sheep. Alleyn sharpened his memory until it could encompass the figure of the woman with whom he had spoken for a few minutes. A tiny woman with a clear and insistent voice and an ugly face. A woman who wished to acquire him as a guest and from whom he had escaped with difficulty. He remembered her sharp stare and her rather too self-confident manner. These recollections remained unchanged by last night's spate of conflicting impressions and it was the wraith of the persistent little woman he had met whom he now conjured up in the dark end of the wool-shed. Where had she stood? From what direction had her assailant come?

"She was going to try her voice, you know," said Fabian at his elbow.

"Yes, but from where? The press? It was full of unpressed wool and open, when the men stopped work the previous night. Did she clamp down the pressing lid or whatever it's called and climb up?"

"That's what we've always supposed."

"Is the new press in exactly the same place?"

"Yes. Under that red show ticket nailed up on the post."

Alleyn walked past the shearing board or floor. The wall opposite was a five-foot-high partition separating the indoor pens from the rest of the shed. Farther along, behind the press, this wall was extended up towards the roof. At some time a nail had been driven through it from the other side and the point, now rusty, projected close to the wool-press. He stooped to look at it. The machines still thrummed and the sheep plunged and skidded as they were hauled out of the pens. The work went on but Alleyn thought that the men knew exactly what he was doing. He straightened up. Above the rusty nail there ran a cross-beam in the wall on which anybody, intending to mount the press, might find foothold. Round the nail they had found a thread of Flossie's dress material. The apex of the tear in her dress had been uppermost, so it had been caused by an upward pull. "As she climbed the press," thought Alleyn, "not when her assailant disposed of the body. It was too securely bound and the press opens from the front. He would truss the body, then clear the tramped wool out of the pack, leaving only the bottom layer, then open the front of the press and get the body into the bale, then would begin the repacking. But where was she when he struck her? A downward blow from behind near the base of the skull and grazing the back of the neck. Was she bent forward, her hands on the press? Stooping to free her dress? Was she in the act of climbing down from the press to speak to him, her feet already on the floor, her back towards him?" That seemed most likely, he thought.

Near the wool-press, a hurricane lantern hung from a nail in the wall. Farther along, to the left, a rough candlestick hammered out of tin was nailed high up on a joist. It held a guttered stump of candle. A box of matches stood beside it. These appointments had been there at the time of the tragedy. Had Flossie lit the lantern or the candle? Surely. It was dusk outside and the wool-shed must have been in darkness. How strange, he thought, as the image of a tiny indomitable woman, lit fantastically, grew in his imagination. There she must have stood, in semi-darkness, shouting out the phrases of which Terence Lynne and Fabian Losse had grown weary, while her sharp voice echoed in the emptiness. "Ladies and Gentlemen!" How far had she got? What did her assailant hear as he approached? Was he—or she—actually an audience, stationed by Flossie at the far end of the shed, to mark the resonant phrases? Or did he creep in under cover of the darkness and wait until she descended? With the branding iron grasped in his right hand? Behind her and to her right, the inside pens had been crowded with sheep waiting for the next day's shearing, too closely packed to do more than shift a little and tap with their small hooves on the slatted floor. Did they bleat at all, Alleyn wondered, when Flossie tried her voice? "Ladies and Gentlemen." "Ba-a-a." From where he stood Alleyn could see slantwise, through the five port-holes and the open doorway at the end of the shearing board. The sun was bright on the sheep pens outside. But when Florence Rubrick stood on the wool-press it had been almost dark outside, the port-holes must have been shut and the sacking curtain dropped over the doorway. The main doors of the shed had been shut that night and a heap of folded wool bales that had fallen across the floor, inside the main entrance, had not been disturbed. The murderer, then, had come in by this sacking door. Did Flossie see the sacking drawn aside and a black silhouette against the dusk? Or did he, perhaps, crawl in through one of the portholes, unobserved? "Ladies and Gentlemen. It gives me great pleasure . . ."

A whistle tooted. Each shearer finished crutching the sheep in hand and loosed it through a port-hole. The engine stopped and the wool-shed was suddenly quiet. The noise from outside became dominant again.

"Smoke-oh," Fabian explained. "Come and meet Ben Wilson."

Ben Wilson was the sorter, boss of the shed, an elderly mild man who shook hands solemnly with Alleyn and said nothing. Fabian explained why Alleyn was there and Wilson looked at the floor and still said nothing. "Shall we move away a bit?" Alleyn suggested, and they walked to the double doors at the far end of the shed and stood there, enveloped in sunshine and the silence of Ben Wilson. Alleyn offered his cigarette case. Mr. Wilson said "Ta," and took one.

"It's the same old story, Ben," said Fabian, "but we're hoping Mr. Alleyn may get a bit further than the other experts. We're lucky to have him." Mr. Wilson glanced at Alleyn and then at the floor. He smoked cautiously, sheltering his cigarette with the palm of his hand. He had the air of a man whose life's object was to avoid making the slightest advance to anybody.

"You were here for the January shearing when Mrs. Rubrick was killed, weren't you, Mr. Wilson?" asked Alleyn.

"That's right," said Mr. Wilson.

"I'm afraid you must be completely fed up with policemen and their questions."

"That's right."

"And I'm afraid mine will be precisely the same set of questions all over again." Alleyn waited and Mr. Wilson, with an extremely smug expression, compounded, it seemed, of mistrust, complacency and resignation, said: "You're telling me."

"All right," said Alleyn. "Here goes, then. On the night of January 29th, 1942 when Mrs. Rubrick was stunned, suffocated, bound, and packed into a wool bale in the replica of the press over there, you were in charge of the shed as usual, I suppose?"

"I was over at Lakeside," Mr. Wilson muttered as if the statement were an obscenity.

"At the time she was murdered? Yes, you probably were. At a dance wasn't it? But (you must forgive me if I've got it wrong) the wool-shed is under your management during the shearing, isn't it?"

"Manner of speaking."

"Yes. And I suppose you have a look round after knock-off time?"

"Not much to look at."

"Those trap-doors or port-holes by the shearing board for instance. Were they shut?"

"That's right."

"But the traps could be raised from outside?"

"That's right."

"And the sacking over the door at the end of the board. Was that dropped?"

"That's right."

"Was it fastened in any way?"

"Fastened?"

"Fastened, yes."

"She's nailed to a bit of three-be-two and we drop it."

"I see. And the pile of sacks or empty bales inside these rolling double doors—were they lying in such a way that anybody coming in or going out would disturb them?"

"I'll say."

"But in the morning, did they look as if they'd been disturbed?"

Mr. Wilson shook his head very slightly.

"Did you notice them particularly?"

"That's right."

"How was that?"

"I'd told the boys to shift them and they never."

"Could the doors have been rolled open from outside?"

"Not a chance."

"Were they fastened inside?"

"That's right."

"Is it remotely possible that there was somebody hiding in here when you knocked off?"

"Not a chance."

"Mrs. Rubrick must have come in by the sacking door?" Mr. Wilson grunted.

"She was very short. She couldn't reach up to fit the baton on the cross-beam where it now rests. So she probably pushed it in a little way. Is that right, should you say?"

"Might be."

"And her murderer must have gained entrance by the same means, if we wash out the possibility of shoving up one of the traps and coming in that way?"

"Looks like it."

"Where was the branding iron left, when you knocked off?"

"Inside the door, on the floor."

"The sacking door, that is. And the pot of paint was there too, wasn't it?"

"That's right."

"Was the iron in its right place the next morning?"

"Young Cliff says it was shifted," said Mr. Wilson in a sudden burst of loquacity.

"Had he put it away?"

"That's right. He says it was shifted. It was him first drew attention to the thing. He put the police on to it."

"Did you notice anything unusual that morning, Mr. Wilson? Anything at all, however trivial?"

Mr. Wilson fixed his pale blue gaze upon a cluster of ewes at the far end of the paddock and said: "Look." Alleyn looked at the ewes. "Listen," Mr. Wilson continued. "I told Sergeant Clark what I seen when I come in and I told Sub-Inspector Jackson and they both wrote it down. The men told them what they seen and they wrote that down too, although it was the same as what I seen."

"I know," said Alleyn, "I know. It seems silly but I would rather like to hear it for myself now I've seen the place. You see, there was nothing new or confusing about a wool-shed to Clark and Jackson. They're New Zealanders, dyed in the wool, and they understand."

Mr. Wilson laughed surprisingly and with unexampled

contempt. "Them?" he said. "They were as much at home in the shed as a couple of ruddy giraffes, those two jokers."

"In that case," said Alleyn with a mental apology to his colleagues, "I should certainly prefer to hear the story from you."

"There isn't a story," said Mr. Wilson piteously. "That's what I keep telling you. There isn't a ruddy story."

"Just give Mr. Alleyn an account of the way you opened up the shed and got going, Ben," said Fabian.

"That's it," Alleyn agreed hurriedly. "I only want to know the routine as you went through with it that morning, step by step. So that I can get an idea of how things went. Step by step," he repeated. "Put yourself in my position, Mr. Wilson. Suppose you had to find out, all of a sudden, exactly what took place at dawn in a—in a pickle factory or a young ladies' boarding-school, or a maternity hospital. I mean—" Alleyn thrust his cigarettes at Mr. Wilson and clapped him nervously on the shoulder. "Be a good chap, for God's sake," he said, "and spit it out."

"Ta," said Mr. Wilson, lighting the new cigarette at the butt of the old one. "Oh, well," he said resignedly, and Alleyn sat down on a wool pack.

Once embarked Mr. Wilson made better showing than might have been hoped for. There was a tendency to skip and become cryptic but Fabian acted as a sort of interpreter and on the whole he did not too badly. A picture of the working day in a wool-shed began to take shape. Everybody had been short-tempered that morning, it seemed. Mr. Wilson himself had a bad attack of some gastric complaint to which he was prone and which had developed during the night on the journey back from the dance. At a quarter to two that morning, when they reached Mount Moon, he was, he said, proper crook, and he had spent the remainder of the night in acute discomfort. No, he said wearily, they'd noticed nothing funny in the wool-shed when they came home. They were not in the mood, Alleyn gathered, to notice anything. The farm lorry had sprung a puncture down by the front gate, and they decided to leave it there until morning. They walked the half mile up to the homestead, with the liquor dying out in them as they did so. They hadn't talked much until they got level with the yards, and there a violent political argument had suddenly developed between two of the shearers. "I told them to pass it up," said Mr. Wilson, "and we all turned in."

They were up again at dawn. The sky was overcast and when Albie Black went down to open up the shed a very light drizzle had set in. If this continued, it meant that when the sheep under cover were shorn, the men would have to knock off until the next batch had dried. This was the last day's shearing and the lorry was to call in the afternoon for the clip which should have been ready before noon. Albie Black went to light the hurricane lantern and found that the boys hadn't filled it with kerosene as he had instructed. He cursed and turned to the candle, only to find it had burnt down to a stump and been squashed out so firmly that the wick had sunk into the wax. He got a fresh piece of candle from another part of the shed, gouged the old stump out and tossed it into the pens. By this time it was light enough to do without it. When Mr. Wilson arrived, Albie poured out his complaints and Mr. Wilson, himself enraged by gastric disorder, gave the boys the sharp edge of his tongue. He was further incensed by finding, as he put it, "a dump of wool in my number two bin that hadn't been there when we knocked off the night before. All mucked up, it was, as if someone had been messing it about and then tried to roll it up proper."

"The wool is put into bins according to its grade?" Alleyn asked.

"That's right. This was number two stuff, all right. I reckoned the broomies had got into the shed when we was over at the dance and started mucking round with the stuff in the press."

The boys, however, had vigorously denied these accusations. They swore that they had filled the lamp and had not meddled with the candle which had been fully five inches long. Tommy Johns arrived and pulled on his overalls which hung on a nail near the shearing board. His foot caught in an open seam in the trousers and tore it wider. He instantly accused Albie Black of having used the overalls, which were new. Albie hotly denied this. Mr. Johns pointed out several dark stains on the front of the overalls and muttered incredulously.

The men started shearing. Damp sheep were crammed under cover to dry off as the already dry sheep thinned out. Fabian and Douglas arrived, anxious about the weather. By this time almost everybody on the place was in an evil temper. One of the shearers, in running across the belly of a sheep, cut it badly and Douglas, who happened to be standing by, trod in a pool of blood. "And did he go crook!" Mr. Wilson ruminated appreciatively.

Arthur Rubrick arrived at this juncture, walking slowly and very short of breath. "And," said Mr. Wilson, "the boss picked things was not too pleasant and asked Tommy Johns what was wrong. Tommy started moaning about nobody being any good on the place. They were standing near the sorting table and I heard what was said."

"Can you remember it?" Alleyn asked.

"I can remember all right, but there was nothing in it."

"May I hear about it? I'm enormously grateful for all this, Mr. Wilson."

"It didn't amount to anything. Tommy's a funny joker. He goes crook sometimes. He said the men were a lot of lazy bastards."

"Anything else?"

"Young Cliff was in trouble about a bottle of booze. Mrs. Rubrick had told him off a couple of nights before. Tommy didn't like it. He was complaining about it."

"What did Mr. Rubrick say?"

"He wasn't too good that morning. He was bad, you could see that. His face was a terrible colour. He was very quiet, and kept saying it was unfortunate. He seemed to think it was very very hot in the shed, and kept moving as if he'd like to clear out. His hands were shaky, too. He was bad, all right."

"How did it end?"

"Young Doug came up—the Captain," Mr. Wilson explained with a hint of irony. "He was in a bit of a mess. Bloody. It seemed to upset the boss and he said quite violent: 'What the devil have you been doing?' and Doug didn't like it and turned his back on him and walked out."

"Now, that's an incident that we haven't got in the files," Alleyn said.

"I never mentioned it. This Sub-Inspector Jackson comes

into my shed and throws his weight about, treating us from the word go as if we're holding back on him. Very inconsiderate, he was. 'I don't want to know what you think. I want you to answer my questions.' All right. We answered his questions."

"Oh, well," said Alleyn pacifically.

"We don't want to hold back on it," Mr. Wilson continued with warmth. "We were as much put out as anyone else when we heard. It's not very nice to think about. When they told Jack Merrywether—he's the presser—what he must of done that morning, he vomited. All over my shearing board before anyone could take any steps about it. It was nearly a month afterwards but that made no difference to Jack."

"Quite," said Alleyn. "How did this visit of Mr. Rubrick's end?"

"It finished up by the boss taking a bad turn. We helped him out into the open. You wasn't about just then, Mr. Losse, and he asked us not to say anything. He carried some kind of medicine on him that he sniffed up and it seemed to fix him. Tommy sent young Cliff for the station car and he drove the boss back to the house. He was very particular we shouldn't mention it. Anxious to avoid trouble. He was a gentleman, was Mr. Rubrick."

"Yes. Now then, Mr. Wilson, about the press. When you knocked off on the previous night it was full of wool, wasn't it? The top half was on the bottom half and the wool had been tramped down but not pressed. Is that right?"

"That's right."

"And that, to all intents and purposes, was what it looked like in the morning?"

"So far as I noticed but I did no more than glance at it, if that. Jack Merrywether never noticed anything."

"When did you finish shearing?"

"Not till six that evening. We cleaned up the sheep that'd been brought in overnight and then there was a hold-up. That was at eleven. The fresh ones we'd brought in hadn't dried off. Then it come up sunny and we turned them out again. Everyone was snaky. Young Doug says the sheep are dry and I say they're not and Tommy Johns says they're not. The lorry turns up and Syd Barnes, he's the driver, he has to shove in his oar and reckon they're dry because he wants to get on with it and make the pub at the Pass before dark. So I tell the whole gang where they get off and by that time the sheep have dried and we start up again. Young Cliff was hanging around the shed doing nothing, and then he slopes off, and his father goes crook when he can't find him. It was lovely."

The whistle tooted and the shed was at once active. Five plunging sheep were dragged in by their hind legs from the pens, machinery whirred, a raw-boned man moved over to the press, spat on his hands, and bore down on the ratchet lever. Mr. Wilson pinched out his cigarette, nodded and walked back to the sorter's table.

Alleyn watched the presser complete his work. The bale was sewn up, removed, and shoved along the floor towards the double doors where he and Fabian still waited. This process was assisted by the use of a short hook which was caught into the corners of the bale. "The lorry backs in here," Fabian said, "and the packs are dumped on board. The floor's the same height as the lorry, or a little higher. There's no lifting. It's the same sort of business in the wool store at the other end."

"Is that the same presser? Jack Merrywether?"

"Yes," said Fabian, "that's Jack. He who was so acutely inconvenienced by the absence of a vomitorium in the wool-shed."

"Is he apt to be sick again, do you imagine, if I put a few simple questions to him?"

"Who can tell? What do you want to ask him?"

"Whether he used one of those hooks when he shifted the crucial bale."

"Ticklish!" Fabian said. "It makes even me a little queasy to think of it. Hi, Jack!"

Merrywether's reaction to his summons was disquieting. No sooner had Fabian spoken his introductory phrases than the presser turned pale and stared at Alleyn with an expression of panic.

"Look," he said. "I wouldn't of come back on this job if it hadn't of been for the war. That's how it affected me. I'd have turned it up only for the war and there being a shortage. 'Look,' I said to Mr. Johns and Ben Wilson, I said, 'not if it's the same outfit,' I said. 'You don't get me coming at the Mount Moon job if it's the same press again,' I said. Then they told me it was a new press and I give in. I come to oblige. Not willing, though. I didn't fancy it and I don't yet. Call me soft if you like but that's how I am. If anybody starts asking me about you-know-what, it catches me smack in the belly. I feel shocking. I don't reckon I'll ever shake it off. Now!"

Alleyn murmured sympathetically.

"Look at it whatever way you like," Merrywether continued argumentatively, "and it's still a fair cow. You think you're mastering the sensation and then somebody comes along and starts asking you a lot of silly questions and you feel terrible again."

"As far as I'm concerned," Alleyn said hurriedly, "there's only one detail I'd like to check." He glanced at the bale hook which Merrywether still grasped in his pink freckled hand. Merrywether followed his glance. His fingers opened and the hook crashed on the floor. With clairvoyant accuracy he roared out: "I know what you mean and I never! It wasn't there. I never touched it with the hook. Now!" And before Alleyn could reply he added: "You ask me why. All right. They'd dumped the hook on me. There you are! Deliberate, I reckon."

"Dumped it on you? The hook? Hid it?"

"That's right. Deliberate. Stuck it up on a beam over there." He gestured excitedly at the far wall of the shed. "There's two of those hooks and that's what they done with them. In that dark corner and high up where I couldn't see them. So what do I do? Go crook at the broomies. Naturally. I get the idea they done it to swing one across me. They're boys and they act like boys. Cheeky. I'd told them off the day before and I reckoned they'd come back at me with this one. 'You come to light with them two hooks,' I said, 'or I'll knock your blocks off you.' Well, of course they says they don't know anything about it and I don't believe them and away we go. And by this time the bins are full and me and my mate are behind on our job."

Alleyn walked over to the wall and reached up. He could just get his hand on the beam.

"So you moved the bales without using hooks?"

"That's right. Now don't ask me if we noticed anything. If we'd noticed anything we'd have said something, wouldn't we? All right."

"When did you find the hooks?"

"That night when we was clearing up, Albie Black starts in again on the boys, saying they never done their job, not filling up the kerosene lamp and fooling round with the candle. So we all look over where the lantern and the candle are on the wall and my mate says they've been swarming up the wall like a couple of blasted monkeys. 'What's that up there?' he howls. He's a tall joker and he walks across and yanks down the bale hooks off of the top beam. The boys reckon they don't know how the hooks got up there and we argue round the point till Tommy Johns has to bring up the matter of who the hell put his foot through his overall pants. Oh, it was a lovely day."

"When the bales were finally loaded on the lorry—" Alleyn began, but at once Merrywether took fright. "Now, don't you start in on me about that," he scolded. "I never noticed nothing. How would I? I never handled it."

"All right, my dear man," said Alleyn pacifically, "you didn't. That disposes of that. Don't be so damned touchy; I never knew such a chap."

"I got to consider my stomach," said Merrywether darkly.

"Your stomach'll have to lump it, I'm afraid. Who stencilled the Mount Moon mark on the bales?"

"Young Cliff."

"And who sewed up the bales?"

"I did. Now!"

"All right. Now the bale with which I'm concerned was the first one you handled that morning. When you started work it was full of wool that apparently had been trampled down but not pressed. You pressed it. You told the police you noticed no change whatever, nothing remarkable or unusual in the condition of the bale. It was exactly as you'd left it the night before."

"So it was the same. Wouldn't I of noticed if it hadn't been?"

"I should have thought so, certainly. The floor, for instance, round the press."

"What about it?" Merrywether began on a high note. Alleyn saw his hands contract. He blinked, his sandy lashes moving like shutters over his light eyes. "What about the floor?" he said less truculently.

"I notice how smooth the surface is. Would that be the natural grease in the fleeces? It's particularly noticeable on the shearing board and round the press where the bales may act as polishing agents when they are shoved across the floor." He glanced at Merrywether's feet. "You wear ordinary boots. The soles must get quite glassy in here, I should have thought."

"Not to notice," he said uncomfortably.

"The floor was in its normal condition that morning, was it? No odd pieces of wool lying about?"

"I told you—" Merrywether began, but Alleyn interrupted him. "And as smooth as ever?" he said. Merrywether was silent. "Come now," said Alleyn, "haven't you remembered something that escaped your memory before, when Sub-Inspector Jackson talked to you?"

"I couldn't be expected—I was crook. The way he kept asking me how could I of shifted a pack with you-know-what inside it. It turned my stomach on me."

"I know. But the floor. Thinking back, now. Was there anything about the floor, round the press, when you arrived here that morning? Was it swept and polished as usual?"

"It was swept."

"And polished?"

"All right, all right, it wasn't. How was I to remember, three weeks later? The way I'd got churned up over what, in all innocence, I done? It never crossed me mind till just now when you brought it up. I noticed it and yet I never noticed it if you can understand."

"I know," said Alleyn.

"But in pity's name, Jack," cried Fabian, who had been silent throughout the entire interview, "what did you notice?"

"The floor was kind of smudged," said Merrywether.

iii

In the men's midday dinner hour, Fabian brought Cliff
Johns to the study. Alleyn felt curious about this boy who
had so unexpectedly refused the patronage of Florence
Rubrick. He had asked Fabian to leave them alone together
and now, as he watched the unco-ordinated movements of
the youth's hands, he wondered if Cliff knew that in defiance
of his alibi he was Sub-Inspector Jackson's pet among the
suspects.

He got the boy to sit down and asked him if he understood
the reason for the interview. Cliff nodded and clenched and
unclenched his wide mobile hands. Behind him, beyond open
windows, glared a noonday garden, the plateau, blank with
sunshine, and the mountains etherealized now by an
intensity of light. Shadows on those ranges appeared
translucent as though the sky beyond shone through. Their
snows dazzled the eyes and seemed to be composed of light
without substance. A nimbus of light rimmed Cliff's hair.
Alleyn thought that his wife would have liked to paint the
boy, and would have found pleasure in reflected colour that
swam in the hollow of his temples and beneath the sharp
arches of his brows. He said: "Are you interested in painting
as well as music?"

Cliff blinked at him and shuffled his feet. "Yes," he said.
"A friend of mine is keen. Anything that—I mean—there
aren't so many people—I mean—"

"I only asked you," Alleyn said, "because I wondered if it
would be as difficult to express this extraordinary landscape
in terms of music as it would be to do so in terms of paint."
Cliff looked sharply at him. "I don't understand music, you
see," Alleyn went on. "But paint does say something to me.
When I heard that music was your particular thing I felt
rather lost. The technique of approach through channels of
interest wouldn't work. So I thought I'd try a switch-over.
Any good or rotten?"

"I'd rather do without a channel of approach, I think," Cliff said. "I'd rather get it over, if you don't mind." But instead of allowing Alleyn to follow his suggestion, he added, half-shamefaced: "That's what I wanted to do. With music, I mean. Say something about this." He jerked his head at the vastness beyond the window and added with an air of defiance: "And I don't mean the introduction of native bird song and Maori *hakas* into an ersatz symphony." Alleyn heard an echo of Fabian Losse in this speech.

"It seems to me," he said, "that the forcible injection of local colour is the catch in any aesthetic treatment of this country. There is no forcing the growth of an art, is there, and, happily, no denying it when the moment is ripe. Is your music good?"

Cliff sank his head between his shoulders and with the profundity of the very young said: "It might have been. I've chucked it."

"Why?"

Cliff muttered undistinguishably, caught Alleyn's eye and blurted out: "The kind of things that have happened to me."

"I see. You mean, of course, the difference of opinion with Mrs. Rubrick, and her murder. Do you really believe that you'll be worse off for these horrors? I've always had a notion that, if his craft has a sound core, an artist should ripen with experience, however beastly the experience may be at the time. But perhaps that's a layman's idea. Perhaps you had two remedies: your music and—" he looked out of the windows—"all this. You chose the landscape. Is that it?"

"They wouldn't have me for the army."

"You aren't yet eighteen are you?"

"They wouldn't have me. Eyes and feet," said Cliff as if the naming of these members were an offence against decency. "I can see as well as anybody and I can muster the high-country for three days without noticing my feet. That's the army for you."

"So you mean to carry on mustering the high-country and seeing as far through a brick wall as the next fellow?"

"I suppose so."

"Do you ever lend a hand at wool sorting, or try to learn about it?"

"I keep outside the shed. Always have."

"It's a profitable job, isn't it?"

"Doesn't appeal to me. I'd rather go up the hill on a muster."

"And—no music?"

Cliff shuffled his feet.

"Why?" Alleyn persisted. Cliff rubbed his hands across his face and shook his head. "I can't," he said. "I told you I can't."

"Not since the evening in the annex? When you played for an hour or more on a very disreputable old instrument. That was the night following the incident over the bottle of whisky, wasn't it?"

More than at anything else, Alleyn thought, more than at the reminder of Florence Rubrick's death, even, Cliff sickened at the memory of this incident. It had been a serio-comic episode. Markins indignant at the window, the crash of a bursting bottle and the reek of spirits. Alleyn remembered that the tragedies of adolescence were felt more often in the self-esteem, and he said: "I want you to explain this whisky story but, before you do, you might just remind yourself that there isn't a creature living who doesn't carry within him the memory of some particular shabbiness of which he's much more ashamed than he would be of a major crime. Also that there's probably not a boy in the world who hasn't at some time or other committed petty larceny. I may add that I personally don't give a damn whether you were silly enough to pinch Mr. Rubrick's whisky or not. But I am concerned to find out whether you told the truth when you said you didn't pinch it and why, if this is so, you wouldn't explain what you were up to in the cellarage."

"I wasn't taking it," Cliff muttered. "I hadn't taken it."

"Bible oath before a beak?"

"Yes. Before anybody." Cliff looked quickly at him. "I don't know how to make it sound true. I don't expect you to believe me."

"I'm doing my best, but it would be a hell of a lot easier if you'd tell me what in the world you were up to."

Cliff was silent.

"Not anything in the heroic line?" Alleyn asked mildly.

Cliff opened his mouth and shut it again.

"Because," Alleyn went on, "there are moments when the heroic line is no more than a spanner in the works of justice. I mean, if you didn't kill Mrs. Rubrick you're deliberately, for some fetish of your own, muddling the trail. The whisky may be completely irrelevant but we can't tell. It's a question of tidying up. Of course if you did kill her you may be wise to hold your tongue. I don't know."

"But you know I didn't," Cliff said and his voice faded on a note of bewilderment. "I've got an alibi. I played."

"What was it you played?"

"Bach's 'Art of Fugue.'"

"Difficult?" Alleyn asked and had to wait a long time for his answer. Cliff made two false starts, checking his voice before it was articulate. "I'd worked at it," he said at last. "Now why," Alleyn wondered, "does he jib at telling me it was difficult?"

"It must be disheartening work, slogging away at a bad instrument," he said. "It is bad, isn't it?"

Again Cliff was unaccountably reluctant. "Not as bad as all that," he muttered and, with a sudden spurt: "A friend of mine in a music shop in town came out for a couple of days and tuned it for me. It wasn't so bad."

"But nothing like the Bechstein in the drawing-room for instance?"

"It wasn't so bad," he persisted. "It's a good make. It used to be in the house here before—before she got the Bechstein."

"You must have missed playing the Bechstein."

"You can't have everything," Cliff said.

"Honour," Alleyn suggested lightly, "or concert grands? Is that it?"

Cliff grinned unexpectedly. "Something of the sort," he said.

"See here," said Alleyn. "Will you, without further ado and without me plodding round the by-ways of indirect attack—will you tell me the whole story of your falling-out with Mrs. Rubrick? You needn't, of course. You can refuse to speak, as you did with my colleagues, and force me to behave as they did: listen to other people's versions of the quarrel. Do you know that the police files devote two foolscap pages to hearsay accounts of the relationship between you and Mrs. Rubrick?"

"I can imagine it," said Cliff savagely. "Gestapo methods."

"Do you really think so?" Alleyn said with such gravity that Cliff looked fixedly at him and turned red. "If you can spare the time," Alleyn went on, "I'd like to lend you a manual of police law. It would give you an immense feeling of security. You would learn from it that I am forbidden to quote in a court of law anything that you tell me about your relationship with Mrs. Rubrick unless it is to read aloud a statement that you've signed before witnesses. And I'm not asking you to do that. I'm asking you to give me the facts of the case so that I can make up my mind whether they have any bearing on her death."

"They haven't."

"Very good. What are they?"

Cliff bent forward, driving his fingers through his hair. Alleyn felt suddenly impatient. "But it is the impatience," he thought, "of a middle-aged man," and he reminded himself of the enclosed tragedies of youth. "Like green figs," he said to himself, "closed in upon themselves. He is not yet eighteen," he thought, growing more tolerant, "and I bring a code to bear upon him." Then, as was habitual with him, he disciplined his thoughts and prepared himself for another assault upon Cliff's over-tragic silence. Before he could speak Cliff raised his head and spoke with simplicity. "I'll tell you," he said. "In a way it'll be a relief. But I'm afraid it's a long story. You see it all hangs on her. The kind of woman she was."

CHAPTER VIII

ACCORDING TO CLIFF JOHNS

"You didn't know her," Cliff said. "That's what makes everything so impossible. You don't know what she was like."

"I'm learning," Alleyn said.

"But it doesn't make sense. I've read about that sort of thing, of course, but somehow I never dropped to it when it was happening to me—I mean not until it was too late to avoid a row. I was only a kid of course. In the beginning."

"Yes," said Alleyn and waited.

Cliff turned his foot sideways and looked at the sole of his boot. Alleyn was surprised to see that he was blushing. "I suppose I'd better explain," he said at last, "that I'm not absolutely positive what the Oedipus complex exactly is."

"And I'm not at all sure that I can help you. Let's just have the whole story, clinical or otherwise, may we?"

"Right-oh, then. You see, when I was a kid she started taking an interest in me. What they said when I used to go to the Lake School over there on the flat—" he jerked his head at the plateau—"about my liking music and so on. I was scared of her at first. You may have the idea that in this country there's no class consciousness but it's there, all right, don't you worry. The station holder's wife taking an interest in the working manager's kid. Accent on *working*. I felt the condescension, all right. Her voice sounded funny to me at first too, but after a bit, when I got used to it, I liked the way she talked. A bit of an English accent. Crisp and clear and not afraid to say straight out what she thought without drawling 'You know' after every other word. The first time she had me over here I was only about ten and I'd never been inside the drawing-room. It seemed very big and white and smelt of flowers and the fire. She played for me. Chopin. Very badly, but I thought it was marvellous. Then she told me to play. I wouldn't at first but she went out of the room and then I touched the keyboard. I felt guilty and silly but nobody came in and I went on striking one note after another, then chords, and then picking out a phrase of the Chopin melody. She left me alone for quite a long time and then she brought me in here for tea. I had ginger beer and cake. That was the beginning."

"You were good friends in those days?"

"Yes, I thought so. You can imagine what it was like for me, coming here. She gave me books and bought new records for the gramophone and there was always the piano. She used to talk a lot about music; terrible stuff, of course, bogus and soulful, but I lapped it up. She began teaching me to 'speak nicely,' too. Dad and my mother used to sling off at me for it, but Mum half liked it all the same. Mum used to buck at Women's Institute meetings about the interest Mrs. Rubrick took in me. Even Dad, for all his views, was a bit tickled at first. Parental vanity. They never saw how socially unsound the whole thing was; that I was just a sort of high-brow hobby and that every penny she spent on me was so much purchase money. Dad must have known of course, but I suppose Mum talked him out of it."

"How did you feel about it?"

"What do you think? It seemed to me that everything I wanted was inside this house. I'd have lived here if I could. But she was very clever. Only one hour every other day, so that the gilt never wore off the gingerbread. She never forced me to do anything too long. I never tired of anything. I can see now what a lot of self-restraint she must have used because by nature she was a slave driver." He paused, tracing back his memories. "Gosh!" he said suddenly. "What a nasty little bit of work I must have been."

"Why?"

"Sucking up to her. Wallowing in second-rate ideas about second-rate music. Telling her what Tchaikovsky made me feel like and slobbering out 'Chanson Triste' on the Bechstein with plenty of soul and wrong notes. Kidding myself as well as her that I didn't like the 'Donkey Serenade.'"

"At the age of ten?" Alleyn murmured incredulously.

"Up to thirteen. I used to write poems too, all about nature and high ideals. 'We must be nothing weak, valleys and hills are ours, from the last lone rocky peak to where the rata flowers.' I set that one to music: 'Tiddely-tum-te-tum. Tiddely-tum-te-te' and wrote it all out and gave it to her for Christmas with a lovely picture in water colour under the dedication. Gosh, I was awful."

"Well," said Alleyn peaceably, "you certainly seem to have been a full-sized *enfant prodigue*. At thirteen you went to boarding-school, didn't you?"

"Yes. At her expense. I was hell-bent on it of course."

"Was it a success?" Alleyn asked and to his surprise Cliff said: "Not bad. I don't approve of the system, of course. Education ought to be the business of the state; not of a lot of desiccated failures whose real object is to bolster up class consciousness. The teaching on the whole was merely comic but there were one or two exceptions." He saw Alleyn raise an eyebrow and reddened. "I suppose you're thinking I'm an insufferable young puppy, aren't you?"

"I'm merely reminding myself rather strenuously that you are probably giving me an honest answer and that you are not yet eighteen. But do go on. Why, after all, was it not so bad?"

"There were things they couldn't spoil. I was bullied at first, of course, and miserable. It's so bracing for one, being made to feel suicidal at the age of thirteen. But I turned out to be a slow bowler and naturally that saved me. I got a bit of kudos at school concerts and I developed a turn for writing mildly indecent limericks. That helped. And I went to a good man for music. I am grateful to her for that. Honestly grateful. He made music clear for me. He taught me what music is about. And I did make some real friends. People I could talk to," said Cliff with relish. The phrase carried Alleyn back thirty years to a dark study and the sound of bells. "In our way," he told himself, "we were just such another clutch of little egoists."

"While you were still at school," he said, "Mrs. Rubrick went to England, didn't she?"

"Yes. That was when it happened."

"When what happened?"

The story developed slowly. Before Florence Rubrick left

for England she visited young Cliff at his school, bearing
down on him, Alleyn thought, as, a few years earlier, she had
borne down on Ursula Harme. With less success, however.
She seemed in the extraordinarily critical eyes of a schoolboy
to make every possible gaffe. She spoke too loudly. She
tipped too lavishly and in the wrong direction. She asked to
be introduced to Cliff's seniors and talked about him, in front
of his contemporaries, to his housemaster. Worst of all she
insisted on an interview with his music teacher, a fastidious
and austere man, at whom she talked dreadfully about
playing with soul and the works of Mendelssohn. Cliff
became morbidly sensitive about her patronage, and
imagined that those boys in his house who came from the
plateau laughed about them both behind his back. He had
committed, he felt, the appalling crime of being different. He
had a private interview with Flossie, who spoke in an
embarrassing manner about his forthcoming confirmation
and even, with a formidable use of botanical parallels, of his
approaching adolescence. In the course of this interview she
told him that her great sorrow was the tragedy of having been
denied (she almost suggested it was by Arthur Rubrick) a
son. She took his face between her sharp large hands and
looked at it until it turned purple. She then reminded him of
all that she had done for him; kindly, breezily, but
unmistakably, and said she knew that he would repay her just
as much as if he really were her own son. "We're real pals,
aren't we?" she said. "Real chums. Cobbers." His blood ran
cold.

   She wrote him long letters from England and brought him
back a marvellous gramophone and a great many records.
He was now fifteen. The unpleasant memory of their last
meeting had been thrust away at the back of his mind. He had
found his feet at school and worked hard at his music. At first
his encounters with his patron after her return from England
were happy enough. Alleyn gathered that he talked about
himself and that Flossie listened.

   In the last term of 1940 Cliff formed a friendship with an
English boy who had been evacuated to New Zealand by his
parents; evidently communistic intellectuals. Their son,
delicate, vehement and sardonic, seemed to Cliff extraordi-

narily mature, a man among children. He devoured everything his friend had to say, became an enthusiastic Leftist, argued with his masters and thought himself, Alleyn suspected, a good deal more of a bombshell than they did. He and his friend gathered round them an ardently iconoclastic group all of whom decided to fight "without prejudice" against fascism, reserving the right to revolt when the war was over. The friend, it seemed, had always been of this mind "but," said Cliff ingenuously, "of course it made a big difference when Russia came in. I suppose," he added, "you are horrified."

"Do you?" said Alleyn. "Then I mustn't disappoint you. The thing is, was Mrs. Rubrick horrified?"

"I'll say she was! That was when the awful row happened. It started first of all with us trying to enlist. This chap and I suddenly felt we couldn't stick it just hanging on at school and—well, anyway, that's what we did. We were turned down, of course. The episode was very sourly received by all hands. That was at the end of 1941. I came home for the Christmas holidays. By that time I realized pretty thoroughly how hopelessly wrong it was for me to play at being a little gentleman at her expense. I realized that if I couldn't get as my right, equally with other chaps, the things she'd given me, then I shouldn't take them at all. I was admitting the right of one class to patronize another. They were short of men all over the high-country and I felt that if I couldn't get into the army I'd better work on the place."

He paused, and with a very shamefaced air muttered: "I'm not trying to make out a flattering case for myself. It wasn't as if I was army-minded. I loathed the prospect. Muddle, boredom, idiotic routine and then carnage. It was just—well, I did honestly feel I ought to."

"Right," said Alleyn. "I take the point."

"She didn't. She'd got it all taped out. I was to go Home to the Royal College of Music. At her expense. She was delighted when they said I'd never pass fit. When I tried to explain she treated me like a silly kid. Then, when I stuck to it, she accused me of ingratitude. She had no right," said Cliff passionately. "Nobody has the right to take a kid of ten and teach him to accept everything without knowing what it means and then use that generosity as a weapon against him. She'd always talked about the right of artists to be free. Free! She'd got vested interests in me and she meant to use them. It was horrible."

"What was the upshot of the discussion?"

Cliff had turned in his chair. His face was dark against the glare of the plateau and it was by the posture of his body and the tilt of his head that Alleyn first realized he was staring at the portrait of Florence Rubrick.

"She sat just like that," he said. "Her hands were like that and her mouth—not quite shut. She hadn't got much expression, ever, and you couldn't believe, looking at her, that she could say the things she said. What everything had cost and how she'd thought I was fond of her. I couldn't stand it. I walked out."

"When was this?"

"The night I got home for the summer holidays. I didn't see her again until—until—"

"We're back at the broken bottle of whiskey, aren't we?"

Cliff was silent.

"Come," said Alleyn, "you've been very frank up to now. Why do you jib at this one point?"

Cliff shuffled his feet and began mumbling. "All very well, but how do I know...not a free agent...Gestapo methods...Taken down and used against you..."

"Nonsense," said Alleyn. "I've taken nothing down and I've no witness. Don't let's go over all that again. If you won't tell me what you were doing with the whisky, you won't, but really you can't blame Sub-Inspector Jackson for taking a gloomy view of your reticence. Let's get back to the bare bones of fact. You were in the dairy-*cum*-cellar with the bottle in your hand. Markins looked through the window, you dropped the bottle, he haled you into the kitchen. Mrs. Duck fetched Mrs. Rubrick. There was a scene in the middle of which she dismissed Mrs. Duck and Markins. We have their several accounts of the scene up to the point when they left. I should now like to have yours of the whole affair."

Cliff stared at the portrait. Alleyn saw him wet his lips and a moment later, give the uncanny little half yawn of nervous expectancy. Alleyn was familiar with this grimace. He had seen it made by prisoners awaiting sentence and by men under suspicion when the investigating officer carried the interrogration towards danger point.

"Will it help," he said, "if I tell you this? Anything that is not relevant to my inquiry will not appear in any subsequent report. I can give you my word, if you'll take it, that I'll never repeat or use such statements if, in fact, they are irrelevant." He waited for a moment. "Well," he said at last, "what about this scene with Mrs. Rubrick in the kitchen? Was it so very bad?"

"You've been told what they heard. The other two. It was bad enough then. Before they went. Almost as if she was glad to be able to go for me. It's as real now as if it had happened last night. Only it's a queer kind of reality. Like the memory of a nightmare."

"Have you ever spoken to anybody about it?"

"Never."

"Then bring the monster out into the light of day and let's have a look at it."

He saw that Cliff half welcomed, half resisted this insistence.

"After all," Alleyn said, "was it so terrible?"

"Not terrible exactly," Cliff said. "Disgusting."

"Well?"

"I suppose I had a kind of respect for her. Partly bogus, I know that. An acceptance of the feudal idea. But partly genuine too. Partly based on the honest gratitude I'd have felt for her if she hadn't demanded gratitude. I don't know. I only know it made me feel sick to see her lips shake and to hear her voice tremble. There was a master at school who used to get like that before he caned us. He got the sack. She seemed to be acting, too. Acting the lady of the house who controlled herself before the servants. It'd have been better if she'd yelled at me. When they'd gone, she did—once. When I said I wasn't stealing it. Then she sort of took hold of herself and dropped back into a whisper. All the same, even then, in a way, I thought she was putting it on. Acting. Really it was almost as if she enjoyed herself. That was what was so particularly beastly."

"I know," said Alleyn.

"Do you? And her being old. That made it worse. I started by being furious because she wouldn't believe me. Then I began to be sorry for her. Then I simply wanted to get away and get clean. She began to—to cry. She looked ghastly. I felt as if I could never bear to look at her again. She held out her hand and I couldn't touch it. I was furious with her for making me feel so ashamed, and I turned round and cleared out of it. I suppose you know about the next part."

"I know you spent the rest of that night, and a good bit of the next day, walking towards the Pass."

"That's right. It sounds silly. A hysterical kid, you'll think. I couldn't help it. I made a pretty good fool of myself. I was out of training and my feet gave out. I'd have gone on, though, if Dad hadn't come after me."

"You didn't make a second attempt."

Cliff shook his head.

"Why?"

"They got on to me at home. Mum got me to promise. There was a pretty ghastly scene when I got home."

"And in the evening you worked it off with Bach on the annex piano? That's how it was, isn't it?" Alleyn insisted, but Cliff was monosyllabic again. "That's right," he mumbled, rubbing the arm of his chair. Alleyn tried to get him to talk about the music he played that night in the darkling room while Florence Rubrick and her household sat in deck-chairs on the lawn. All through their conversation it had persisted, and through the search for the brooch. Florence Rubrick must have heard it as she climbed up her improvised rostrum. Her murderer must have heard it when he struck her down and stuffed her mouth and nostrils with wool. "Murder to Music," thought Alleyn, and saw the words splashed across a news bill. Was it because of these associations that Cliff would not speak of his music? Was it because this, theatrically enough, had been the last time he played? Or was it merely that he was reluctant to speak of music with a Philistine? Alleyn found himself satisfied with none of these theories.

"Losse," he said, "tells me you played extremely well that night."

"*What's he mean!*" Cliff stopped dead, as if horrified at his own vehemence. "I'd worked at it," he said indistinctly. "I told you."

"It's strange to me," Alleyn said, "that you don't go on with your music. I should have thought that not to go on would be intolerable."

"Would you?" he muttered.

"Are you sure you are not a little bit proud of your abstinence?"

This seemed to astonish Cliff. "Proud!" he repeated. "If you only realized . . ." He got up. "If you've finished with me," he said.

"Almost, yes. You never saw her again?"

Cliff seemed to take this question as a statement of fact. He moved towards the French window. "Is that right?" Alleyn said, and he nodded. "And you won't tell me what you were doing with the whisky?"

"I can't."

"All right. I think I'll just take a look at this annex. I can find my way. Thank you for being so nearly frank."

Cliff blinked at him and went out.

ii

The annex proved to be grander than its name suggested. Fabian had told Alleyn that it had been added to the bunk-house by Arthur Rubrick as a sort of common-room for the men. Florence, in a spurt of solicitude and public-spiritedness, had urged this upon her husband, and, on acquiring the Bechstein, had given the men her old piano and a radio set, and had turned the house out for odd pieces of furniture. "It was when she stood for Parliament," Fabian explained acidly. "She had a photograph taken with the station hands sitting about in exquisitely self-conscious attitudes and sent it to the papers. You'll find a framed enlargement above the mantelpiece."

The room had an unkempt look. There was a bloom of dust on the table, the radio and the piano. A heap of old radio magazines had been stacked untidily in a corner of the room and yellowing newspapers lay about the floor. The top of the piano was piled with music; ballads, student song-books and dance tunes. Underneath these he found a number of classical works with Cliff's name written across the top. Here at the bottom was Bach's "Art of Fugue."

Alleyn opened the piano and picked out a phase from Cliff's music. Two of the notes jammed. Had the Bach been full of hiatuses, then, or had the piano deteriorated so much in fifteen months? Alleyn replaced the "Art of Fugue" under a pile of song sheets, brushed his hands together absently, closed the door and squatted down by the heap of radio magazines in the corner.

He waded back through sixty-five weeks of wireless programs that had been pumped into the air from all the broadcasting stations in the country. The magazines were not stacked in order and it was a tedious business. Back to February, 1942: laying them down in their sequence. The second week in February, the first week in February. Alleyn's hands were poised over the work. There were only half a dozen left. He sorted them quickly. The last week in January, 1942, was missing.

Mechanically he stacked the magazines up in their corner and, after a moment's hesitation, disordered them again. He walked up and down the room whistling a phrase of Cliff's music. "Oh, well!" he thought. "It's a long shot and I may be off the mark." But he stared dolefully at the piano and presently began again to pick out the same phrase, first in the treble and then, very dejectedly, in the bass, swearing when the keys jammed. He shut the lid at last, sat in a rakish old chair and began to fill his pipe. "I shall be obliged to send them all away on ludicrous errands," he muttered, "and get a toll call through to Jackson. Is this high fantasy, or is it murder?"

The door opened. A woman stood on the threshold.

She looked dark against the brilliance of sunshine outside. He could see that the hand with which she had opened the door was now pressed against her lips. She was a middle-aged woman, plainly dressed. She was still for a moment and then stepped back. The strong sunshine fell across her face, which was heavy and pale for a country-woman's. She said breathlessly: "I heard the piano. I thought it was Cliff."

"I'm afraid Cliff would not be flattered," Alleyn said. "I lack technique!" He moved towards her.

She backed away. "It was the piano," she said again. "Hearing it after so long."

"Did the men never play it?"

"Not in the daytime," she said hurriedly. "And I kind of remember the tune." She tidied her hair nervously. "I'm sure I didn't mean to intrude," she said. "Excuse me." She was moving away when Alleyn stopped her.

"Please don't go," he said. "You're Cliff's mother aren't you?"

"That's right."

"I'd be grateful if you would spare me a moment. It won't be much more than a moment. Really. My name, by the way, is Alleyn."

"Pleased to meet you," she said woodenly.

He stood aside, holding back the door. After a little hesitation she went into the room and stood there, staring straight before her, her fingers still moving against her lips. Alleyn left the door open. "Will you sit down?" he said.

"I won't bother, thanks."

He moved the chair forward and waited. She sat on the edge of it, unwillingly.

"I expect you've heard why I'm here," Alleyn said gently. "Or have you?"

She nodded, still not looking at him.

"I want you to help me, if you will."

"I can't help you," she said. "I don't know the first thing about it. None of us do. Not me, or Mr. Johns or my boy." Her voice shook. She added rapidly with an air of desperation: "You leave my boy alone, Mr. Alleyn."

"Well," said Alleyn, "I've got to talk to people, you know. That's my job."

"It's no use talking to Cliff. I tell you straight, it's no use. It's something cruel what those others done to Cliff.

Pestering him, day after day, and him proved to be innocent. They proved it themselves with what they found out and even then they couldn't let him alone. He's not like other lads. Not tough. Different."

"Yes," Alleyn agreed, "He's an exceptional chap, isn't he?"

"They broke his spirit," she said, frowning, refusing to look at him. "He's a different boy. I'm his mother and I know what they done. It's wicked. Getting on to a bit of a kid when it was proved he was innocent."

"The piano?" Alleyn said.

"Mrs. Duck saw him. Mrs. Duck who cooks for them down there. She was out for a stroll, not having gone to the dance, and she saw him sit down and commence to play. They all heard him and they said they heard him, and me and his Dad heard him too. On and on, and him dead-beat, till I couldn't stand it any longer and come over myself and fetched him home. What more do they want?"

"Mrs. Johns," Alleyn began, "what sort—" He stopped short, feeling that he could not repeat once more the too-familiar phrase. "Did you like Mrs. Rubrick?" he said.

For the first time she looked sharply at him. "Like her?" she said unwillingly. "Yes, I suppose I did. She was kind. Always the same to everyone. She made mistakes as I well know. Things didn't pan out the way she reckoned."

"With Cliff?"

"That's right. There's been a lot of rubbish talked about the interest she took in my boy. People are funny like that. Jealous." She passed her roughened hand over her face with a movement that suggested the wiping away of a cobweb. "I don't say I wasn't a bit jealous myself," she said grudgingly. "I don't say I didn't think it might make him discontented like with his own home. But I saw what a big thing it was for my boy and I wouldn't stand in his light. But there it is. I won't say I didn't feel it."

She said all this with the same air of antagonism, but Alleyn felt a sudden respect for her. He said: "But this feeling didn't persist?"

"Persist? Not when he grew older. He grew away from her, if you can understand. Nobody knows a boy like his mother and I know you can't drive Cliff. She tried to drive him and in the finish she set him against her. He's a good boy," said Mrs. Johns coldly, "though I say it, but he's very unusual. And sensitive."

"Did you regret taking her offer to send him to school?"

"Regret it?" she repeated, examining the word. "Seeing what's happened, and the cruel way it's changed him—" She pressed her lips together and her hands jerked stiffly in her lap. "I wish she'd never seen my boy," she said with extraordinary vehemence and then caught her breath and looked frightened. "It's none of his doing or of hers, poor lady. They were devoted to each other. When it happened there was nobody felt it more than Cliff. Don't let anyone tell you different. It's wicked, the way an innocent boy's been made to suffer. Wicked."

Her eyes were still fixed on the wall, beyond Alleyn and above his head. They were met, but so wooden was her face that her tears seemed to be accidental and quite inexpressive of sorrow. She ended each of her speeches with such an air of finality that he felt surprised when she embarked on a new one.

"Mrs. Johns," he said, "what do you make of this story about the whisky?"

"Anybody who says my boy's a thief is a liar," she said. "That's what I make of it. Lies! He never touched a drop in his life."

"Then what do you think he was doing?"

At last she looked full at him. "You ask the station cook what he was doing. Ask Albert Black. Cliff won't tell you anything, and he won't tell me. It's my idea and he'd never forgive me if he knew I'd spoken of it." She got up and walked to the door, staring out into the sunshine. "Ask them," she said. "That's all."

"Thank you," said Alleyn looking thoughtfully at her. "I believe I shall."

iii

Alleyn's first view of the station cook was dramatic and incredible. It took place that evening, the second of his stay at Mount Moon. After their early dinner, a silent meal at which the members of the household seemed to be suffering from a carry-over from last night's confidences, Fabian suggested that he and Alleyn should walk up to the men's quarters. They did so but, before they left, Alleyn asked Ursula to lend him the diamond clip that Florence Rubrick had lost on the night she was murdered. He and Fabian walked down the lavender path as the evening light faded and the mountains began their nightly pageant of violet and gold. The lavender stalks were grey sticks, now, and the zinnias behind them isolated mummies crowned with friable heads. "Were they much the same then," Alleyn asked, "as far as visibility goes?"

"The lavender was green and bushy," Fabian replied, "but the thing was under one of the zinnias and had no better cover than there would be now. They don't flourish up here and were spindly-looking apologies even when they did their stuff."

Alleyn dropped the clip, first in one place and then in another. It glittered like a monstrously artificial flower on the dry earth. "Oh, well," he said, "let's go and see Cookie."

They passed through the gate that Florence had used that night and, like her, turned up the main track that led to the men's quarters.

Long before they came within sight of their objective, they heard a high-pitched, raucous voice raised in the unmistakable periods of oratory. They passed the wool-shed and came within full view of the bunk-house and annex.

A group of a dozen men, some squatting on their heels, others leaning, relaxed, against the wall of the building, listened in silence to an empurpled man, dressed in dirty white, who stood on an overturned box and loudly exhorted them.

"I howled unto the Lord," the orator bawled angrily.

"That's what I done. I howled unto the Lord."

"That's Cookie," Fabian murmured, "in the penultimate stage of his cups. The third and last stage is delirium tremens. It's a regular progression."

"...and the Lord said unto me: 'What's biting you, Perce?' And I answered and said: 'Me sins lie bitter in me belly,' I says. 'I've backslid,' I says, 'and the grade's too hot for me.' And the Lord said: 'Give it another pop, Perce.' And I give it another pop and the Lord backed me up and I'm saved."

Here the cook paused and, with extreme difficulty, executed a peculiar gesture, as if writing on the air. "The judgement's writ clear on the wall," he shouted, "for them as aren't too shickered to read it. It's writ clear as it might be on that bloody bunk-'ouse be'ind yer. And what does it say? It says in letters of flame: 'Give it another pop.' Hallelujah."

"Hallelujah," echoed a small man who sat in an attitude of profound dejection on the annex step. This was Albie Black, the roustabout.

"A couple more brands to be snatched from the burning," the cook continued, catching sight of Alleyn and Fabian, and gesturing wildly towards them. "A couple more sheep to be cut out from the mob and baled up in the pens of salvation. A couple more dirty two-tooths for the Lord to shear. Shall we gather at the river?" He and the roustabout broke into a hymn, the melody of which was taken up by an accordion player inside the bunk-house. Fabian indicated to the men that he and Alleyn would like to be left alone with the cook and Albie Black. Ben Wilson, who was quietly smoking his pipe and looking at the cook with an air of detached disapproval, jerked his head at him and said: "He's fixed all right." He led the way into the bunk-house, the accordion stopped abruptly, and Alleyn was left face to face with the cook, who was still singing, but half-heartedly and in a melancholy key.

"Pretty hopeless, isn't it?" Alleyn muttered, eyeing him dubiously.

"It's now or never," Fabian rejoined. "He'll be dead to the world to-morrow and we're supposed to ship him down-country the next day. Unless, of course, you exercise your authority and keep him here. Perce!" he said loudly, placing himself in front of the cook. "Come down off that. Here's somebody wants to speak to you."

The cook stepped incontinently off his box into midair and was caught like an unwieldy ballerina by Alleyn. "Open up your bowels of compassion," he said mildly and allowed them to seat him on the box.

"Shall I leave you?" asked Fabian.

"You stay where you are," said Alleyn. "I want a witness."

The cook was a large man with pale eyes, an unctuous mouth and bad teeth. "Bare your bosom," he invited Alleyn. "Though it's as black as pitch it shall be as white as snow. What's your trouble?"

"Whisky," said Alleyn.

The cook laid hold of his coat lapels and peered very earnestly into his face. "You're a pal," he said. "I don't mind if I do."

"But I haven't got any," Alleyn said. "Have you?"

The cook shook his head mournfully and, having begun to shake it, seemed unable to leave off. His eyes filled with tears. His breath smelt of beer and of something that at the moment Alleyn was unable to place.

"It's not so easily come by these days, is it?" Alleyn said.

"I ain't seen a drop," the cook whispered, "not since—" he wiped his mouth and gave Alleyn a look of extraordinary cunning—"not since you-know-when."

"When was that?"

"Ah," said the cook profoundly, "that's telling." He looked out of the corners of his eyes at Fabian, leered, and, with a ridiculously Victorian gesture, laid his finger alongside his nose. Albie Black burst into loud meaningless laughter. "Oh, dear!" he said and buried his head in his arms. Fabian moved behind the cook and pointed suggestively in the direction of the house.

"Haven't they got some of the right stuff down there?" Alleyn suggested.

"Ah," said the cook.

"How about it?"

The cook began to shake his head again.

Alleyn took a deep breath and fired point-blank. "How about young Cliff?" he suggested. "Any good?"

"Him!" said the cook and, with startling precision, uttered a stream of obscenities.

"What's the matter with Cliff?" Alleyn asked.

"Ask him," the cook said and looked indignantly at Albie Black. "They're cobbers, them two ——s."

"You shut your face," said Albie Black, suddenly furious. He broke into a storm of abuse to which the cook listened sadly. "You shut your face, or I'll knock your bloody block off. Didn't I tell you to forget it? Haven't you got any sense?" He pointed a shaking finger at Alleyn. "Don't you pick what he is? D'you want to land us both in the cooler?"

The cook sighed heavily. "I thought you said you'd got the fine work in with young Cliff," he said. "You know. What you seen that night. I thought you'd fixed him. You know."

"You come away," said Albie in great alarm, "I'm not as sozzled as what you are and I'm telling you. You come away."

"Wait a minute," said Alleyn, but the cook had taken fright. "Change and decay in all around I see," he said, and, rising with some difficulty, flung one arm about the neck of his friend. "See the hosts of Midian," he shouted, waving the other arm at Alleyn. "How they prowl around. It's a lousy life. Let's have a little wee drink, Albie."

"No, you don't!" Alleyn began, but the cook turned until his face was pressed into the bosom of his friend and, by slow degrees, slid to the ground.

"Now see what you done," said Albie Black.

CHAPTER IX

ATTACK

The cook being insensible and, according to Fabian, certain to remain so for many hours, Alleyn suffered him to be removed and concentrated on Albert Black.

There had been a certain speciousness about the cook but Albert, he decided, was an abominable specimen. He disseminated meanness and low cunning. He was drunk enough to be truculent and sober enough to look after himself. The only method, Alleyn decided, was that of intimidation. He and Fabian withdrew with Albert into the annex.

"Have you ever been mixed up in a murder charge before?" Alleyn began with the nearest approach to police-station truculence of which he was capable.

"I'm not mixed up in one now," said Albert, showing the whites of his eyes. "Choose your words."

"You're withholding information in a homicidal investigation, aren't you? D'you know what that means?"

"Here!" said Albert. "You can't swing that across me."

"You'll be lucky if you don't get a pair of bracelets swung across you. Haven't you been in trouble before?" Albert looked at him indignantly. "Come on, now," Alleyn persisted. "How about a charge of theft?"

"Me?" said Albert. "Me, with a clean sheet all the years I bin 'ere! Accusing me of stealing! 'Ow dare yer?"

"What about Mr. Rubrick's whisky? Come on, Black, you'd better make a clean breast of it."

Albert looked at the piano. His dirty fingers pulled at his underlip. He moved closer to Alleyn and peered into his face. "It's methylated spirits they stink of," Alleyn thought.

"Got a fag on yer?" Albert said ingratiatingly and grasped him by the coat.

Alleyn freed himself, took out his case and offered it, open, to Albert.

"You're a pal," said Albert and took the case. He helped himself fumblingly to six cigarettes and put them in his pocket. He looked closely at the case. "Posh," he said. "Not gold though, d'you reckon, Mr. Losse?"

Fabian took it away from him.

"Well," Alleyn said. "How about this whisky?"

Albert jerked his head at the piano. "So he got chatty after all, did he?" he said. "The little bastard. O.K. That lets me out." He again grasped Alleyn by the coat with one hand and with the other pointed behind him at the piano. "What a Pal," he said. "Comes the holy Jo over a drop of Johnny Walker and the next night he's fixing the big job."

"What the hell are you talking about!" Fabian said violently.

"Can—you—tell—me," Albert said, swaying and clinging to Alleyn, "how a little bastard like that can be playing the ruddy piano and at the same time run into me round the corner of the wool-shed? There's a mystery for you if you like."

Fabian took a step forward. "Be quiet, Losse," said Alleyn.

"It's a very funny thing," Albert continued, "how a nindividual can be in two places at oncet. And he knew he oughtn't to be there, the ruddy little twister. Because all the time I sees him by the wool-shed he keeps on thumping that blasted pianna. Now then!"

"Very strange," said Alleyn.

"Isn't it? I knew you'd say that."

"Why haven't you talked about this before?"

Albert freed himself, spat, and wiped his mouth with the back of his hand. "Bargain's a bargain, isn't it? Fair dos. Wait till I get me hands on the little twister. Put me away, has he? Good-oh! And what does he get? Anywhere else he'd swing for it."

"Did you hear Mrs. Rubrick speaking in the wool-shed?"

"How could she speak when he'd fixed her? That was earlier: 'Ladies and Gentlemen.' Gawd, what a go!"

"Where was he?"

"Alleyn, for God's sake—" Fabian began and Alleyn turned to him. "If you can't be quiet, Losse, you'll have to clear out. Now Black, where was Cliff?"

"Aren't I telling you? Coming out of the shed."

Alleyn looked through the annex window. He saw a rough track running downhill, past the yards, past a side road to the wool-shed, down to a narrow water race above the gate that Florence Rubrick came through when she left the lavender path and struck uphill to the wool-shed.

"Was it then that you asked him to say nothing about the previous night when he caught you stealing the whisky?" Alleyn held his breath. It was a long shot and almost in the dark.

"Not then," said Albert.

"Did you speak to him?"

"Not then."

"Had you already spoken about the whisky?"

"I'm not saying anything about that. I'm telling you what he done."

"And I'm telling you what you did. That was the bargain, wasn't it? He found you making away with the bottles. He ordered you off and was caught trying to put them back. He didn't give you away. Later, when the murder came out and the police investigation started, you struck your bargain. If Cliff said nothing about the whisky, you'd say nothing about seeing him come out of the shed?"

Albert was considerably sobered. He looked furtively from Alleyn to Fabian. "I got to protect myself," he said. "Asking a bloke to put himself away."

"Very good. You'd rather I tell him you've blown the gaff and get the whole story from him. The police will be interested to know you've withheld important information."

"All right, all right," said Albert shrilly. "Have it your own way, you blasted cow," and burst into tears.

ii

Fabian and Alleyn groped their way down the hill in silence. They turned off to the wool-shed where Alleyn paused and looked at the sacking-covered door. Fabian watched him miserably.

"It must have been in about this light," Alleyn said. "Just after dark."

"You can't do it!" Fabian said. "You can't believe a drunken sneak thief's story. I know young Cliff. He's a good chap. You've talked to him. You can't believe it."

"A year ago," Alleyn said, "he was an over-emotionalized, slightly hysterical and extremely unhappy adolescent."

"I don't give a damn! Oh God!" Fabian muttered. "Why the hell did I start this?"

"I did warn you," Alleyn said with something like compassion in his voice.

"It's impossible, I swear—I formally swear to you that the piano never stopped for more than a few seconds. You know what it's like on a still night. The cessation of a noise like that hits your ears. Albie was probably half tight. Good Lord, he said himself that the piano went on all the time. Of course it wasn't Cliff that he saw. I'm amazed that you pay the smallest attention to his meanderings." Fabian paused. "If he saw anyone," he added, and his voice changed, "I admit that it was probably the murderer. It wasn't Cliff. You yourself pointed out that it was almost dark."

"Then why did Cliff refuse to talk about the whisky?"

"Schoolboy honour. He'd struck up a friendship with the wretched creature."

"Yes," said Alleyn. "That's tenable."

"Then why don't you accept it?"

"My dear chap, I'll accept it if it fits. See here. I want you to do two things for me. The first is easy. When you go indoors, help me to get a toll call through in privacy. Will you?"

"Of course."

"The second is troublesome. You know the pens inside the shearing shed? With the slatted floor where the unshorn sheep are huddled together?"

"Well?"

"You've finished crutching to-day, haven't you?"

"Yes."

"I'm afraid I want to take that slatted floor up."

Fabian stared at him. "Why on earth?"

"There may be something underneath."

"There are the sheep droppings of thirty years underneath."

"So I feared. Those of the last year are all that concern me. I'll want a sieve and a spade and if you can lay your hands on a pair of rejected overalls, I'd be grateful."

Fabian looked at Alleyn's hands. "And gloves if it could be managed," Alleyn said. "I'm very sorry about taking up the floor. The police department will pay the damage, of course. It may only be one section—the one nearest the press. I think you might warn the others when we go in."

"May I ask what you hope to find?"

"A light that failed," said Alleyn.

"Am I supposed to understand that?"

"I don't see why you shouldn't." They had reached the gate into the lavender walk. Alleyn turned and looked back at the track. He could see the open door into the annex where they had left Albie Black weeping off the combined effects of confession, betrayal and the hangover from wood alcohol.

"Was it methylated spirit they'd been drinking?" he asked. "He and the cook?"

"I wouldn't put it past them. Or Hokanui."

"What's that?"

"The local equivalent of potheen."

"Why do you keep him?"

"He doesn't break out very often. We can't pick our men in war-time."

"I'd love to lock him up," Alleyn said. "He stinks. He's a toad."

"Then why do you listen to him?"

"Do you suppose policemen only take statements from

people they fall in love with? Come in. I want to get that call through before the Bureau shuts."

They found the members of the household assembled in the pleasant colonial-Victorian drawing-room, overlooking the lawn on the wool-shed side of the house.

"We rather felt we couldn't face the study again," Ursula said. "After last night, you know. We felt it could do with an airing. And I'm going to bed at eight. If Mr. Alleyn lets me, of course. Does everyone realize we got exactly five and a half hours of sleep last night?"

"I should certainly prefer that Flossie's portrait did not preside over another session," Fabian agreed. "If there was to be another session, of course. Having never looked at it for three years I've suddenly become exquisitely self-conscious in its presence. I suppose, Ursy darling, you wouldn't care to have it in your room?"

"If that's meant to be a joke, Fabian," said Ursula, "I'm not joining in it."

"You're very touchy. Mr. Alleyn is going to dash off a monograph on one of the less delicious aspects of the merino sheep, Douglas. We are to take up the floor of the wool-shed pens."

Alleyn, standing in the doorway, watched the group round the fire. Mrs. Aceworthy wore her almost habitual expression of half-affronted gentility. Terence Lynne, flashing the needles in her scarlet knitting, stared at him, and drew her thin brows together. Ursula Harme, arrested in the duelling mood she kept for Fabian, paused, her lips parted. Douglas dropped his newspaper and began his usual indignant expostulation: "What in heaven's name are you talking about, Fab? Good Lord—!"

"Yes, Douglas my dear," said Fabian, "we know how agitating you find your present condition of perpetual astonishment, but there it is. Up with the slats and down goes poor Mr. Alleyn."

Douglas retired angrily behind his newspaper. "The whole thing's a farce," he muttered obscurely. "I always said so." He crackled his paper. "Who's going to do it?"

"If you'll trust me," said Alleyn, "I will."

"I don't envy you your job, sir."

"The policeman's lot," Alleyn said lightly.

"I'll tell the men to do it," Douglas grunted ungraciously from behind his paper. He peeped round the corner of it at Alleyn. The solitary, rather prominent eye he displayed was reminiscent of Florence Rubrick's in her portrait. "I'll give you a hand, if you like," he added.

"That's the spirit that forged the empire," said Fabian. "Good old Douggie."

"If you'll excuse me," Alleyn said and moved into the hall. Fabian joined him there.

"The telephone's switched through to the study," he said. "I promise not to eavesdrop." He paused reflectively. "Eavesdrop!" he muttered. "What a curious word! To drop from eaves. Reminds one of the swallows and, by a not too extravagant flight of fancy, of your job for the morrow. Give one long ring and the exchange at the Pass may feel moved to answer you."

When Alleyn lifted the receiver it was to cut in on a cross-plateau conversation. A voice angrily admonished him: "Working!" He hung up and waited. He could hear Fabian whistling in the hall. The telephone gave a brief tinkle and he tried again, this time with success. The operator at the Pass came through. Alleyn asked for a police station two hundred miles away, where he hoped Sub-Inspector Jackson might possibly be on duty. "I'll call you," said the operator coldly. "This is a police call," said Alleyn, "I'll hold the line." "Aren't you Mount Moon?" said the operator sharply. "Yes, and it's still a police call, if you'll believe me." "Not in trouble up there, are you, Mr. Losse?" "I'm as happy as a lark," said Alleyn, "but in a bit of a hurry." "Hold the line," giggled the operator. A vast buzzing set up in his ear, threaded with ghost voices. "That'll be good-oh, then, Bob." "Eh?" "I said, that'll be jake." The operator's voice cut in omnipotently. "There you are, Mr. Losse. They're waiting."

Sub-Inspector Jackson was not there but P.C. Wetherbridge, who had been detailed to the case in town, answered the telephone and was helpful. "The radio programs for the last week in January, '42, Mr. Alleyn? I think we can do that for you."

"For the evening of Thursday the 29th," Alleyn said,

"between eight and nine o'clock. Only stations with good reception in this district."

"It may take us a wee while, Mr. Alleyn."

"Of course. Would you tell the exchange at the Pass to keep itself open and call me back?"

"That'll be O.K., sir."

"And Wetherbridge. I want you to get hold of Mr. Jackson. Tell him it's a very long chance, but I may want to bring someone in to the station. I'd very much like a word with him. I think it would be advisable for him to come up here. He asked me to let him know if there were developments. There are. If you can find him, he might come in on the line when you call me back."

"He's at home, sir. I'll ring him. I don't think I'll have much trouble over the other call."

The voice faded, and Alleyn caught only the end of the sentence... "a cobber of mine... all the back numbers... quick as I can make it."

"Three minutes, Mr. Losse," said the operator. "Will I extend the call?"

"Yes—no! All right, Wetherbridge. Splendid. I'll wait."

"Working?" demanded a new voice.

"Like a black," said Alley crossly, and hung up.

He found Fabian sitting on the bottom step of the stairs, a cigarette in his mouth. He hummed a dreary little air to himself.

"Get through?" he asked.

"They're going to call me back."

"If you're very very lucky. It'll be some considerable time, at the best, if I know Toll. I'm going up to the workroom. Would you care to join me? You can hear the telephone from there."

"Right." Alleyn felt in his breast pocket. "Damn!" he said.

"What's up?"

"My cigarette case."

"Did you leave it in the drawing-room?"

"I don't think so." He returned to the drawing-room. Its four occupants, who seemed to be about to go to bed, broke off what appeared to be a lively discussion and watched him. The case was not there. Douglas hunted about politely, and

Mrs. Aceworthy clucked. While they were at this employment there was a tap on the door and Cliff came in with a rolled periodical in his hand.

"Yes?" said Douglas.

"Dad asked me to bring this in," said Cliff. "It came up with our mail by mistake. He says he's sorry."

"Thank you, Cliff," they murmured. He shuffled his feet and said awkwardly, "Good night, then."

"Good night, Cliff," they said and he went out.

"Oh Lord!" Alleyn said. "I've remembered. I left it in the annex. I'll run up there and fetch it."

He saw Terence Lynne's hands check at their work.

"Shall I dodge up and get it?" Douglas offered.

"Not a bit of it, thanks Grace. I'll do my own tedious job. I'm sorry to have disturbed you. I'll get a coat and run up there."

He returned to the hall. Cliff was in the passage heading to the kitchen. Fabian had gone. Alleyn ran upstairs. A flashlight bobbed in the long passage and came to rest on the workroom door. Fabian's hand reached out to the lock. "Hi," Alleyn called down the passage, "you had it." The light shone in his eyes."

"What?"

"My cigarette case. You took it away from the unspeakable Albert."

"Oh, help! I put it on the piano. It'll be all right."

"I think I'll get it. It's rather special. Troy—my wife—gave it to me."

"I'll get it," Fabian said.

"No, you're going to work. It won't take me a moment."

He got his overcoat from his room. When he came out he found Fabian hovering uncertainly on the landing. "Look here," he said, "you'd better let me—I mean—"

The telephone in the study gave two long rings. "There's your call," Fabian said. "Away with you. Lend me your coat, will you, it's perishing cold."

Alleyn threw his coat to him and ran downstairs. As he shut the study door he heard the rest of the party come out of the drawing-room. A moment later the front door banged.

The telephone repeated its double ring.

"There you are, Mr. Losse," said the operator. "We've kept open for you. They're waiting."

It was P.C. Wetherbridge. "Message from the Sub-Inspector, sir. He's left by car and ought to make it in four hours."

"Gemini!"

"I beg your pardon, Mr. Alleyn."

"Great work, Wetherbridge. Hope I haven't cried Wolf."

"I don't get you too clear, sir. We've done that little job for you. I've got it noted down here. There are three likely stations."

"Good for you," said Alleyn warmly.

"Do you want to write the programs out, Mr. Alleyn?"

"No, no. Just read them to me."

Wetherbridge cleared his throat and began: "Starting at seven-thirty, sir, and continuing till nine." His voice droned on through a list of items. "...Syd Bando and the Rhythm Kids...I Got a Big Pink Momma...Garden Notes and Queries...Racing Commentary...News Summary...Half an Hour with the Jitterbugs...Anything there, Mr. Alleyn?"

"Nothing like it so far, but carry on. We're looking for something a bit high-brow, Wetherbridge."

"Old Melodies Made New?"

"Not quite. Carry on."

"There's only one other station that's likely to come through clearly, up where you are."

Alleyn thought: "I hope to God we've drawn a blank."

"Here we go, sir. Seven-thirty, Twenty-first instalment of 'The Vampire.' Seven forty-five, Reading from Old Favourites. Eight-five, An Hour with the Masters."

Alleyn's hand tightened on the receiver. "Yes?" he said. "Any details?"

"There's a lot of stuff in small print. Wait a jiffy, sir, if you don't mind. I'm putting on my glasses." Alleyn waited. "Here we are," said Wetherbridge, and two hundred miles away a paper crackled. "Eight twenty-five," said Wetherbridge, "'Polonaise' by Chopping but there's a lot more. Back," said Wetherbridge uncertainly, "or would it be Bark? The initials are J. S. It's a pianna solo."

"Go on please."

"'The Art of Fewje,'" said Wetherbridge. "I'd better spell that, Mr. Alleyn. F for Freddy, U for Uncle, G for George, U for Uncle, E for Edward? Any good?"

"Yes."

"It seems to have knocked off at eight fifty-seven."

"Yes."

"Last on the list," said Wetherbridge. "Will that be the article we're looking for, sir?"

"I'm afraid so," said Alleyn.

iii

After they'd rung off he sat on for a minute or two, whistling dolefully. His hand went automatically to the pocket where he kept his cigarette case. It was quite ten minutes since Fabian went out. Perhaps he was waiting in the hall.

But the hall was empty and very still. An oil lamp, turned low, burnt on the table. Alleyn saw that only two candles remained from the nightly muster of six. The drawing-room party had evidently gone to bed. Fabian must be upstairs. Using his torch, Alleyn went quietly up to the landing. Light showed under the doors of the girls' rooms, and farther down the passage, under Douglas'. There was none under Fabian's door. Alleyn moved softly down the passage to the workroom. No light in there. He waited, listening, and then moved back towards the landing. A board creaked under his feet.

"Hullo!" called Douglas. "That you, Fab?"

"It's me," said Alleyn quietly.

Douglas' door opened and he looked out. "Well, I wondered who it was," he said, eyeing Alleyn dubiously. "I mean it seemed funny."

"Another night prowler? Up to no good?"

"Well, I must say you sounded a bit stealthy. Anything

you want, sir?"

"No," said Alleyn. "Just sleuthing. Go to bed."

Douglas grinned and withdrew his head. "Enjoy yourself," Alleyn heard him say cheekily, and the door was shut.

Perhaps Fabian had left the cigarette case in his room and was already asleep. Odd, though, that he didn't wait.

There was no cigarette case in his room. "Blast!" Alleyn muttered. "He can't find it! The miserable Albert's pinched it. Blast!"

He crept downstairs again. A faint glimmer of light showed at the end of the hall. A door into the kitchen passage was open. He went through it, and met Markins in the silver pantry, candle in hand.

"Just locking up, sir," said Markins. "Were you wanting me?"

"I'm looking for Mr. Losse."

"Wasn't he up by the men's quarters with you, Mr. Alleyn? About ten minutes ago."

"He was probably there, but I wasn't."

"That's funny," Markins said, staring at him. "I'd 'ave sworn it was you."

"He was wearing my coat."

"Is that the case? Who was the other gentleman, then?"

"Not me. What other gentleman?"

Markins set his candle down and shut the door. "I was going up to the manager's cottage," he said. "I wanted to have a word with Mr. Johns. Cliff had just gone back there. The cottage is up the hill at the back of the annex, you know. When I came out of the back door here, I thought I saw you on the main track to the men's quarters, going towards the annex. I thought I'd cut across and see you, and I started up the path from the back door. You lose sight of the other track for a bit. I heard you call out something and I sung out 'Hullo, sir?' Then I heard you run downhill. When I came up to where you can see the track, you weren't in sight."

Alleyn took the tip of his nose between thumb and forefinger. "Not me," he said. "Mr. Losse."

"It sounded like you, sir. I thought you must have been talking to someone else."

"And apparently, on the telephone, I sounded like Mr.

Losse. Damn it then," Alleyn said irritably, "where is he? If he ran downhill why didn't he come in? And who was he singing out to? Young Cliff?"

"No, sir. Cliff was home by then. When I got up to the cottage I asked him if he'd seen you and he said he hadn't seen anybody. What was Mr. Losse doing, sir?"

Alleyn told him. "Come on," he said. "I don't like this. Let's hunt him out."

"There's half a dozen things he might be doing, Mr. Alleyn."

"What sort of things? We'll go through your kitchen, Markins. Lead the way. I've got a torch."

"Well," said Markins, moving off, "letting water out of the truck radiator. It's going to be a hard frost."

"Would he run downhill to do that?"

"Well, no. The garage is up by the sheds."

"What was it he called out?" asked Alleyn, following Markins into a dark warm kitchen that smelt of pine wood and fat.

"I couldn't say, really. He just shouted. He sounded surprised. Just a moment if you please, Mr. Alleyn. I've bolted the door. Ever since that young Cliff played up with the whisky, I've shut up careful."

"Cliff didn't play up. It was the unspeakable Albie."

"I caught him with the bottle in his hand!"

"He was putting it back."

"He never was!" Markins cried out with almost lady-like incredulity.

"Albie's admitted it. The boy was saving his disgusting face for him."

"Then why the hell couldn't he say so?" Markins demanded in a high voice. "I'd better stick to valeting and cut out the special stuff," he added disgustedly. "I can't pick petty larceny when it's under my nose. Come on, sir."

It was pitch-dark outside and bitingly cold. Markins, using Alleyn's torch, led the way up a steep path. Grass was crisp under their feet and frost scented the air. Ice seemed to move against their faces as they climbed. The sky was clear and full of winking stars.

"Where are we going, Mr. Alleyn?"

"To the annex."

"This path comes out above the buildings, but we can cut across to the track. It's not too rough, but it's steepish."

Clods of earth broke icily under Alleyn's shoes. He and Markins skated and slithered. "Kick your heels in," Markins said. A sense of urgency, illogically insistent, plagued Alleyn. "Where's this cursed track?" he grunted.

They mounted a rise and a dim rectangular blackness showed against a hillside that must be white with frost. "Here we are," Markins said. "There's a wire fence, sir. No barbs." The wire clanged as they climbed through. The flashlight played on frozen cart tracks.

"There's no light in the annex," Alleyn said.

"Shall we call out, sir?"

"No. If he was about he'd have heard us. We don't want the men roused up. Is this where the branch track goes down to the shearing shed? Yes, there it goes. Downhill. *Wait a moment.*"

Markins turned quickly, flashing his light on Alleyn, who stood facing towards the shearing shed. "Give me the torch, Markins, will you?"

He reached out his hand, took the torch, and flashed it down the branch track. Points of frost glittered like tinsel. The circle of light moved on and came to rest on a sprawling mound.

"My God!" Markins said loudly. "What's he bin and done to 'imself?"

"Keep off the track." Alleyn stepped on the frozen turf beside it and moved quickly down towards the wool-shed. The torchlight now showed him the grey shepherd's plaid of his own overcoat with Fabian's legs, spread-eagled, sticking out from under the skirts, Fabian's head, rumpled and pressed face downwards in a frozen rut, and his arms stetched out beyond it as if they had been raised to shield it as he fell.

Alleyn knelt beside him, giving the torch to Markins.

Fabian's hair grew thick over the base of his head, which, like the nape of his thin and delicately grooved neck, looked boyish and vulnerable. Alleyn parted the hair delicately.

Behind him, holding the torch very steadily, Markins whispered a thin stream of blasphemy.

"A downward blow," said Alleyn. He thrust one hand swiftly under the hidden face, raised the head, and with the other hand, like a macabre conjurer, pulled out of Fabian's mouth a gaily coloured silk handkerchief.

iv

"He's not—?"

"No, no, of course not." Alleyn's hands were busy. "But we must get him out of this damnable cold. It's not more than twelve yards to the wool-shed. There are no other injuries I fancy. Think we can do it? We mustn't go falling about with him."

"O.K., O.K."

"Steady then. I'll get that sacking door opened first."

When they lifted him, Fabian's breathing was thick and stertorous. Little jets of vapour came from his mouth. When they reached the open door and Alleyn lifted his shoulders to the level of the raised floor, he groaned deeply.

"Gently, gently," Alleyn said. "That's the way, Markins. Good. I've got his head. Slide him in. The floor's like glass. Now, drop the door and I'll get some of those bales."

The light darted about the wool-shed, on the press, the packed bales, and the heap of empty ones. They bedded Fabian down in strong-smelling sacking.

"Now the hurricane lamp and that candle. I've a notion," said Alleyn grimly as he hunted for them, "that they'll be in order this time. Wrap his feet up, won't you?"

"This place is as cold as a morgue," Markins complained. "Not meaning anything unpleasant by the comparison."

The lantern and home-made candlestick were in their places on the wall. Alleyn took them down, lit them, and brought them over to Fabian. Markins built a stack of bales over him and slid a folded sack under his head.

"He's not losing blood," he said. "What about his

breathing, Mr. Alleyn?"

"All right, I think. The handkerchief, my handkerchief it is, was only a preliminary measure, I imagine. You saved his life, Markins."

"I did?"

"I hope so. If you hadn't called out—perhaps not, though. Perhaps when this expert fetched the bag in here and had a look at— It all depends on whether Losse recognized his assailant."

"By God, I hope he did, Mr. Alleyn."

"And, by God, I'm afraid he didn't."

Alleyn pushed his hand under the bales and groped for Fabian's wrist. "His pulse seems not too bad," he said presently, and a moment later, "He'd been to the annex."

"How do you get that, sir?"

Alleyn drew out his hand and held up a flat cigarette case. "Mine. He went up there to fetch it. It was in the pocket."

"What's our next move?"

Alleyn stared at Fabian's face. The eyes were not quite closed. Fabian knitted his brows. His lips moved as if to articulate, but no sound came from them. "Yes," Alleyn muttered, "what's best to do?"

"Fetch the Captain?"

"If I was sure he'd be all right, we'd fetch nobody. But we can't be sure of that. We can't risk it. No, don't rouse them yet, down at the house. Go first of all to the men's hut and check their numbers. What they are doing and how long they've been at it. Be quick about this. They'll probably be in bed. Then go on up to the cottage and tell them there's been an accident. No more than that. Ask them for hot-water bottles and blankets, and something that will do as a stretcher. Ask Mr. Johns—and Cliff—to come here. Then use their telephone and try to get through somehow to Mr. Losse's doctor for instructions."

"The Bureau won't open till the morning, Mr. Alleyn."

"Damn. Then we'll have to use our common sense. Away you go, Markins. And—" Alleyn raised his head and looked at Markins. "Just say an accident. I want Cliff to come with his father and with you. And if he's there when you go in, watch him."

Markins slipped out of the door.

Alleyn waited in a silence that seemed to be compounded of extreme cold and of the smells of the wool-shed. He sat on his heels and watched Fabian, whose head, emerging like a kernel from its husk of sacking, lay in a pool of yellow light. Portentously he frowned and moved his lips. Sometimes he would turn his head and then he would make a little prosaic grunting sound. Alleyn took a clean handkerchief from his pocket and slid it under the base of Fabian's skull. The frosty air outside moved and a soughing crept among the rafters. Alleyn turned his torch on the press. It was empty, but near it were ranged bales packed with the day's crutchings. "Was there to be a complete repetition?" he wondered. "Was one of them to be unpacked and was I to take Florence Rubrick's journey down-country to-morrow?" He looked at Fabian. "Or rather you," he added, "if you'd been so inconsiderate as to die?" Fabian turned his head. The swelling under his dark thatch was now visible. Very delicately, Alleyn parted and drew back the strands of hair. He shone his torch light on a thick indented mark behind the swelling. He rose and hunted along the pens. Near the door, in its accustomed niche, was the branding iron, a bar with the Mount Moon brand raised on its base. Alleyn squatted down and looked closely at it. He had a second handkerchief in his pocket and he wrapped it round the shaft of the iron before carrying it over to Fabian.

"I think so," he said, looking from the iron to Fabian's scalp. He shifted the lantern along the floor and, groping under the bales that covered Fabian, pulled out the skirts of his own overcoat, first on one side, then on the other. On the left-hand skirt he found a kind of scar, a longish mark with the rough tweed puckered about it. He took out his pocket lens. The surface of the tweed was burred and stained brown.

"And where the devil," said Alleyn, addressing the branding iron, "am I going to stow you away?"

Still muffling his hand, he carried the iron farther along the shed, spread his handkerchief over it and dropped a sack across the whole. He stood in the dark, looking absently at the pool of light round Fabian's head. It seemed a long way away, an isolated island, without animation, in a sea of dark. Alleyn's gaze turned from it and wandered among the shadows, seeing, not them, but the fork in the track, where it branched off to the wool-shed, the frosty bank that overhung it, the scrubby bush that cast so black a shadow behind it.

"That's funny," someone said loudly.

Alleyn's skin jumped galvanically. He stood motionless, waiting.

"And what the devil are you up to? Running like a scalded cat."

There was a movement inside the island of yellow light. The heap of bales shifted.

"Hurry! Hurry!" An arm was flung up. "All right when I'm up. Sleep," said the voice, dragging on the word. "To die. To sleep. Go on, blast you. Up. Oh, dear. Oh, God," it whispered very drearily. "So *bloody* tired."

Alleyn began to move quietly towards Fabian.

"You would butt in," Fabian chuckled. "You won't be popular." Alleyn stopped. "Funny old thing," said Fabian affectionately. "Must have found the damned object. Hullo," he added a moment later and then, with disgust and astonishment, "Terry! Oh, Lord! I do wish I hadn't got up here. Silly old man."

He sat up. Alleyn moved quickly to him and knelt down. "It's all right," he said, "you can go to sleep now, you know."

"Yes, but why run like that? Something must have happened up there."

"Up where?"

"Well, you heard what she said. You will be unpopular. Where was it?"

"In the lavender walk," Alleyn said. Fabian's eyes were open, staring past Alleyn under scowling brows.

"Who found it?"

"Uncle Arthur."

"Well, you must be pretty fit. I couldn't . . . I'm so hellish tired. I swear I'll drop off into the sea. It's that damned piano. If only he'd shut up. Excelsibloodyor! Up!"

He fought Alleyn off, his eyes on the wall with its cross-beams. "Come on, chaps," he said. "It's easy. I'll give you a lead."

Alleyn tried to quieten him, but he became so frenzied

that, to hold him, Alleyn himself would have been obliged to use violence, and indeed stood in some danger of being knocked out.

"I'm trying to help you, you goat," Alleyn grumbled.

"Think I don't know a Jerry, when I get one," Fabian panted. "Not yet, Fritzy darling. I'm for Home." He lashed out, caught Alleyn on the jaw, flung himself forward and, clawing at the beams on the wall, tried to climb it. Alleyn wrapped his arms round his knees. Without warning, Fabian collapsed. They fell together on the floor, Fabian uppermost.

"Thank God," Alleyn thought, "his head didn't get another rap," and crawled out. Fabian lay still, breathing heavily. Alleyn, himself rather groggy, began to cover him up again.

"Oh, Ursy, you celestial imbecile," Fabian said miserably and after a moment sighed deeply and, turning on his side, fell sound asleep.

"If this is amnesia," Alleyn muttered, nursing his jaw, "yet there's method in it."

He went to the doorway and, pulling aside the sacking, looked out into the cold. His head buzzed. "Damn the fellow," he thought irritably and then: "Not altogether, though. Do they hark back to a former bout? And is it evidence? Up the side of a ship. Up a gate. Up a companion-way. But up *what* in the vegetable garden?" He stared down at the dark bulk of the house. Beyond it, out to the right, a giant Lombardy poplar made a spear-like pattern against the stars. "That can't be far from the marrow patch," Alleyn thought. "He said his pants were dirty. He was under a tree. Oh, Lord, what's the good of a pair of pants that were dirty over a year ago?"

The thrumming in his head cleared. He shivered violently. "I'll catch the thick end of a cold before the night's out," he muttered and the next second had shrunk back into the shadow of the doorway.

The night was so quiet that the voice of the Moon River, boiling out of its gorge beyond a shoulder of the mountain, and sweeping south to a lake out on the plateau, moved like a vague rumour behind the silence and was felt in the ear-drums rather than heard. Alleyn had been aware of it once or twice that night, and he heard it now as he listened for the nearer sound that had caught his attention. Down the main track, it had been, a tiny rustle, a slipping noise, followed by a faint thud. He remembered how he and Markins had skidded and fallen on the icy ground. He waited and heard a faint metallic clang. "That's the fence," he thought, "a moment, and whoever it is will come up the track. Now what?"

At that moment, above the men's quarters, there was a rattle of chains. The Mount Moon dogs, plunging by their kennels, broke into clamorous barking. A man's voice cursed them: "Lie down, Jock! By God, I'll warm your hide!" The chains rattled and, a faint metallic echo, the wire fence down the track twanged again. A light came bobbing round the annex.

"Hell and damnation!" said Alleyn violently. "Am I never to get a clear run!"

CHAPTER X

NIGHT PIECE

Tommy Johns and his son Cliff followed Markins through the sacking door and stood blinking in the lamplight. Tommy nodded morosely at Alleyn. "What's the trouble?" he said.

"There it is."

He moved forward. Cliff said loudly: "It's Fabian."

"Yes," said Alleyn.

"What's happened to him?" He turned to Markins. "Why didn't you say it was Fabian? What's wrong with you?"

"Orders," said Markins and Tommy Johns looked sharply at Alleyn.

"Whose orders?" Cliff demanded. "Has he had another of his queer turns?" His voice rose shrilly. "Is he dead?"

"No," said Alleyn. Cliff strode forward and knelt by Fabian.

"You keep clear of this," said his father.

"I want to know what's happened to him. I want to know if he's been hurt."

"He's been hit over the head," said Alleyn, "with the branding iron."

Cliff cried out incoherently and his father put his hand on his shoulder.

"I don't want you to say so when he's conscious again," Alleyn went on. "Remember that please, it's important. He's had a nasty shock and for the moment he's to be left to put his own interpretation on it. Tell nobody."

"The branding iron," said Tommy Johns. "Is that so?" He

looked across to the corner where the iron was usually kept.
Cliff said quickly: "It wasn't there. It was left over by the
press."

"Where is it now?" Johns demanded.

"Safely stowed," said Alleyn.

"Who done it?"

In reply to this classic, Alleyn merely shook his head.

"I checked up on the men, sir," said Markins. "They're all
in their bunks. Ben Wilson was awake and says nobody's
gone or come in for over an hour. Albie's dead to the world.
Soaked."

"Right. Have you got a stretcher?"

"Yes, sir," said Markins. "It's the one Mrs. R. had for her
first-aid classes."

"Have you been down to the house?" Alleyn asked
sharply.

"No. It was stowed away up above. Come on, Tommy."

They had dumped a pile of grey blankets inside the door.
Markins brought in the stretcher. The three men covered it,
moved Fabian on to it, and laid the remaining blankets over
him. Cliff, working the palms of his hands together, looked
on unhappily.

"What about this damned icy track?" Alleyn muttered.
"You've got nails in your boots, Johns. So's the boy. Markins
and I are smooth-soled."

"It's not so bad on the track, sir," said Markins.

"Did you come up the kitchen path?" Tommy Johns
demanded.

"Ready?" asked Alleyn before Markins could reply.

They took their places at the corners of the stretcher.
Fabian opened his eyes and looked at Cliff.

"Hullo," he said clearly. "The Infant Phenomenon."

"That's me," said Cliff unevenly. "You'll be all right, Mr.
Losse."

"Oh Lord," Fabian whispered, "have I been at it again?"

"You've taken a bit of a toss," said Alleyn. "We'll get you
into bed in a minute."

"My head."

"I know. Nasty crack, you got. Ready?"

"I can walk," Fabian protested. "What's all this nonsense!

I've always walked before."

"You're riding this time, damn your eyes," said Alleyn cheerfully. "Up we go, chaps. Keep on the grass if you can."

"Easier going on the track," Tommy Johns protested.

"Nevertheless, we'll try the grass. On the left. Keep to the left."

And as they crept along, flashing their torches, he thought: "If only I could have been sure he'd be all right for a bit in the wool-shed. A nice set of prints there'll be with this frost and here we go, all over Tom Tiddler's ground tramping out gold and silver."

It was less slippery on the verge than it had been on the steep hillside, and when they reached the main track the going was still easier. The French windows into the drawing-room were unlocked and they took Fabian in that way, letting the stretcher down on the floor while Markins lit the lamps. Fabian was so quiet that Alleyn waited anxiously to see him, wondering he he had fainted. But when the lamplight shone on his face his eyes were open and he was frowning.

"All right?" Alleyn asked gently. Fabian turned his head aside and muttered: "Oh yes. Yes."

"I'll go upstairs and tell Grace what you've been up to. Markins, you might get a kettle to boil. You others wait, will you?"

He ran upstairs to be confronted on the landing by Ursula in her dressing-gown, holding a candle above her head and peering into the well.

"What's happened?" she said.

"A bit of an accident. Your young man's given himself a crack on the head but he's doing nicely."

"Fabian?" Her eyes widened. "Where is he?"

"Now, don't go haring off, there's a good child. He's in the drawing-room and we're putting him to bed. Before you go down to him, put a couple of hot-water bottles in his bed and repeat to yourself some appropriate rune from your first-aid manual. He'll do, I fancy."

They were standing outside Terence Lynne's door and now it opened. She too came out with a candle. She looked very sleek and pale in her ruby silk dressing-gown.

"Fabian's hurt," said Ursula, and darted back into her own room.

Miss Lynne had left her door open. Alleyn could see where a second candle burnt on her bedside table above an open book, a fat notebook it seemed to be, its pages covered in a fine script. She followed the direction of his gaze and, with a swift movement, shut her door. Ursula returned with a hot-water bag and hurried down the passage to Fabian's room.

Miss Lynne examined Alleyn by the light of her own candle.

"You've been fighting," she said.

He touched his jaw. "I ran into something in the shed."

"It's bleeding."

"So it is. Can you give me a bit of cotton wool or something?"

She hesitated. "Wait here a moment," she said and slipped through the door, shutting it behind her.

Alleyn tapped and entered. She was beside her dressing-table but in a flash had moved to the bed and shut the book. "I asked you to wait," she said.

"I'm extremely sorry. Would you lend your hot-water bottle? Take it along to his room, would you? Ah, there's the cotton wool. Thanks so much."

He took it from her and turned to her glass. As he dabbled the wool on his jaw he watched her reflection. Her back was towards him. She stooped over the bed. When she moved aside, the bedclothes had been pulled up and the book was no longer on the table.

"Here's the bottle," she said, holding it out.

"Will you be an angel and take it yourself? I'm just fixing this blasted cut."

"Mr. Alleyn," she said loudly, and he turned to face her. "I'd rather you staunched your wounds in your own room," said Miss Lynne.

"Please forgive me, I was trying to save my collar. Of course."

He went to the door. "Terry!" Ursula called quietly down the passage.

"I'm off," said Alleyn. He crossed the landing to his own

room. "Terry!" Ursula called again. "Yes, coming," said Miss Lynne, and carrying the candle and her hot-water bottle she moved swiftly down the passage, observed by Alleyn through the crack of his own door.

"Every blasted move in the game goes wrong," he thought and darted back to her room.

The book, a stoutly bound squat affair, had been thrust well down between the sheets. It fell open in his hands and he read a single long sentence.

February 1st, 1942. Since I am now assured of her affection towards me I must confess that the constant unrest of this house and (if I am to be honest in these pages, of Florence herself) under which I have for so long been complaisant, is now quite intolerable to me.

Alleyn hesitated for a moment. A card folder slipped from between the pages. He opened it and saw the photograph of a man with veiled eyes, painfully compressed lips, and deep grooves running from his nostrils to beyond the corners of his mouth. The initials "A.R." were written at the bottom in the same fine strokes that characterized the script in the book.

"So that was Arthur Rubrick," Alleyn thought and returned the photograph and the diary to their hiding place.

ii

Before he left Miss Lynne's room, Alleyn took an extremely rapid look at her shoes. All except one pair were perfectly neat and clean. Her gardening brogues, brushed, but unpolished, were dry. He closed the door behind him as the voices of the two girls sounded in the passage. He found them at the head of the stairs in conference with Mrs. Aceworthy, a formidable figure in mottled flannel, which she drew unhappily about her when she saw Alleyn. He persuaded her, with some difficulty, to return to her room.

"I am going to Fabian," said Ursula. "How are we going to carry him upstairs?"

"I think he will be able to walk up," Alleyn said. "Take him gently. I'll get Grace to help put him to bed. Is he awake, do you know?"

"Not Douglas," said Terence Lynne. "He sleeps like a log."

Ursula said: "Has Fabian had another blackout, Mr. Alleyn?"

"I think so. Wait for me before you bring him."

"Damn!" said Ursula. "Now, of course, he'll think he can't marry me. Come on, Terry."

Terence went; not, Alleyn thought, over-willingly.

He knocked on Douglas Grace's door and, receiving no answer, walked in and flashed his torch on a tousled head.

"Grace!"

"Wha-aa?" The clothes were flung back with a convulsive jerk and Douglas stared at him. "What d'you want to make me jump like that for?" he asked angrily and then blinked. "Sorry, sir. I was back at an advanced gun post. What's up now?"

"Losse had had another blackout."

Douglas gazed at Alleyn with his familiar air of affronted incredulity. "He will now," Alleyn thought crossly, "repeat the last word I have uttered whenever I pause to draw breath."

"Blackout," said Douglas faithfully. "Oh, hell! How? When? Where?"

"Up near the annex. Half an hour ago. He went up there to collect my cigarette case."

"I remember that," cried Douglas triumphantly. "Is he still all out? Poor old Fab."

"He's conscious again, but he's had a nasty crack on the head. Come and help me get him upstairs, will you?"

"Get him upstairs?" Douglas repeated, looking very startled. He reached for his dressing-gown. "I say," he said. "This is pretty tough luck, isn't it? I mean, what he said about Ursy and him?"

"Yes."

"Half an hour ago," said Douglas, thrusting his feet into

his slippers. "That must have been just after we came up. I went out to the side lawn to have a look at the weather. He must have been up there then, good Lord."

"Did you hear anything?"

Douglas gaped at him with his mouth open. "I heard the river," he said. "That means there's a southerly hanging round. Sure sign. You wouldn't know."

"No. Did you hear anything else?"

"Hear anything? What sort of thing?"

"Voices or footsteps."

"Voices? Was he talking? Footsteps?"

"Let it pass," said Alleyn. "Come on."

They went down to the drawing-room.

Fabian was lying on the sofa with Ursula on a low stool beside him. Tommy Johns and Cliff stood awkwardly by the French windows looking at their boots. Markins, with precisely the correct shade of deferential concern, was setting out a tea tray with drinks. Terence Lynne stood composedly before the fire, which had been mended, and flickered its light richly in the folds of her crimson gown.

"Here, I say," said Douglas. "This is no good, Fab. Damn bad luck."

"Extremely tiresome," Fabian murmured, looking at Ursula. He was still covered by grey blankets and Ursula had slid her hand beneath them. "Give the stretcher-bearers a drink, Douglas. They must need it."

"You mustn't," said Ursula.

"See section four. Alcohol after cerebral injuries, abstain from."

Markins moved away with decorum. "You must have a drink, Markins," said Fabian weakly. Douglas looked scandalized.

"Thank you very much, sir," said Markins primly.

"You'll have whisky, won't you, Tommy? Cliff?"

"I don't mind," said Tommy Johns. "The boy won't take it, thank you."

"He looks as if he wants it," said Fabian, and indeed Cliff was very white.

"He doesn't take whisky, thank you," said his father, with uncomfortable emphasis.

"I think you ought to get to bed, Fab," fussed Douglas. "Don't you agree, Mr. Alleyn?"

"We'll drink to your recovery when we've finished the job," Alleyn said.

"I'm not going to be carried upstairs and don't you think it."

"Well then, you shall walk and Grace and I will see you up."

"O.K.," said Douglas amiably.

"One's enough," Fabian said peevishly. "I tell you, I'm all right. You give these poor swine a drink, Douglas. Mr. Alleyn started the rescue squad, didn't he? He might like to finish the job."

He sat up and grimaced. He was very white and his hands trembled.

"Please Fab, go slow," said Ursula. "I'll come and see you."

"Come on," Fabian said to Alleyn. He grinned at Ursula. "Thank you, darling," he said. "I'd like you to come but not just yet, please."

When they were outside in the hall, Fabian took Alleyn's arm. "Sorry to appear churlish," he said. "I wanted to talk to you. God, I do feel sick."

Alleyn got him to bed. He was very docile. Remembering Markins' story of the medicine cupboard in the bathroom, Alleyn raided it and found dressings. He clipped away the thick hair. The wound, a depression, swollen at the margin and broken only at the top, was seen to be clearly defined. He cleaned it and was about to put on a dressing when Fabian, who was lying face downwards on his pillow, said: "I didn't get that by falling, did I? Some expert's had a crack at me, hasn't he?"

"What makes you think so?" said Alleyn, pausing with the lint in his fingers.

"After a fashion I can remember. I was on my feet when I got it. Where the main track branches off to the wool-shed. It felt just like the bump I got at Dunkirk only, thank the Lord, it's not on the same spot. I think I called out. You needn't bother to deny it. Somebody cracked me."

"Any more ideas?"

"It was where that bank with a bit of scrub on it overhangs the track. I was coming back from the annex. There's always water or ice lying about on the far side so I walked close in to the bank. Whoever it was must have been lying up there, waiting. But why? Why me?"

Alleyn dropped the lint over the wound and took up a length of strapping. "You were wearing my coat," he said.

"Stay me with flagons!" Fabian whispered. "So I was." And he was silent while Alleyn finished his dressing. He was comfortable enough lying on his side with a thick pad of cotton wool under his head. Alleyn tidied his room and when he turned back to the bed Fabian was already dozing. He slipped out.

Before going downstairs he visited the other bedrooms. There were no damp shoes in any of them. Douglas' and Fabian's working boots were evidently kept downstairs. "But it was something quieter than working boots," Alleyn muttered and returned to the drawing-room.

He found the two Johnses on the point of departure and Markins about to remove the tray. Douglas, lying back in an armchair with his feet in the hearth and a pipe in his mouth, glanced up with evident relief. Terence Lynne had unearthed her inevitable knitting and, erect on the sofa, her feet to the fire, flashed her needles composedly. Ursula, who was speaking to Tommy Johns, went quickly to Alleyn.

"Is he all right? May I go up?"

"He's comfortably asleep. I think it will be best to leave him. You may listen at his door presently."

"We'll be going," said Tommy Johns. "Good night all."

"Just a moment," said Alleyn.

"Hullo!" Douglas looked up quickly. "What's up now?" And before Alleyn could answer, he added sharply: "He is all right, isn't he? I mean, shall I go down-country for a doctor? I could get back inside four hours if I stepped on it. We don't want to take any risks with an injury to the head."

"No," Alleyn agreed, "we don't. If you feel you want to do something of the sort, of course you may, but I fancy he'll do very well. I'm sure his skull is not injured. It seems to have been a glancing blow."

"A blow?" Terence Lynne's voice struck harshly. Her

mouth was open. The muscle of the upper lip was contracted, showing her teeth in the parody of a smile.

"But didn't he fall on his head?" Douglas shouted.

"He fell on his face because he'd been struck on the back of the skull."

"D'you mean someone attacked him?"

"I do."

"Good God," Douglas whispered.

Ursula stood before Alleyn, her hands jammed down in the pockets of her dressing-gown. Her voice shook but she held her chin up and looked squarely at him. "Does that mean somebody wanted to kill Fabian?" she said.

"It was a dangerous assault," Alleyn said.

"But—" She moved quickly to the door. "I'm going to him," she said. "He mustn't be left alone."

"Please stay here, Miss Harme. The house is locked up and I have the key of his door in my pocket. You see," Alleyn said, "we are all in here, so he is quite safe."

It was at this point that Terence Lynne, winding her hands in her scarlet knitting, broke into a fit of screaming hysteria.

iii

Police officers are not unfamiliar with hysterics. Alleyn dealt crisply with Miss Lynne. While Tommy Johns and Douglas turned their backs, Cliff looked sick and Markins interested; Ursula, with considerable aplomb, offered to fetch a jug of cold water and pour it over the patient. This suggestion, combined with Alleyn's less drastic treatment, had its effect. Miss Lynne grew quieter, rose, and walking to the far end of the room seemed to fight down savagely her own incontinence.

"Really, Terry," Ursula said, "you of all people!"

"Shut up, Ursy," said Douglas.

"Well, after all, Douglas darling, he's my young man."

Douglas glared at her and, after a moment's hesitation, went to Terence Lynne and spoke to her in a low voice. Alleyn heard her say: "No! Please leave me alone. I'm all right. Please go away." He returned, looking discomfited and portentous.

"I think Terence should be let off," he said to Alleyn.

"I'm extremely sorry," Alleyn returned, "but I'm afraid that's impossible." He moved to the fire-place and stood with his back to it, collecting their attention. It was an unpleasantly familiar moment and he was struck by the resemblance of all frightened people to each other. There was always a kind of blankness in their faces. They always watched him carefully, yet turned aside their gaze when he looked directly at them. There was always a tendency to draw together, to make a wary little mob of themselves, leaving him isolated.

He was isolated now, a tall figure, authoritative and watchful, unaware of himself, closely attentive to their self-consciousness.

"I'm afraid," he said, "that I can't let anybody off. I should tell you that at the moment it seems unlikely that this attack was made by one of the outside men. Each of you, therefore, will be well advised, in your own interest, to give an account of your movements since I left this room to go up to the annex for my cigarette case."

"I can't believe this is true," said Ursula. "You sound exactly like a detective. For the first time."

"I'm afraid I must behave like one. Will you all sit down? Suppose we start with you, Captain Grace."

"Me? I say, look here, sir..."

"What did you do when I left the room?"

"Yes, well, what did I do? I was sitting here reading the paper when you came in, wasn't I? Yes, well, you went out and I said: 'D'you think I ought to go up with him—' meaning you—'and help him look for his blasted case?' and nobody answered and I said: 'Oh, well, how about a bit of shut-eye?' and I wound up my watch and everybody pushed off. I went out on the side lawn here and had a squint at the sky. I always do that, last thing. Freshens you up. I think I heard you bang the back door." Douglas paused and looked baffled. "At least I suppose it was really Fabian, wasn't it, because you say he went. Well, I mean he must have gone if you found him up there, mustn't he? Someone was moving up the track beyond the side fence. I thought it was probably one of the men. I called out 'Good night' but they didn't answer. Well, I just came in and the others had gone, so I put the screen in front of the fire, got my candle and went upstairs. I tapped on Terry's door and said good-night. I had a bath and went to my room, and then I heard you snooping about the passage and I wondered what was up because I've been a bit jumpy about people in the passage ever since..." Here Douglas paused and glanced at Markins. "However!" he said. "I called out: 'Is that you, Fab?' and you answered, you'll remember, and I went to bed."

"Any witnesses?" asked Alleyn.

"Terence. I told you I tapped on her door."

"Did you hear him?" Alleyn asked Ursula.

"Yes. I heard," she said. "I heard other people come upstairs, too, and move about after I went to bed, but I didn't take any particular notice. I heard the pipes gurgle. I went to sleep almost at once. I was awakened by the sound of voices and boots downstairs, and I sort of knew something was wrong and came out on the landing where I met you."

"Did you all go up together? You and Miss Lynne and Mrs. Aceworthy?"

"No, we straggled. The Ace-pot went first and I know she had a bath because she was in it when I wanted to brush my teeth. I remember hearing the telephone give our ring just before I came out of this room and I was going to answer it when I heard Fabian speaking. At least, I thought it was Fabian. You see I saw—I thought I saw you whisk out of doors."

"You saw my overcoat whisk out."

"Well," said Ursula, "it's very dark in the hall."

She looked fixedly at Alleyn. "You swear he's all right?"

"He was perfectly comfortable and sound asleep when I left him and he's safe from any further assault. You can ring up a doctor when the Bureau opens in the morning, indeed I should like to get a medical opinion myself, or—is there anyone near the Pass on your party line?"

"Four miles," said Douglas.

"If you're anxious, couldn't you get these people to drive over the Pass and ring up a doctor? I don't think it's necessary but isn't it possible?"

"Yes, I suppose it is," said Ursula. "If I could just see him," she added.

"Very well. When I've finished, you may go in with me, wake him up and ask him if he's all right."

"You can be rather a pig," said Ursula, "can't you?"

"This is a serious matter," said Alleyn without emphasis.

She flushed delicately and he thought she was startled and bewildered by his disregard of her small attempt at lightness. "I know it is," she said.

"You heard me answer the telephone, didn't you, and thought I was Losse? You caught sight of him going out and mistook him for me. What did you do then?"

"I called out 'Good night' to Terry, lit my candle and went upstairs. I undressed and when the Ace-pot came out of the bathroom I washed and brushed my teeth and went to bed."

"Seeing nobody?"

"Only her—Mrs. Aceworthy."

"And you, Miss Lynne? You were after Miss Harme?"

She had moved forward and stood behind Ursula. Douglas was close beside her but she seemed to be unaware of him. When he slipped his hand under her arm she freed herself, but with a slight movement as if she loosed a sleeve that had caught on a piece of furniture. She answered Alleyn rapidly, looking straight before her: "It was cold. Douglas had left the French window open. He was on the lawn. I said good-night to him and asked him to put the screen in front of the fire. He called out that he would. I went into the hall and lit my candle. I heard a voice in the study and was not sure if it was yours or Fabian's. I went up to my room. Douglas came upstairs and tapped on my door. He said good-night. I put away some things I had been mending and then undressed. I heard someone come out of the bathroom, it was Mrs. Aceworthy's step. Ursula said something to her. I—I read for a minute or two and then I went to the bathroom and returned and got into bed."

"Did you go to sleep?"

"Not at once."

"You read, perhaps?"

"Yes. For a—yes, I read."

"What was your book?"

"Really," said Ursula impatiently, "can it possibly matter?"

"It was some novel," said Terence. "I've forgotten the title. Some spy story, I think it is."

"And you were still awake when I came upstairs and spoke to Miss Harme?"

"I was still awake."

"Yes, your candles were alight. Were you still reading?"

"Yes," she said, after a pause.

"The spy story must have had some merit," Alleyn said with a smile. She ran her tongue over her lips.

"Did you hear anyone other than Mrs. Aceworthy and Miss Harme come upstairs?"

"Yes. More than one person. I thought I heard you speaking to Fabian or Douglas. Or it might have been Fabian speaking to Douglas. Your voices are alike."

"Anyone on the backstairs?"

"I couldn't hear from my room."

"Did you use the backstairs at all, during this period, Markins?"

"No, sir," said Markins woodenly.

"I'd like to hear what Markins was doing," said Douglas suddenly.

"He has already given me an account of his movements," Alleyn rejoined. "He was on his way up the back path to the track when he thought he saw me. Later he heard a voice which he mistook for mine. He continued on his way and met nobody. He visited the manager's cottage and returned. I met him. Together we explored the track and discovered Losse, lying unconscious on the branch track near the wool-shed."

"So," said Douglas, raising an extremely obvious eyebrow at Alleyn, "Markins was almost on the spot at the critical time." Alleyn heard Markins sigh windily. Tommy Johns said quickly: "He was up at our place, Captain, and I talked to him. There's nothing funny about that."

"Supposing we take you next, Mr. Johns," said Alleyn.

"Were you at home all the evening?"

"I went down to the ram paddock after tea—about half-past six, it was, and I looked in at the men's quarters on my way back. That lovely cook of theirs has made a job of it this time, Captain. Him and Albert are both packed up. Singing hymns and heading for the willies."

"Tcha!" said Douglas.

"And then?" Alleyn asked.

"I went home. The half-past seven program started up on the radio just after I got in. I didn't go out again."

"And Markins arrived—when?"

"Round about a quarter to eight. The eight o'clock program came on just as he left."

"It was a quarter to eight by radio when I left here, sir," said Markins, "and five past when I got back and wound the kitchen clock."

"You seem to have taken an interest in the time," said Douglas, staring at him.

"I always do, sir. Yes."

"Mr. Johns," said Alleyn, "have you witnesses that you stayed at home from half-past seven onwards?"

Tommy Johns drew down his brows and stuck out his upper lip. "He *is* like a monkey," Alleyn thought.

"The wife was about," said Tommy. "Her and Mrs. Duck. Mrs. Duck dropped in after she'd finished here."

"Ah, yes," Alleyn thought. "The wife!" And aloud he said: "They were in the room with you?"

"They were in the front room. Some of the time. I was in the kitchen."

"With Cliff?"

"That's right," said Tommy Johns quickly.

"Except for the time when you sent Cliff down here with the paper?"

Cliff made a brusque movement with his hands.

"Oh that!" said Tommy loudly, too easily. "Yes, that's right, he ran down with it, didn't he? That's right. Only away a minute or two. I'd forgotten."

"You came here," Alleyn said to Cliff, "while I was in the room. You went away as I was saying I'd left my cigarette case in the annex and would go and fetch it."

"I never heard that," said Cliff. He cleared his throat and added hurriedly, as if the words were irrelevant: "I went straight back. I went out by the kitchen door. Mr. Markins saw me. I was home when he came up a few minutes later. I never heard anything about anybody going out from here."

"Did you hear or see Mr. Losse, or anyone at all, as you went back?"

"How could I? He left after me. I mean," said Cliff, turning very white, "he must have left after me because he was here when I went away."

"No. He was upstairs."

"I mean upstairs. He was going upstairs when I came out."

"I see. Which way did you take going home?"

"The kitchen path. Then I cut across the hill and through the fence. That brings you out on the main track, just below the fork off to the wool-shed."

"And you heard nothing of anyone else?"

"When I got above the annex I heard a door slam down below. That would be Mr. Markins coming out. He turned up at our place a couple of minutes after I got in. He followed me up."

"Was it to you that Captain Grace called 'Good night' from the lawn?" Cliff looked at Douglas and away again.

"Not to me," he said. "Anyway I didn't think so."

"But you heard him?"

"I did just hear."

"Why didn't you answer?"

"I didn't reckon it was me he called out to. I was away up on the kitchen path."

"Did you hear anyone on the track?"

"I didn't notice."

"Someone was there," said Douglas positively and stared at Markins.

"Well, I didn't hear them," Cliff insisted.

His father scowled anxiously. "You want to be sure of that," he said. "Look, could you swear you didn't hear somebody on the track? Put it that way. Could you swear?"

"You'd make a good barrister, Mr. Johns," said Alleyn with a smile.

"I don't know anything about that," said Johns angrily,

"but I reckon Cliff needs a lawyer to stand by before he says anything else. You close down, and don't talk, son."

"I haven't done anything, Dad."

"Never mind that. Keep quiet. They'll trip you into making a fool of yourself."

"I've only one more question in any case, Cliff," said Alleyn. "Once at home, did you go out again?"

"No. I sat in the kitchen with Dad and Mr. Markins. I was still there when Markins came back the second time to say there'd been an accident."

"All right." Alleyn moved away from the fire-place and sat on the arm of the sofa. His audience also shifted a little, like sheep, he thought, keeping an eye on the dog.

"Well," he said. "That about covers the collective questions. I'd like to see some of you individually. I think, Grace, that you and I had better have a consultation, hadn't we?"

"By all means," said Douglas, looking a little as if he had been summoned to preside over a court-martial. "I quite agree, sir."

"Perhaps we could move into the study for a moment. I'd like you all to stay here, if you don't mind. We shan't be long."

The study was piercingly cold. Douglas lit a lamp and the fire, and they sat together on the wooden fender while, above them, Florence Rubrick's portrait stared at nothing.

"I don't think Losse ought to be bothered with a plan of action, just yet," Alleyn said. "Do you?"

"Oh, no. Good Lord, no."

"I wanted to consult you about our next move. I'll have to report this business to the police, you know."

"Oh, God!"

"Well, I'll have to."

"They're such hopeless chaps, sir. And to have them mucking about again with notebooks! However! I quite see. It's not altogether your affair, is it?"

"Only in so far as I was the intended victim," said Alleyn dryly.

"You know," Douglas muttered with owlish concern, "I'd come to that conclusion myself. Disgraceful, you know."

Alleyn disregarded this quaint reflection on the ethics of attempted murder.

"They may," he said, "ask me to carry on for a bit, or they may come fuming up here themselves, but the decision rests with them."

"Quite. Well, I jolly well hope they do leave it to you. I'm sure we all feel like that about it."

"Including the assailant, do you suppose?"

Douglas pulled his moustache. "Hardly," he said. "That joker would be quite a lot happier without you, I imagine." He laughed heartily.

"Evidently. But of course he may choose to have another whack at me."

"Don't you worry, sir," said Douglas kindly. "We'll look after that."

His complacency irritated Alleyn. "Who's we?" he asked.

"I'll make it my personal responsibility—"

"You," said Alleyn warmly. "My dear man, you're a suspect. How do I know you won't come after me with a bludgeon?"

Douglas turned scarlet. "I don't know if you're serious, Mr. Alleyn," he began, but Alleyn interrupted him.

"Of course I'm serious."

"In that case," said Douglas grandly, "there's no more to be said."

"There's this much to be said. If you'll prove to me that you couldn't have dodged up that blasted track and had a whack at poor Losse, I'll be profoundly grateful to you. There are too many suspects in this case. The house is littered with them."

"I've told you," said Douglas, who seemed to hover between alarm and disapproval. "I've told you what I did. I went out on the lawn and I came upstairs and knocked at Terry's door. I said good-night."

"Most unnecessary. You'd already said good-night to her. You might have been establishing an alibi."

"Good God, you saw me yourself when you came upstairs!"

"Fully ten minutes later. Longer."

"I was in my pyjamas," Douglas shouted.

"I saw you. Your pyjamas prove nothing. I'm completely unmoved by your pyjamas."

"Look here, this is too much. Why would I want to go for Fabian? I'm fond of him. We're partners. Good Lord," Douglas fumed, "you can't mean what you're saying! Haven't I urged him to be careful over the work? Why should I go for old Fab?"

"For me."

"Damn! For you, then. You're supposed to be the blasted expert."

"And as an expert, God save the mark, I'm keeping my eye on the whole boiling of you, and that's flat."

"Well I don't think you put it very nicely," said Douglas, staring at him, and he added angrily, "What's the matter with your face?"

"Somebody hit it. It's very stiff and has probably turned purple."

Douglas gaped at him. "Hit you!" he repeated.

"Yes, but it's of the smallest consequence, now you've appointed yourself my guardian."

"Who hit you?"

"It's a secret at the moment."

"Here!" said Douglas loudly. "Are you pulling my leg?" He looked anxiously at Alleyn. "It's a funny sort of way to behave," he said dubiously. "Oh, well," he added, "I'm sorry if I got my rag out, sir."

"Not a bit," said Alleyn. "It's always irritating to be a suspect."

"I wish you wouldn't keep on like that," said Douglas fretfully. "It's damned unpleasant. I hoped I might be allowed to help. I'd like to help."

"We're talking in circles. Beat me up a respectable alibi, with witnesses, for the murder of your aunt and the attack on Losse and I'll take you to my professional bosom with alacrity."

"By God," said Douglas with feeling, "I wish I could."

"In the meantime, will you, without prejudice, undertake to do three things for me?"

"Of course!" he said stiffly. "Anything at all. Naturally."

"The first is to see I get a fair field and no interference in the wool-shed, from daybreak to-morrow until I let you know I've finished. I can't do any good there at night, by the light of a farthing dip."

"Right-o, sir. Can do."

"The second is to tell the others in confidence that I propose to spend the night in the wool-shed. That'll prevent any unlawful espials up there, and give me a chance to get the tag end of a night's sleep in my room. Actually, I can't start work until daybreak, but they're not to know that. After daybreak we'll keep the shed, the track and the precincts generally clear of intruders, but you need say nothing about that. Let them suppose I'm going up there now and that you oughtn't to tell them. Let them suppose that I want them to believe I'm going to my room."

"They won't think that kind of thing very like me," said Douglas solemnly. "I'm not the sort to cackle, you know."

"You'll have to do a bit of acting. Make them understand that you're not supposed to tell them. That's most important."

"O.K. What's the third duty?"

"Oh," said Alleyn wearily, "to lend me an alarm clock or knock me up before the household's astir. Unless somebody shakes me up I'll miss the bus. I wish to heaven you'd carried your electricity over to the shed. There's important evidence lying there for the taking, but I must have light. Are you sure you follow me? Actually I'm going to my room. They are to suppose I'm going to the wool-shed, but want to be thought in bed."

"Yes," said Douglas. "I've got that. Jolly subtle."

"Will you give me an alarm clock, or call me?"

"I'll call you," said Douglas, who had begun to look portentous and tolerably happy again.

"Good. And now ask Miss Lynne to come in here, will you?"

"Terry? I say, couldn't you . . . I mean . . . well she's had a pretty rough spin to-night. Couldn't you . . ."

"No," said Alleyn very firmly. "With homicide waiting to be served up cold on a plate, I'm afraid I couldn't. Get her, like a good chap, and deliver your illicit information. Don't forget Markins."

Douglas moved unhappily to the door. Here he paused and a faint glint of complacency appeared on his face.

"Markins, what?" he said. His eyes travelled to Alleyn's jaw. "I'm not one to ask questions out of my turn," he said, "but I bet it was Markins."

iv

Terence was some time coming. Alleyn built up the fire and thawed himself out. He was caught on a wave of nostalgia: for Troy, his wife; for London; for Inspector Fox with whom he was accustomed to work; for his own country and his own people. If this had been a routine case from the Yard he and Fox would, at its present stage, have gone into one of their huddles, staring at each other meditatively over their pipes. He could see old Fox, now; his large unspeaking face, his grave attentiveness, his huge passive fists. And when it was over, there would be Troy, hugging her knees on the hearthrug and bringing him a sense of peace and communion. "She *is* nice," he thought. "I do like my wife," and he felt a kind of panic that he was so far away from her. With a sigh, he dismissed his mood and returned to the house on the slopes of Mount Moon and felt again the silence of the plateau beyond the windows and the austerity of the night.

A door banged and someone crossed the hall. It was Terence Lynne.

She made a sedate entrance, holding herself very erect, and looking straight before her. He noticed that she had powdered her face and done her lips. Evidently she had visited her room. He wondered if the book was still tucked down between the sheets.

"All right now?" he asked and pushed a chair up to the fire.

"Quite, thank you."

"Sit down, won't you? We'll get it over quickly."

She did as he suggested, at once, stiffly, as if she obeyed an order.

"Miss Lynne," Alleyn said, "I'm afraid I must ask you to let me read that diary."

He felt her hatred, as if it were something physical that she secreted and used against him. "I wasn't mistaken after all," she said. "I was right to think you would go back to my room. That's what you're like. That's the sort of thing you do."

"Yes, that's the sort of thing I do. I could have taken it away with me, you know."

"I can't imagine why you didn't."

"Will you please wait here, now, while I get it?"

"I refuse to let you see it."

"In that case I must lock your room and report to the police in the morning. They will come up with a search warrant and take the whole thing over themselves."

Her hands trembled. She looked at them irritably and pressed them together in the folds of her gown. "Wait a minute," she said. "There's something I must say to you. Wait."

"Of course," he said and turned away.

After perhaps a minute she began to speak slowly and carefully. "What I am going to tell you is the exact truth. Until an hour ago I would have been afraid to let you see it. There is something written there that you would have misinterpreted. Now you would not misinterpret it. There is nothing in it that could help you. It is because the thought of your reading it is distasteful to me that I want to keep it from you. I swear that is all. I solemnly swear it."

"You must know," he said, "that I can't act on an assurance of that sort. Surely you must know." She leant forward, resting her forehead on her hand and pushing her hair back from it. "If it is as you say," Alleyn continued, "you must try to think of me as something quite impersonal, as indeed I am. I have read many scores of such documents, written for one reader only, and have laid them aside and put them from my mind. But I must see it or, if I don't, the police must do so. Which is it to be?"

"Does it matter?" she said harshly. "You then. You know where it is. Go and get it, but don't let me see it in your hands."

"Before I go, there is one question. Why, when we discussed the search for the brooch, did you tell us you didn't meet Arthur Rubrick in the long walk below the tennis-court?"

"I still say so."

"No, no. You're an intelligent person. You heard what Losse and Grace said about the search. It was obvious you must have met him." He paused, and the memory returned to him of Fabian muttering: "Terry! Oh Lord, I do wish I hadn't got up here. Silly old man!" He sat on the wooden fender, facing Terence Lynne. "Come," he said, "there was an encounter, wasn't there? A significant encounter? Something happened that would speak for itself to an observer at some distance."

"Who was it? Was it Douglas? Ursula?"

"Tell me what happened."

"If you know as much as this," she said, "you know, unless you're trying to trap me, that he—he put his arms about me and kissed me. There's nothing left. Everything has been coarsened now, and made common."

"Isn't there something unsound in a happiness that fades in the light? I know this particular light is harsh and painful for you but it is a passing thing. When it's gone you will still have your remembrances—" He broke off for a moment and then added deliberately, "Whatever happens."

She said impatiently: "Within the last hour everything has altered. I told you. You don't understand."

"I've got an inkling," he said. "Within the last hour there has been an attempt at a second murder. You think, don't you, that I'm saying to myself: 'This attempt follows, in character, the attack on Mrs. Rubrick. Therefore it has been made by Mrs. Rubrick's assailant!'"

Terence looked attentively at him, a wary sidelong glance. She seemed to take alarm and rose quickly, facing him. "What do you mean..."

"You think," said Alleyn, "that because Arthur Rubrick is dead, I cannot suspect him of the murder of his wife."

CHAPTER XI

ACCORDING TO ARTHUR RUBRICK

There was nothing further to be got from Terence Lynne. Alleyn went upstairs with her and stood in the open doorway while she fetched Arthur Rubrick's diary from its hiding place. She gave it to him without a word and the last glimpse he had of her was of an inimical face, pale, framed in its loosened wings of black hair. She shut the door on him. He went downstairs and called Cliff Johns and Markins into the study. It was now ten o'clock.

Cliff was nervous, truculent, and inclined to give battle.

"I don't know why you want to pick on me again," he said. "I don't know anything, I couldn't have done anything, and I've had just about enough of these sessions. If this is the Scotland Yard method, I don't wonder at what modern psychiatrists say about British justice."

"Don't you talk silly," Markins admonished him and added hurriedly: "Beg pardon, sir, I'm sure."

"It's absolutely mediaeval," Cliff mumbled.

"Now, see here," Alleyn said. "I heartily agree that you and I have had more than enough of these interviews. In the course of them you have refused to give me certain information. I have now got that information from another source. I am going to repeat it to you and ask for your confirmation or denial. You're in a difficult position. Indeed it is my duty to tell you that what you say will be taken down and may be used in evidence against you."

Cliff wetted his lips. "But that's what they say when—that means—"

"It means that you'll be well advised either to tell the truth or to say nothing at all."

"I didn't kill her. I didn't touch her."

"Let us start with this business of the whisky. Is it true that you caught Albert Black in the act of stealing it and were yourself in the act of replacing it when Markins found you?"

Markins had moved behind Cliff to the desk. He sat at it, opened his pocket-book and produced a stump of pencil from his waistcoat.

"Anything to say about that?" Alleyn asked Cliff. "True or untrue?"

"Did he tell you?"

Alleyn raised an eyebrow. "I extracted it from his general manner. He admitted it. Why did you refuse to give this story to Mrs. Rubrick?"

"He wouldn't hand it over until I promised. He'd have got the sack and might have got jailed. A year before, one of the chaps on the place pinched some liquor. They searched his room and found it. She got the police on to him and he did a week in jail. Albie was a bit tight when he took it. I told him he was crazy."

"I see."

"I told you it hadn't anything to do with the case," Cliff muttered.

"But hasn't it? We'll go on to the following night, the night Mrs. Rubrick was murdered, the night when you, dog-tired after your sixteen-mile tramp, were supposed to have played difficult music very well for an hour on a wreck of a piano."

"They all heard me," Cliff cried out. "I can show you the music."

"What happened to that week's instalment of the published radio programs?"

As Cliff's agitation mounted, he seemed to grow younger. His eyes widened and his lips trembled like a small boy's.

"Did you burn it?" Alleyn asked.

Cliff did not answer.

"You knew, of course, that a Chopin 'Polonaise' was to be broadcast, followed by the 'Art of Fugue.' You had started to work at the Bach and perhaps, while you waited for the program to begin at eight-five P.M., played the opening passages. You saw him playing, Markins, didn't you?"

"Yes sir," said Markins, still writing. Cliff started violently at the sound of his voice.

"But at eight-five you stopped and turned up the radio, which was probably already tuned to the station you wanted. From then, until just before your mother came, when you began to play again, the radio didn't stop. But at some time during that fifty minutes you went to the wool-shed. It was almost dark when you came out. Albert Black saw you. He was drunk, but he remembered and when, three weeks later, Mrs. Rubrick's body was found, and the police inquiry began, he used his knowledge for blackmail. He was afraid that when the whisky incident came to light, you would speak the truth. He drove a bargain with you. Now. Why did you go down to the wool-shed?"

"I didn't touch her. I didn't plan anything. I didn't know she was going to the shed. It just happened."

"You sat in the annex with the door open. If, after you stopped playing and the radio took up the theme, you sat on the piano chair, you would be able to see down the track. You would be able to see Mrs. Rubrick come through the gate at the end of the lavender path and walk up the track towards you. You'd see her turn off to the wool-shed and then she would disappear. I don't for a moment suggest that you expected to see her. You couldn't possibly do so. I merely suggest that you did see her. The door was open, otherwise they would not have been able to hear the Bach from the tennis lawn. Why did you leave the 'Art of Fugue' and follow her to the wool-shed?"

Watching Cliff, Alleyn thought: "When people are afraid, how little their faces express. They become wooden, dead almost. There's only a change of colour and a kind of stiffness in the mouth."

"Is there to be an answer?" he asked.

"I am innocent," said Cliff, and this gracious phrase came strangely from his lips.

"If that's true, wouldn't it be wise to tell me the facts? Do you want the murderer to be found?"

"I haven't got the hunter's nose," said Cliff harshly.

"At least, if you're innocent, you want to clear yourself."

"How can I? How can I clear myself when there's only me

to say what happened! She's dead, isn't she?" His voice rose shrilly. "And even if the dead could talk, she might still bear witness against me. If she had a moment to think, to realize she'd been hit, she may have thought it was me that did it. That may have been the last thought that flashed up in her mind before she died—that I was killing her."

As if drawn by an intolerable restlessness, he moved aimlessly about the room, blundering short-sightedly against chairs. "That's a pretty ghastly idea to get into your head, isn't it? Isn't it!" he demanded, his back to Alleyn.

"Then she was alive when you went into the shed? Did you speak to her?"

Cliff turned on him. "Alive? You must be crazy. Alive! Would I feel like this if I'd been able to speak to her?" His hands were closed on the back of a chair and he took in a shuddering breath. "Now," Alleyn thought, "it's coming."

"Wouldn't it have been different," Cliff said rapidly, "if I could have told her I was sorry, and tried to make her believe I wasn't a thief? That's what I wanted to do. I didn't know she was going to the shed. How could I? I just wanted to hear the Bach. I started off thinking I might try playing in unison with the radio, but it didn't work, so I stopped and listened. Then I saw her come up the track and turn off to the shed. I wanted, suddenly, to tell her I was sorry. I sat by the radio for a long time listening and thinking about what I could say to her. I couldn't make up my mind to go. Then, almost without properly willing it, I got up and walked out, leaving the music still going. I went down the hill, turning the phrases over in my mind. And then . . . to go in—into the dark—expecting to find her there and . . . I actually called out to her, you know. I wondered what she could be doing, standing so quiet somewhere in the dark. I could hear the music quite clearly. I called out: 'Mrs. Rubrick, are you there?' and my voice cracked. It hadn't broken properly then, and it cracked and sounded rotten. I walked on, deeper into the shadow."

He rubbed his face with a shaking hand.

"Yes?" Alleyn said. "You went on?"

"There was a heap of empty bales beyond the press. I was quite close to it by then. It was so queer, her not being there. I don't know what I thought about. I don't know really, if I'd any sort of idea about what was coming, but it seems to me now that I had got a kind of intuition. Like one of those nightmares, when something's waiting for you and you have to go on to meet it. But I don't know. That may not be true. It may not have happened till my foot touched hers."

"Under the empty bales?"

"Yes, yes. Between the press and the wall. They were heaped up. I think I wondered what they were doing there. I suppose it was that. And then, in the dark, I stumbled into them. It's very queer, but I knew at once that it was Mrs. Rubrick and that she was dead."

"What did you do?" Alleyn said gently.

"I jumped back and bumped into the press. Then I didn't move for a long time. I wanted to but I couldn't. I kept thinking: 'I ought to look at her.' But it was dark. I stooped down and grabbed up an armful of bales. I could just see something bright. It was that diamond thing. The other one was lost. Then I listened and there wasn't any sound. And then I put down my hand and it touched soft dead skin. My arms threw the bales down without my knowing what they did. I swear I meant to go and tell them. I swear I never thought, then, of anything else. It wasn't till I was outside and he called out that I had any other idea."

"Albert Black called out?"

"He was up the track a bit. He was drunk and stumbling. He called out: 'Hey, Cliff, what have you been up to?' Then I felt suddenly like—well, as if I'd turned to water inside. It's a lie to say people think when things like this happen to them. They don't. And you don't control your body either. It acts by itself. Mine did. I didn't reason out anything, or tell myself what to do. It wasn't really me that ran uphill, away from the track and round the back of the bunk-house. It was me, afterwards, thawing back into my body, going to the annex and beginning to think with the radio still playing. It was me remembering the row we'd had and what I'd said to her. It was me switching off the radio and playing, when I heard the door of our house bang and the dogs start barking. It was me, next day, when nobody said anything, and the next and the next. And the next three weeks, wondering where they'd put it, and whether it was somewhere near. I thought about that much more often than I thought about who had done it. Albie had the wind up, he thought I'd say he'd taken the whisky, and they'd start wondering if he had a grudge against her. She'd wanted Mr. Rubrick to sack him. When he was drunk he used to talk as if he'd give her the works. Then, when they found her, he talked to me just like you said. He thought I did it, he still thinks I did it, and he was afraid I'd try and put it across him and say he was tight and went for her."

He lurched round the chair and flung himself clumsily into it. His agitation, until now precariously under control, suddenly mastered him and he began to sob, angrily, beating his hand on the chair arm. "It's gone," he stammered. "It's gone. I can't even listen now. There isn't any music."

Markins eyed him dubiously. Alleyn, after a moment's hesitation, went to him and touched him lightly on the shoulder. "Come," he said, "it's not as bad as all that. There will be music again."

ii

"There's as neat a case against that boy as you'd wish to see," said Markins. "Isn't that right, sir? He's signed a statement admitting he did go into the shed and we've only his word for it that the rest of the yarn's not a taradiddle. D'you think they'll take his youth into consideration and send him to a reformatory?"

Alleyn was prevented from answering this question by the entrance of Tommy Johns, white to the lips and shaking with rage.

"I'm that boy's father," he began, standing before Alleyn and lowering his head like an angry monkey, "and I won't stand for this third-degree business. You've had him in here and grilled him till he's broke down and said anything you liked to put into his mouth. They may be your ways, wherever you come from, but they're not ours in this country and we won't take it. I'll make a public example of you. He's out there, poor kid, all broke up and that weak and queer he's not responsible for himself. I told him to keep his trap shut, silly young tyke, and as soon as he gets out of my sight this is what you do to him. Has anything been took down against him? Has he put his name to anything? By God, if he has, I'll bring an action against you."

"Cliff has made a statement," Alleyn said, "and has signed it. In my opinion it's a true statement."

"You've no right to make him do it. What's your standing? You've no bloody right."

"On the contrary I am fully authorized by your police. Cliff has taken the only possible course to protect himself. I repeat that I believe him to have told the truth. When he's got over the effects of the experience he may want to talk to you about it. Until then, if I may advise you, I should leave him to himself."

"You're trying to swing one across me."

"No."

"You reckon he done it. You're looking for a case against him."

"Without much looking, there is already a tenable case against him. At the moment, however, I don't think he committed either of these assaults. But, as you are here, Mr. Johns—"

"You're lying," Tommy Johns interjected with great energy.

"—I feel I should point out that your own alibis are in both instances extremely sketchy."

Tommy Johns was at once very still. He leant forward, his arms flexed and hanging free of his body, his chin lowered. "I'd got no call to do it," he said. "Why would I want to do it? She treated me fair enough according to her ideas. I've got no motive."

"I imagine," Alleyn said, "it's fairly open secret on the place that the work Captain Grace and Mr. Losse have been doing together is of military importance. That it is, in fact, an experimental war job and, as such, has been carried out in secrecy. You also know that Mrs. Rubrick was particularly interested in anti-espionage precautions."

"I don't know anything about that," Tommy Johns

began, but Alleyn interrupted him.

"You don't see a windmill put up at considerable expense to provide an electric supply for one room only, and that a closely guarded workroom, without wondering what it's in aid of. Mrs. Rubrick herself seems to have adopted a somewhat obvious attitude of precaution and mystery. The police investigation was along unmistakable lines. You can't have failed to see that they were making strenuous efforts to link up murder with possible espionage. To put it bluntly, your name appears in the list of persons who might turn out to be agents in the pay of an enemy power, and therefore suspects in the murder of Mrs. Rubrick. Of course there's a far more obvious motive: anger at Mrs. Rubrick's attitude towards your son in the matter of the stolen whisky, and fear of any further steps she might take."

Tommy Johns uttered an extremely raw expletive.

"I only mention it," said Alleyn, "to remind you that Cliff's 'grilling,' as you call it, was in no way peculiar to him. Your turn may come, but not to-night. I've got to start work at five, and I must get some sleep. You pipe down like a sensible chap. If you and your boy had no hand in these assaults, you've nothing to worry about."

"I'm not so sure," Tommy Johns said, blinking. "The wife's had about as much as she can take," he added indistinctly, and looked at Alleyn from under his jutting brows. "Oh, well," he said.

"Murder takes it out of all hands," Alleyn murmured, piloting him to the door. Johns halted in front of Markins. "What's he doing in here?" he demanded.

"I'm O.K., Tommy," said Markins. "Don't start in on me, now."

"I haven't forgot it was you that put the boy away with her in the first instance," said Johns. "The boy asked us not to let it make an unpleasantness so we didn't. But I haven't forgot. You're the fancy witness in this outfit, aren't you? What's he pay you for it?"

"He's not in the least fancy," said Alleyn. "He's going to see you and the boy home in about ten minutes. In the meantime I want you all to wait in the drawing-room."

"What d'you mean, see us home?"

"In case there are any more murders and you're littered about the place without alibis." He nodded to Markins, who opened the door. "You might ask Miss Harme to come in," Alleyn said, and they went away.

iii

"I wanted to see you by yourself," said Ursula. "I never have, you know."

"I'm afraid there'll be no marked improvement," said Alleyn.

"Well, I rather like you," she said, "and so does Fab. Of course I'm terribly pleased that the murderer didn't kill you, and so will Fab be when he's better, but I must say I do wish he could have missed altogether and not caught my poor boy-friend on his already very tricky head."

"It may all turn out for the best," Alleyn said.

"I don't quite see how. Fabian will almost certainly consider himself well below C3 as a marrying man and turn me down flat."

"You'll have to insist."

"Well, so I will if I can, but it's a poor prospect. I wanted to ask you. Was he at all peculiar while he was unconscious? Did he want to go swarming up the walls or anything?"

Alleyn hesitated before answering this startlingly accurate description. "I see he did," said Ursula quickly. "Then it did get to the old spot. I'd hoped not. Because, you know, he was hit behind the ear when he was climbing up into the boat at Dunkirk and this is at the back of his head."

"Perhaps it's just because he was unconscious."

"Perhaps," she said doubtfully. "Did he talk about dropping into the sea, and did he do the sort of gallant young leader number for the men who were with him? 'Come on, you chaps. Excelsibloodyor.'"

"Exactly that."

"Isn't it difficult!" Ursula said gloomily. "I had a frightful set-to with him in the ship. Up the companion-way like greased lightning and then all for shinning up the rigging only fortunately there was no rigging very handy. But to do him justice I must say he didn't fight me. Although concussed I supposed he knew a lady when he saw one and remained the little gent."

"Does he ever call you 'funny old thing'?"

"Never. That's not at all his line. Why?"

"He called somebody that when he was talking."

"You perhaps?"

"Positively not. He merely hit me."

"Well, it would be a man."

"Are you at all interested in the shearing process?"

Ursula stared at him. "Me?" she said. "What do you mean?"

"Do you ever help in the shed? Pick up fleeces or anything?"

"Good heavens, no. Women don't, though I suppose we'll have to if the war goes on much longer. Why?"

"Then you couldn't tell me anything about sorting?"

"Of course not. Ask Douglas or Fab or Tommy Johns. Or why not Ben Wilson? It's frightfully technical."

"Yes. Do you suppose Fabian tried to climb anything when he blacked-out on the night of the search?"

"I'm quite sure he did," said Ursula soberly.

"You are? Why?"

"I had a good look at him, you know. You remember I guessed he'd had another go. The palms of his hands were stained as if he'd held on to things like branches. I sent his white trousers to the wash. They had green lines on them."

"You're a very good sensible girl," said Alleyn warmly, "and if you want to marry him, you shall."

"I don't see what you can do about it, but it's nice of you all the same. Why are you so excited about Fabian climbing the tree?"

"Because if he did he had a view of the lay-out."

"Did he say anything?"

"Yes. Scarcely evidence, I'm afraid. The only way to get that would be to knock him neatly over the head in the witness-box and I don't suppose you'd allow that. He'll have forgotten all about his blackouts, as usual, when he comes round. It seems that when they happen he is at once aware of the previous experiences and returns in memory to them."

"Isn't it rum?" said Ursula.

"Very. I think you may go to bed now. Here is the key of Losse's room. You may open the door and look at him if you like. If he wakes, whisper some pacific reassurance and come away."

"I suppose I couldn't sit with him for a bit?"

"It's half-past ten. I thought it was to be an early night."

"I'd like to. I'd be as still as a mouse."

"Very well. I'll leave the key in your charge. What did you decide about a doctor?"

"We're going to nip up when the Bureau opens."

"Very sensible. Good night to you."

"Good night," said Ursula. She took hold of his coat lapels. "You're terribly attractive," she said, "and you're a darling because you don't think it was us. Any of us. I'm sorry he hit you." She kissed him and walked soberly out of the room.

"A baggage!" Alleyn said to himself, meditatively stroking the side of his face. "A very notable baggage."

Markins came in. "That's the lot, sir," he said. "Unless you want me to wake up Mrs. Aceworthy and Mrs. Duck."

"They can wait till the morning. Send the others to bed, Markins. Escort the Johns brace to their cottage and then join me in the wool-shed."

"So you are going."

"I'm afraid so. We can't wait, now. I've told Captain Grace."

"And he told us. 'Strewth, he's a beauty, that young fellow. 'Officially,' he says, 'Mr. Alleyn's going to bed. Between ourselves, he's not letting the grass grow under his feet. You needn't say I said so, but he's going up to the wool-shed to work on the scene of the crime!' Could you beat it? Goes and lets it out."

"He was under orders to do so."

Markins looked thoughtfully at his superior. "Inviting them to come and have another pop at you, sir? Is that the lay? Taking a risk aren't you?"

"You go and do your stuff. Make sure nobody sees you go

into the wool-shed. I shan't be long."

"Very good, sir." Markins went out but reopened the door and put his head round it.

"Excuse me, Mr. Alleyn," he said, wrinkling up his face, "but it's nice to be working with someone—after all these years on me pat—especially you."

"I'm delighted to have you, Markins," said Alleyn, and when the little man had gone, he thought: "He's not old Fox, but he's somebody. He's a nice little bloke."

He heard the others come out of the drawing-room. Douglas called out importantly: "Good night, Tommy; good night, Cliff. Report to me first thing in the morning, remember. You too, Markins."

"Certainly sir," said Markins, briskly. "I'll lock up, sir."

"Right."

Alleyn went into the hall. Douglas and Terence were lighting their candles. The two Johnses and Markins were in the back passage.

"Captain Grace," Alleyn said not too loudly, "is there such a thing as a paraffin heater on the premises? Sorry to be a nuisance, but I'd be glad of one—for my room."

"Yes, yes, of course," said Douglas. "I quite understand, sir. There's one somewhere about, isn't there, Markins?"

"I'll get it out for Mr. Alleyn, sir, and take it up?"

"No. Just leave it in the hall here, will you? When you come back."

Alleyn looked at Douglas who instantly winked at him. Terence Lynne stood at the foot of the stairs, shielding her candle with her hand. She was an impressive figure in her ruby-red gown. The flame glowed through her thin fingers, turning them blood red. Her face, lit from below, took on the strangely dramatic air induced by upward-thrown shadows. Her eyes, sunk in black rings above the brilliant points of her cheek-bones, seemed to fix their gaze on Alleyn. She turned stiffly and began to mount the stairs, a dark figure. The glow of her candle died out on the landing.

Alleyn lit one of the candles. "Don't wait for me," he said to Douglas, "I want to see that Markins comes in. I'll lock my door. Don't forget to batter on it at four-thirty, will you?"

"Not I, sir." Douglas jerked his head complacently. "I

think they're quite satisfied that you're spending the night in the shed," he whispered. "Markins and Tommy and Co. Rather amusing."

"Very," said Alleyn dryly, "but please remember that Miss Lynne and Miss Harme are both included in the deception."

"Oh—er, yes. Yes. All right."

"It's important."

"Quite."

"Thanks very much, Grace," said Alleyn. "See you, alas, at four-thirty."

Douglas lowered his voice: "Sleep well, sir," he chuckled.

"Thank you. I've a job of writing to do first."

"And don't forget to lock your door."

"No, no. I'll come up quietly in a moment."

"Good night, Mr. Alleyn."

"Good night."

"I'm sorry," Douglas muttered, "that I didn't take it better in there. Bad show."

"Not a bit. Good night."

Alleyn waited until he heard a door bang distantly upstairs and then went up to his room. He brought two sweaters and a cardigan out of his wardrobe, put them all on, and then wedged himself into a tweed jacket. The candle he had used the previous night was burned down to less than a quarter of an inch. "Good for twenty minutes," he thought and lit it. He heard Douglas come along the passage to the landing, go into the bathroom, emerge, and tap on Terence Lynne's door. "Damn the fellow!" thought Alleyn. "Are we never to be rid of his amatory gambits?" He heard Douglas say: "Are you all right, Terry?... Sure? Promise? Good night again, then, bless you." He creaked away down the passage. Here, it seemed, he ran into Ursula Harme emerging from Fabian's room. Alleyn watched the encounter through the crack between the hinges of his open door. Ursula whispered and nodded, Douglas whispered and smiled. He patted her on the head. She put her hand lightly on his and came tiptoe with her candle past Alleyn's door to her own room. Douglas went into his and in a minute or two all was quiet. Alleyn put his torch in one pocket and Arthur Rubrick's diary in the other. He then went quietly downstairs. A paraffin heater was set out in the hall. He left it behind him with regret and once more went out into the cold. It was now five minutes to eleven.

iv

Alleyn shone his torch on Markins. Sitting on a heap of empty bales with one pulled about his shoulders, he looked like some chilly Kobold. Alleyn squatted beside him and switched off his torch.

"It'll be nice when we can converse in a normal manner with no more stage whispers," he muttered.

"I've been thinking things over, sir. I take it your idea is to lay a trap for our joker. Whoever he is—say 'he' for argument's sake—he thinks the Captain's let the cat out of the bag about you coming up here and that you'd be off guard and wide-open to another welt on the napper? I'm to lie low, cut in at the last moment, and catch him hot."

"Just a second," said Alleyn. He pulled off his shoes and thudded to the press. "We've got to stow ourselves away."

"Both of us?"

"Yes. It may be soon and it may be a hellish long wait. You'll get in the wool press. Into that half. The one with the door. Be ready to open the front a crack for a view. I'm going to lie alongside it. I'll get you to cover me with these foul sacks. It sounds idiotic but I think it's going to work. Don't disturb the sacks that Mr. Losse was lying on. Now, then."

Alleyn, remembering Cliff's narrative, spread three empty sacks on the floor behind the press. He lay on them with Arthur Rubrick's diary open under his chin. Markins dropped several more packs over him. "I'll put my torch on," Alleyn whispered. "Can you see any light?"

"Wait a bit, sir." A further weight fell across Alleyn's shoulders and head. "O.K., now, sir." Alleyn stretched himself like a cat and relaxed his muscles systematically until his body lay slack and resistless on its hard bed. It was abominably stuffy and there was some danger of the dusty hessian inducing a sneeze. If his nose began to tickle he'd have to plug it. Close beside him the press creaked. Markins' foot rapped against the side. He thudded down into his nest.

"Any good?" Alleyn whispered.

"I'm tying a bit of string to the side," said a tiny voice. "I can let it open then."

"Good. Don't move unless I do."

After a silence of perhaps a minute, Alleyn said: "Markins?"

"Sir?"

"Shall I tell you my bet for our visitor?"

"If you please."

Alleyn told him. He heard Markins give a thin ghost of a whistle. "Fancy!" he whispered.

Alleyn turned his torch on the open pages of Arthur Rubrick's diary. On closer inspection it proved to be a well-made, expensively bound affair, with his initials stamped on the cover. On the fly-leaf was an enormous inscription: "Arthur with fondest love from Florence, Christmas 1941."

Alleyn read with some difficulty. The book was no more than five inches from his nose, and Rubrick had written a tiny and delicate script. His curiously formal style appeared in the first line and continued for many pages without interruption or any excursions into modernity. It was in this style or one more antique, Alleyn supposed, that he had written his essays.

December 28th, 1941 [Alleyn read]. I cannot but think it a curious circumstance that I should devote these pages, the gift of my wife, to a purpose I have long had in mind, but have been too lanquid or too idle to pursue. Like an unstudious urchin I am beguiled by the smoothness of paper and the invitation of pale blue lines, to accomplish a task to which a common ledger or exercise book could not beguile me. In short, I intend to keep a journal. In my judgement there is but one virtue in such a practice: the writer must consider himself free; nay, rather, bound to set down impartially those thoughts, hopes, and secret burdens of the heart which, at all other times, he may not disclose. This, then, I propose to do and I believe those persons who study the ailments of the mind would applaud my intention as salutary and wise.

Alleyn paused in his stuffy confinement and listened for a moment. He heard only the sound of his pulse and when he moved his head the scratch of hessian against his shoulders.

. . . That I had been mistaken in my choice was too soon apparent. We had not been married a year before I wondered at the impulse that had led me into such an unhappy union and it seemed to me that some other than I had acted so precipitately. Let me be just. The qualities that had invoked the admiration I so rashly mistook for affection were real. All those qualities, indeed, which I am lacking are hers in abundance: energy, intelligence, determination and, above all, vitality . . .

A rat scuttled in the rafters.
"Markins?"
"Sir?"
"Remember, no move until you get your cue."
"Quite so, sir."
Alleyn turned a page.

. . . Is it not a strange circumstance that admiration should go hand in hand with faded love? Those qualities for which I most applaud her have most often diminished, indeed prevented altogether, my affection. Yet I believed my indifference to be caused, not so much by a fault in her or in myself, as by the natural and unhappy consequence of my declining health. Had I been more robust, I thought, I would, in turn, have responded more easily to her energy. In this belief I might have well continued for the remainder of our life together, had not Terence Lynne come upon me in my solitude.

• • •

Alleyn rested his hand upon the open book and called to his mind the photograph of Arthur Rubrick. "Poor devil!" he thought. "What bad luck!" He looked at his watch. Twenty minutes past eleven. The candle in his bedroom would soon gutter and go out.

. . . It is over a fortnight now since I engaged to keep this journal. How can I describe my emotions during this time? "I attempt from love's sickness to fly," and (how true): "I cannot raise forces enough to rebel," Is it not pitiful that a man of my age and sad health should fall a victim of this other distemper? Indeed, I am now become an antic, a classical figure of fun, old Sir Ague who languishes upon a pretty wench. At least she is ignorant of my dotage and, in her divine kindness, finds nothing but gratitude in me.

Alleyn thought: "If, after all, the diary gives no inkling, I shall think myself a toad for having read it."

January 10th. Florence came to me to-day with a tale of espionage at which I am greatly disquieted, the more so that her suspicions are at war with her inclining. I cannot, I will not believe what my judgement tells me is possible. Her very astuteness (I have never known her at fault in appraisement of character), and her great distress, combine to persuade me of that which I cannot bring myself to set down in detail. I am the more uneasy that she is determined to engage herself in the affair. I have entreated her to leave it in the hands of authority and can only hope that she will pursue this course and that they will be removed from Mount Moon and placed under a more careful guard as indeed would sort well with their work. I am pledged to say nothing of this and, truth to tell, am glad to be so confined. My health is so poor a thing nowadays that I have no stomach for responsibility and would be rid, if I might, of all emotions, yet am not so, but rather the more engaged. Yet I must ponder the case and find myself, upon consideration, woefully persuaded. Circumstance, fact, and his views and character all point to it.

Alleyn read this passage through again. Markins, inside the press, gave a hollow little cough and shifted his position.

January 13th. I cannot yet believe in my good fortune. My emotion is rather one of humility and wonder than of exaltation. I cannot but think I have made too much of her singular kindness, yet when I recollect, as I do continually, her sweetness and her agitation, I must believe she loves me. It is very strange, for what a poor thing I am, creeping about with my heart my enemy: her equal in nothing but my devotion and even in that confused and uncertain. I mistrust Florence. She interpreted very shrewdly the scene she interrupted and I fear she may conclude it to be the latest of many; she cannot believe it to be, as in fact it is, the first of its kind.... Her strange and most unwelcome attentiveness, the watch she keeps upon me, her removal of Terence; these are signs that cannot be misread.

Alleyn read on quickly, reaching the sentence he had lighted upon when he first opened the book. Behind the formal phrases he saw Arthur Rubrick, confused and desperately ill, moved and agitated by the discovery of Terence Lynne's attachment to him, irked and repelled by his wife's determined attentions. Less stylized phrases began to appear at the end of the day's record. "A bad night" ... "Two bad turns, to-day." A few days before his wife was killed, he had written: "I have been reading a book called *Famous Trials.* I used to think such creatures as Crippen must be monsters; unbalanced and quite without the habit of endurance by which custom inoculates the normal man against intolerance, but am now of a different opinion. I sometimes think that if I could be alone with her and at peace I might recover my health...." On the night of Florence's death he had written: "It cannot go on like this. I must not see her alone. To-night, when we met by chance, I was unable to obey the rule I had set myself. It is too much for me."

There were no other entries.

Aileyn closed the book, shifted his position a little and switched off his torch. Cautiously he adjusted the covering over his head to leave a peep-hole for his right eye and, like a trained actor, dismissed all senses but one from his mind. He listened. Markins, a few inches away, whispered: "Now then, sir."

v

The person who moved across the frozen ground towards the wool-shed did so very slowly. Alleyn was aware not so much of footsteps as of interruptions in the silence, interruptions that might have been mistaken for some faint disturbance of his own ear-drums. They grew more definite and were presently accompanied by a crisp undertone when occasionally the advancing feet brushed against stivered grass. Alleyn directed his gaze through his peep-hole toward that part of the darkness where the sacking should be.

The steps halted and were followed, after a pause, by a brushing sound. A patch of luminous blue appeared and widened until a star burned in it. It opened still wider and there hung a patch of glittering night sky and the shape of a hill. Into this, sidelong, edged a human form, a dark silhouette that bent forward, seeming to listen. The visitor's feet were still on the ground below, but, after perhaps a minute, the form rose quickly, mounting the high step, and showed complete for a moment before the sacking door fell back and blotted out the picture. Now there were three inhabitants of the wool-shed.

How still and how patient was this visitor to wait so long! No movement, no sound but quiet breathing. Alleyn became aware of muscles in his own body that asked for release, of a loose thread in the packing that crept down and tickled his ear.

At last a movement. Something had been laid down on
the floor. Then two soft thuds. A disk of light appeared,
travelled to and fro across the shearing board and halted. The
reflection from its beam showed stockinged feet and the dim
outline of a coat. The visitor squatted and the light fanned
out as the torch was laid on the floor. A soft rhythmic noise
began. Gloved hands moved in and out of the region of light.
The visitor was polishing the shearing board.

It was thoroughly done, backwards and forwards with
occasional shifting of the torch, always in the direction of the
press. There was a long pause. Torch-light found and played
steadily upon the heap of packs where Fabian had rested. It
moved on.

It found a single empty pack that Alleyn had dropped
over the branding iron. This was pulled aside by a gloved
hand, the iron was lifted and a cloth was rubbed vigorously
over the head and shaft. It was replaced and its covering
restored. For a blinding second the light shone full in Alleyn's
right eye. He wondered how quickly he could collect himself
and dive. It moved on and the press hid it.

Holding his breath, Alleyn writhed forward an inch. He
could make out the visitor's shape, motionless in the shadow
beyond the press. The light now shone on a tin candlestick
nailed to a joist, high up on the wall.

Alleyn had many times used the method of reconstruction
but this was the first time it had been staged for him by an
actor who was unaware of an audience. The visitor reached
up to the candle. The torch moved and for a brief space
Alleyn saw a clear silhouette. Gloved fingers worked, a hand
was drawn back. The figure moved over to the pens.
Presently there was the sound of a sharp impact, a rattle and
a soft plop. Then silence.

"This is going to be our cue," thought Alleyn.

The visitor had returned to the shearing board. Suddenly
and quite clearly a long thin object was revealed, lying near
the doorway. It was taken up and Alleyn saw that it was a
green branch. The visitor padded back to the sheep pens. The
light jogged and wavered over the barrier and was finally
directed inside. Alleyn began to slough his covering. Now he
squatted on his heels with the press between himself and the

light. Now he rose until he crouched behind it and could look
with his left eye round the corner. The visitor fumbled and
thumped softly. The light darted eccentrically about the walls
and, for a brief flash, revealed its owner astride the barrier. A
movement and the figure disappeared. Alleyn looked over
the edge of the press into blackness. He could hear Markins
breathing. He reached down and his fingers touched short
coarse hair.

"When you hear me," he breathed, and a tiny voice
replied, "O.K."

He slipped off his too tight jacket and moving sideways
glided across the shed and along the wall, until his back was
against the port-holes. He peered across the shearing board
towards the pens, now faintly lit by reflected light from the
visitor's torch. A curious sound came from them, a mixture
of rattle and scuffle.

Alleyn drew his breath. He was about to discover whether
the post-mortem on Florence Rubrick's character, the
deductions he had drawn from it, and the light it had seemed
to cast on her associates, were true or false. The case had
closed in upon a point of light still hidden from him. He felt
an extraordinary reluctance to take the final step. For a
moment time stood still. "Get it over," he thought, and lightly
crossed the shearing board. He rested his hand on the
partition and switched on his torch.

It shone full in the eyes of Douglas Grace.

EPILOGUE

ACCORDING TO ALLEYN

Part of a letter from Chief Detective-Inspector Alleyn to Detective-Inspector Fox.

... You asked for the works, Br'er Fox, and you'll get them. I enclose a copy of my report but it may amuse you to have the pointers as I saw them. All right. First pointer. The leakage of information through the Portuguese journalist.

Not being a believer in fairies or in stories of access to sealed rooms you'll have decided that Fabian Losse, Douglas Grace and, possibly, Florence Rubrick, were the only persons who had a hope of extracting blueprints and handing them on. Remembering they were copies, not originals, you'll see that Florence Rubrick is ruled out. She hadn't the ability to make copies or the apparatus to photograph originals.

So our enemy agent, murderer or not, looked like Douglas Grace or Fabian Losse. Both had free access to the stuff and means of passing it on. My job was to find the agent. As a working proposition I supposed he was also the murderer. If, then, the murderer was the agent and the two likeliest bets for the agent were Losse and Grace, which of them shaped up best as the murderer? Grace. Grace put the coat with the diamond clips over Mrs. Rubrick's shoulders and leant over her chair on the tennis lawn. Grace, therefore, could most easily remove one of the clips. It was obvious that the thing would have been found if it had lain glittering on bare earth under a scraggy zinnia. I tried it and it showed up like a lighthouse.

Grace egged on his aunt to organize a search-party and take herself off to the wool-shed. I wondered if he'd pinched the clip in order to bring about this situation and dropped it among the zinnias for Arthur Rubrick to find when Grace himself had finished the job in the wool-shed. If so, he was a quick thinker and a bold customer altogether. He'd hatched the whole project between the time Mrs. Rubrick said she was going to the wool-shed and the moment when she actually left.

Grace had gone up to the house during the search and had answered the telephone and fetched two torches. This would give him a chance to bolt out by the dining-room windows and up the track to the wool-shed. On his return he could hang out the placard on Mrs. Rubrick's bedroom door. This placard is important. You'll have noticed that he was the only member of the party who had the opportunity to do this.

You'll notice, too, that the disposal of the body must, unless our expert was Markins, Albert Black, or the quite impossible Mrs. Duck, have been interrupted by a period not shorter than the interval between the end of the search and the going to bed of the household and the cottage; and not longer than that between the assault and the onset of *rigor mortis*. Now, the abominable Black gouged out the candle stump which had been pressed down, almost certainly by the murderer, and chucked it into the pens. If he was guilty he would hardly have volunterred this information.

But suppose Grace was our man?

The pressing out of the light suggests a hurried movement. The men returning from the dance came quietly up the hill until they reached the shed, when they broke into a violent altercation. If you want to put out a candle quietly and quickly you don't blow, you press. When I told these people I wanted to yank up the slatted floor, Grace hid behind his paper and said he'd give orders to the men to do the job and that he himself would help. I'd have prevented this, of course, but the offer was suggestive. All right.

You remember the presser told me that the floor round the press was smudged. With what? Florence Rubrick, poor thing, had lost no blood. Grace and Losse wore tennis shoes. If you tramp about on a glassy surface on rubber soles it gets smudged.

The bale hooks were hidden on a very high beam. It was

just within my reach and certainly not within the reach of any suspect but Grace. There's no easily movable object, in the shed, by which a shorter person could have gained access to this hiding place, but Douglas was as tall as I.

Next, Br'er Fox, we come to the wool that was found in number-two bin next morning. It hadn't been there overnight. It was tangled and bitty and not in the least like the neatly rolled fleece in the sorter's rack. But it was in the correct bin. Had it been put there by someone who knew about wool sorting? Fabian Losse, Douglas Grace or possibly Arthur Rubrick? It was, of course, the wool that the body had replaced. A piece of it dropped from the murderer when, late that night, he returned to Florence Rubrick's room to hide away her suitcase. The notice was already on the door and remember, only Grace could have put it there.

Next, there was his character. There was his legend. He was accepted by the two girls on Fabian's estimate. Fabian thought him an amiable goat with a knack for mechanics.

But Grace was no fool. He'd got a resourceful and a bold mind. He was determined and inventive. Look at his handling of poor old Markins. Without a doubt he guessed that Markins was watching him and, with a flourish, struck first. You've got to admire his cheek. Of course it was Grace himself who was abroad on the night when Markins heard something in the passage. Again, he coolly nipped in the complaint to his aunt that Markins was up to no good and she ought to get rid of him. But he reckoned without his Flossie. Flossie didn't behave according to pattern. The woman who emerged from our post-mortem was nothing if not shrewd. Even Terence Lynne, whose opinion, poor girl, was distorted by jealousy, admitted her astuteness. I fancy Mrs. Rubrick was brisk enough to have her doubts about Douglas Grace. His popularity waned after their quarrel over Markins and again, since they were bound to tell me of this, Grace got in first with his version. It is in his underestimation of Florence Rubrick that we see, for the first time, that brittle, cast-iron habit of thinking that his earlier German training probably bred in him. He was one of the clutch of young foreign *Herrenvolk*, small, thank God, but infernal, who did their worst to raise Cain when they returned, bloated with fascism, to their own countries.

At this point, Br'er Fox, you'll raise your eyebrows and begin to look puffy. You will say that so far I've presented a very scrubby case against this young man. I agree. If he had come to trial we'd have been on tenterhooks, but as you have seen by the report, Grace did not come to trial.

It was with the object of forcing an exposure that I lay for him. I let him know that I proposed to hunt for the candle which Albert Black threw into the pens. This evidently shook Master Douglas. We've found the candle and it has got his prints, but of course they wouldn't have been conclusive evidence. However, he'd probably decided I was a nuisance on general grounds, and that my liquidation would be to the greater glory of the Fatherland.

When I said I'd go to the annex for my cigarette case he made one of his snap decisions. He would follow me, get the branding iron from the wool-shed, apply the proved method, and send me down-country with the crutchings. Losse, wearing my overcoat, came in for the cosh.

I was now pretty sure of Grace. By dint of a rigmarole so involved that I myself nearly got bogged in it, I induced him to tell the others that I'd be working in the shed all night, and, at the same time, to believe himself that I was going to do no such thing. He had been interrupted by the stretcher party in his first attempt to return and tidy up any prints he'd left. And he must have left some when he fetched and replaced the branding iron. Persuaded that the shed would be deserted, and alarmed by my elephantine hints of clues to be discovered at daybreak, he made his fatal slip. He waited until he thought I was asleep, and then up he came to go over the ground for himself. He took off his slippers (he'd dried them at the drawing-room fire after the assault on Losse) and polished the wool-shed floor. He had another go at the branding iron which he'd already wiped on my overcoat. Then, harking back to his earlier intention, he gouged out the existing candle stump, leaving no prints on it, and dropped it into the pens. He then climbed into the pens and scuffled a branch between the slats until he'd covered the new candle end. It was odds on we'd find it before the one that Albert Black had chucked into the pens nearly a year and a half ago.

I'd counted on a show-down and got more than I bargained for.

It all happened quickly and, until the last moment, very quietly. It was a rum scene. I flashed the torch on him and he blinked and peered at me over the partition while Markins scudded across the shed looking for a fight. There wasn't one. Boxed up in there, he hadn't a hope. The whole affair suddenly became very formal. Grace drew himself up to attention and waited for me to make the first move. He didn't speak. I was never to hear him speak again. I gave him the official warning, told him the police would arrive in two hours and said that if he liked to give his parole under temporary arrest we'd all move to warmer quarters.

He bowed. He bent stiffly from the waist. This made an extraordinary impression on me because in that moment, when he was queerly lit by two torches, Markins and I having turned both ours upon him, I saw him as a Nazi. He would now, I thought, play the role to which he was naturally suited. He would be formal and courageous, a figure from a recognizable pattern. He would exhibit correct manners because these are the coachwork of the Nazi machine. He would betray nothing.

Then I saw his hand move to his side pocket.

His eyes widened and his lips were compressed. I yelled out: "Stop that!"

If he'd been slower I'd have gone with him. As it was I'd got my foot on a beam in the partition, but it was still between us. It seemed to belly out and hit me amidships in a flare of white light. The last sensation I had was of an intolerable noise and of my body hurtling through space and striking itself crazily against a wall. I was, in effect, blown into the middle of next week. He went considerably further and is now among the eternal *Herrenvolk*.

There wasn't much left. However we did find enough to show how he'd provided for the last emergency. His work on shells may have given him the idea but I fancy he was under orders, in event of a final exit, to take me with him. We found the wreck of a cigarette case showing traces of an explosive and a detonator that had been wired to a torch cell. The cigarette case, we think, was in his breast pocket and the cell in his side pocket.

We shall never hear the story of his engineering days in
Germany, of his association with other correct and terrible
youths. We shall never know what oaths he took or to what
intensive training he submitted himself before he was sent
back to await the end of 1939 and the moment when he would
enlist with our forces and begin to be useful.

Fabian Losse talks of building a new wool-shed.

ii

*Part of a letter from Chief Detective-Inspector Alleyn to his
    wife:*

...almost midnight and I am in the study with only poor
Flossie Rubrick's portrait for company. I'm afraid, my love,
that you would be very much put out by this painting and,
indeed, it is a dreadfully slick and glossy piece of work. Yet
with its baleful assistance and the post-mortem on her
character I feel as if I had known her very well. In a sense
Fabian Losse was right when he said the secret of her end lay
in her own character. Who but Florence Rubrick would have
practised a speech in the dark to a handful of sheep during a
search for her own diamonds? Who but she, having made up
her mind that her nephew was an enemy agent, would have
informed her husband, bound him to secrecy, and
decided to tackle the job herself? That it was Douglas Grace
she suspected, and not Markins, is clear enough when one
remembers that Rubrick clung to Markins after her death
and that after her interview with Grace, her manner toward
him altered and she subsequently climbed down over Fabian
Losse's engagement to Ursula Harme. She said nothing of
her precise suspicions to anyone else. She played a lone hand
and she hadn't a chance. Down she went, that ugly little

woman, with all her obstinacy, arrogance, generosity, shrewdness and energy, down she went before an idea that was too strong for her.

It's all over. Already the inhabitants of Mount Moon are beginning to readjust themselves. Fabian Losse, who is fast recovering from the whack on his head, is naturally shocked and horrified by the discovery that his partner gave it to him and appalled to think that for years he has been confiding his dearest secret to his country's enemy. Grace's death is no more than additional cause for bewilderment. It's poor consolation for Fabian that the Portuguese journalist was intercepted. He feels he's been criminally blind and stupid. He doesn't think Grace managed to get any information away. I'm not so sure, but at all events there's no sign of the enemy using the Losse aerial magnetic fuse. Fabian will recover. Ursula Harme will make nonsense of his scruples. They will be married and he will become an important but unknown expert, one of the "boys in the back room." Miss Lynne will composedly follow her neat destiny and will never forgive herself or me for her one outburst. Young Cliff, who, of the entire set-up, would most interest you, will, I hope, grow out of his megrim and return to his music. He was suffering from chronic fear, and psychological constipation. The cause has been removed. His father will doubtless continue to draft sheep and eat fire with perfect virtuosity. I've persuaded Losse to get rid of the abominable Albert.

I almost dare to say I may soon come home. I've just taken up my pen again after stopping to ruminate and fill my pipe. When you pause at midnight in this house, the landscape comes in through the windows and sends something exciting down your spinal column. Out there are the plateau, the cincture of mountains, the empty sparkling air. To the north, more mountains, a plain, turbulent straits, another island, thirteen thousand miles of sea and at the far end, you.

The case is wound up but as I stretch my cold fingers and look once again at the portrait of Florence Rubrick I regret very much that I didn't accept her invitation and come, before she was dead, for a week-end at Mount Moon.